Covering Kendall

Also by Julie Brannagh

Covering Kendall

A LOVE AND FOOTBALL NOVEL

JULIE BRANNAGH

AVONIMPULSE
An Imprint of HarperCollinsPublishers

Excerpt from *Beauty and the Brit* copyright © 2014 by Lizbeth Selvig.

Excerpt from *The Governess Club: Sara* copyright © 2014 by Heather Johnson.

Excerpt from *Caught in the Act* copyright © 2014 by Sara Jane Stone.

Excerpt from *Sinful Rewards 1* copyright © 2014 by Cynthia Sax.

Excerpt from *When the Rancher Came to Town* copyright © 2014 by Gayle Kloecker Callen.

Excerpt from *Learning the Ropes* copyright © 2014 by Tina Klinesmith.

EPub Edition OCTOBER 2014 ISBN: 9780062363817

Print Edition ISBN: 9780062363824

JV 10 9 8 7 6 5 4 3 2 1

To my mom, who believed in me when
I wasn't sure I believed in myself.
I miss you every day.

Acknowledgments

I'D LIKE TO thank my agent, Sarah Younger of Nancy Yost Literary Agency, and my editor, Amanda Bergeron of Avon Impulse. They went above and beyond for me and this book, and I appreciate them both (and all of their hard work) so much.

Thank you to everyone at Avon Impulse for their extra effort on my books. As always, a special shout-out to Jonathan Baker of the copyediting group, who makes me look like I actually know something about grammar and punctuation and checks my football research.

Thank you to the staff and the owners of the Bellevue, Washington, Cupcake Royale, who continue to harbor the Cupcake Crew each week.

Thank you to Jessi Gage and Amy Raby of the Cupcake Crew, my critique partners and my friends. I am so lucky to have you both in my life.

Thank you to my husband, Eric, who took on a lot

more than his fair share so that I could write. I love you, honey.

Thank you to Susan Mallery, who continues to offer great advice and encouragement.

Thank you to Mike Freeman of Bleacher Report for patiently answering my questions on Twitter and making me laugh every day. He's forgotten more about pro football than I'll ever know. Follow him on Twitter at @mikefreemanNFL, won't you?

Thank you to the Super Bowl Champions Seattle Seahawks (that NEVER gets old!) for interviews they've given in various forms of media, which were a huge help with my research.

Speaking of research, the research for this book was challenging. Women still aren't being hired for front office jobs in the NFL in most franchises. I believe this will change, especially since forty-eight percent of women from nineteen to forty-eight identify as NFL fans. I'm looking forward to seeing how the league will address this.

Thank YOU for buying and reading my books. I hope you'll enjoy them as much as I love writing them! If you want to learn a little more about me, I'm at www.juliebrannagh.com, on Facebook, and on Twitter at @julieinduvall.

Go Sharks!

Chapter One

DREW MCCOY DODGED pouring rain as he darted through a puddle-infested parking lot and into the entrance of the biggest bookstore in Bellevue. As he shook off the rain and jammed his hands into the pockets of his black North Face fleece jacket, he nodded at a familiar bookstore employee.

He spent enough time here that the staff knew who he was, despite the fact he always kept his long blond ponytail tucked out of sight beneath a slouchy knit hat. He didn't mind because they kept a respectful distance, but he was occasionally recognized by another customer. It looked like his luck was about to run out.

As he passed the Women's Fiction aisle he overheard a woman say to the employee he'd nodded at, "Wasn't that Drew McCoy that just walked by? From the Sharks?"

Drew darted into Gardening/Home Improvement and braced himself to be exposed.

"That guy looks a lot like him, huh?" the employee said. "A football player probably doesn't like to browse in the Women's Fiction section of the store, though."

"You're right," the woman said and laughed a little. "He's probably not into books."

He sighed with relief. Peeking around the end display, he saw the woman walk away in the opposite direction. He waited until she got in line at the checkstand and doubled back to find the store employee who'd misdirected her.

The employee glanced up from his work in surprise. Drew stuck out his hand. The guy shook it. He wore a nametag: CRAIG. Drew would be stopping by next week with autographed team merchandise for him.

"Thanks, man," Drew said.

"Anytime." The guy grinned at him. "Go Sharks."

Drew continued on to the history section. A freestanding sign caught his eye, and he paused to take a closer look. Carl Sagan's latest biographer would be speaking in fifteen minutes about his new book on the famed astronomer.

Drew had a couple of hours before he needed to get his ass home and get ready for this weekend's Sharks game. He'd enjoy listening to what the guy had to say, and he could grab a couple of books on his way out the door too. He glanced around to see a few rows of empty chairs in front of a lectern. Another bookstore employee was unpacking books to stack on a table for the author to sign.

A deserted book signing: bad for the author, but great for Drew. He could geek out to his heart's content in anonymity. He loved what he did. He loved the Sharks' fans. He didn't love the inability to move freely in public, however. He relished any situation in which he was just another bookworm.

He threaded his way into the middle row of chairs. There was plenty of room to spread out, so he sat down mid-aisle. The front row was too conspicuous. The back row was for those who wanted to catch a nap. He hoped the author didn't mind a few questions from the audience, either.

The only way things could be more perfect for Drew at that moment was if the bookstore sold beer on tap.

KENDALL TRACY STOOD in the parking lot of the bookstore wrestling with an umbrella blown inside-out as the heavens opened up. She'd been sitting in meetings all day. Stepping out of a warm, dry hotel conference room into a ferocious rainstorm wasn't the best idea she'd ever had. She attempted to pull the umbrella back into working shape while she clutched the hood she wore with her other hand. Needless to say, she was getting smacked in the face with rain and wind, and the umbrella was unsalvageable.

She wasn't used to torrential downpours accompanied by strong winds. The weather was perfect when she flew out of San Francisco last night. It might get a little windy at times, but she'd be more likely to don additional layers than get soaked there. She'd been heading to a restaurant a few doors down for a glass of wine, but now she reversed course. A bookstore would be a great place to wait until the storm let up a bit.

She dropped the ruined umbrella next to the front door of the bookstore and found herself propelled through the entrance by a gust of wind. A few other people followed her inside. They milled around the tables stacked with books, crowded aisles, and a few hurried into the attached Starbucks to warm up. She had a digital reader, but it might be nice to find something new to read while she curled up in yet another hotel bed for the night.

She was in Seattle on business a few times a year with her employers, the San Francisco Miners. The football team and front office personnel typically stayed closer to the airport, but she was happy for the opportunity to get out and walk a little. She would have been flat-out thrilled if the weather cooperated. Despite the storm, she was safe, indoors, and there were plenty of books available. She hurried over to the Women's Fiction section but halted mid-aisle at a free-standing sign.

There was a book signing in ten minutes by a guy who'd written a book about Carl Sagan. Her dad loved astronomy. He'd shown her VCR tapes of Carl Sagan's show as a kid too. Maybe the author would sign one of his books for her dad. Kendall glanced over at a grand total of one guy sitting in the four rows of chairs set up for the event. She could spend a few minutes listening to the author's comments. She'd buy a book or two and make a dash for the hotel again.

DREW GLANCED UP as a tall, curvy woman in dress clothes sat down a few chairs away from him. She shoved the hood of her jacket off, and it was all he could do not to stare. Her black hair was cut in a shiny cap around her face. Her skin was palest alabaster, dewy with what must have been rainwater, and her mouth was the shade of juicy summertime cherries. When she glanced over at him and smiled, he noted her eyes were dark gray. Those yes roamed over his face. She rested her handbag on the chair between them.

The bookstore employee hurried away for some reason, and they were left alone. She clasped her hands in her lap while she waited. He quickly checked for rings: She didn't wear one. He was getting a bit warm, but if he took off his jacket and the knit hat he wore, every football fan in the building would recognize him. He also wanted to speak to the woman two seats away from him.

She smelled like green apples—fresh, delicious, and tempting. He cleared his throat, and she glanced up at him.

"Hello," he said.

"Hi." She treated him to another smile.

"The author must be a little late this evening." Normally, he'd think of something witty and memorable to say to a woman he'd just met. Right now, it was all he could do to remember the English language, let alone string sufficient words together to form a sentence.

"Maybe he's caught in traffic. It's awful out there," she said.

"Yes, it is," he said. There were a hundred things he'd like to say to her right now, but he went for the safest. He stuck out his hand. "I'm Drew," he said. "It's nice to meet you."

"I'm Kendall." He clasped her smaller hand in his. Her skin was cool and dry. She wore red nail polish, and he hated letting go of her. "Nice to meet you as well, Drew."

"Do you live in Bellevue?"

"Actually, I don't. I'm here on business this week. I live in Santa Clara, which is just outside of San Francisco."

"Sounds like a great place to live."

"Yes, it is." He saw her lips curve into a smile again, and the flash of perfect teeth. Her eyes sparkled. "I'm guessing you live here."

"My house is a couple of miles away."

She glanced over at him again. "Hopefully, you didn't walk to the store."

He chuckled a little. "It sounded like a great idea at the time." He nodded at the dampness of her coat. "I'm guessing you did too." He slipped his arm around the back of the chair between them while slouching to stretch his legs out a little. She didn't move away. This was a very good sign.

Silence fell. He sifted through the hundred things he'd like to ask her about. A woman that looked like her had heard a line from every guy she came into contact with, so he'd have to come up with something original and appealing. She glanced around the store and gave him another smile. Unless he was really wrong, she wanted to keep talking.

"It looks like we're the only Sagan fans in the bookstore tonight," he said.

To his surprise and delight, she made accompanying

arm gestures as she imitated Sagan's trademark line: "Billions and billions . . ."

"Did you watch the show, or did you watch *Saturday Night Live* reruns?"

"A little of both," she admitted. "My dad was really into it."

The bookstore employee raced out of one of the aisles and hurried over to the author's table. She glanced at the empty chairs surrounding Drew and Kendall and grabbed one of the boxes she'd been unpacking books out of less than ten minutes ago.

"I'm so sorry," she told them. "The author just called. His flight has been on a ground hold in San Francisco due to high winds, and it's just been cancelled. He won't be able to be here tonight. He is very sorry."

Kendall gave her a polite nod and picked up her handbag. Drew leaned forward in his chair. "I'd like to buy a copy of his book anyhow."

"Of course," the employee said, handing him one of the books.

"I'll take one too," Kendall said. Her dad would enjoy it, autographed or not.

Drew turned to face her.

"Kendall, would you like to have a cup of coffee with me?"

A FEW MINUTES later, Drew and Kendall sat down at a table in the Starbucks next door. She set the plastic bookstore bag and her handbag next to her chair. The typically crowded, noisy coffee shop was now almost deserted. The employees had even dimmed the overhead lights a bit. She took a sip of the green tea latte Drew had bought for her and watched him gently nudge the plate holding a couple of cookie bars toward her.

"How about a blueberry oatmeal bar? I whipped it up myself."

She let out a laugh, and his lips moved into a grin. His smile softened chiseled facial features that wouldn't have been out of place on a Viking: strong brow, high cheekbones, deep-set cornflower-blue eyes flecked with silver, square chin, straight white teeth, and blond stubble. He must have been taking a break from the wenching and pillaging tonight. The laugh lines around his eyes and his mouth that appeared when he smiled told her he was most likely a happy person.

She knew she'd seen him somewhere before. She couldn't put her finger on *where*, though. His shoulders were broad and the fleece jacket he wore concealed what she imagined were bulging muscles. When he unzipped his coat, he revealed a black thermal-type Henley. She spent so much time looking at professional athletes that a guy with his build wasn't out of the ordinary to her. It was kind of cute that he didn't take off his knit hat, though.

Maybe he'd got a bad haircut and he felt a little shy about it. His eyebrows were dark blond. His hair must be as well.

"All this, and you bake?" she said.

"Wait until you see what's in the oven right now." The look in his eyes as he held hers was confident.

"Lucky me." She twirled the protective sleeve on her cup with her fingers, and he raised an eyebrow. "So, Drew, what are you up to when you're not baking or rescuing women in bookstores?"

He took a sip of his chai tea. "Working, reading, the usual."

She wanted to ask him what he did, but she could almost guess: personal trainer, or he ran a gym. Guys didn't get those muscles from sitting at a desk in a software firm twelve hours a day.

She wasn't about to tell him what she did. Whenever she told a man where she worked, he spent the rest of the night peppering her with questions about the NFL, about the San Francisco Miners, or how she managed to get along with a volatile head coach known around the league for being difficult to deal with on a daily basis. When the guy wasn't demanding inside information, he was subtly (or not) hinting around for free game tickets.

San Francisco was Seattle's archrival, but she was pretty sure guys here weren't above scoring some tickets and team merchandise, either.

She took another sip of her drink. "I'm guessing it won't be a surprise to you that I love to read as well."

"What's the last book you read?"

She eyed the saucer in front of them. Should she be good and select the blueberry oatmeal bar, or should she pick the one she really wanted: sea salt chocolate caramel? She slid the chocolate caramel bar onto a napkin in front of her.

"How did you know I wanted the blueberry oatmeal one?" Drew said.

"I hoped you didn't want chocolate," she said. "The last book I read? Hmm." She pretended to think for a minute. She wasn't about to tell him she'd spent most of a night earlier this week reading Loretta Chase's latest. She typically relaxed after a day spent dealing with her hyper-masculine colleagues by immersing herself in the love stories of fictional characters that lived almost two hundred years ago. She also read current non-fiction bestsellers as well, and she'd just finished one. "I read Malcolm Gladwell's *David and Goliath*. I wonder why some people succeed beyond their wildest dreams despite setbacks in life, and I thought his conclusions were interesting."

She nibbled at the chocolate caramel bar. It tasted even better than it looked. Drew gave her a nod.

"How is it?"

"Unbelievable. You'll have to give me the recipe."

"I'll work on that," Drew teased, raising one eyebrow. "In the meantime, I have a question. Do you think you've succeeded in life beyond your wildest dreams?"

He reached out for the oatmeal blueberry bar and took a bite. She had a job she'd been seriously pursuing (and working toward) since she got out of college, but she wanted more. Anyone who was ambitious wanted the most they could attain from life—the most success, the most money, the most recognition by their colleagues. She wasn't any different. She wasn't sure how he would react to this, so she kept it light.

"I didn't have a lot of setbacks in life, so I had to come up with my own motivation, but yes. I think so. I'm working in a job I really enjoy, and I like to think I've helped others achieve their goals as well. What about you? Do you believe you've succeeded in the things you've set out to do?" Kendall said.

She was surprised at Drew's questions. Most guys might be asking about her hobbies (besides reading, she really didn't have a lot), if she'd been on vacation lately, or about her relationship status. He seemed more interested in finding out who she was. She'd like to find out a few things about him, most especially why she had the nagging feeling that she'd seen him before. Somewhere, somehow, she knew who he was, and she couldn't quite remember.

Maybe she was having one of those déjà vu moments. She'd read about the chemical in the brain that made a person feel like they'd been somewhere before and they really hadn't. She took another bite of the chocolate caramel bar. She'd be doing some extra time in the gym for it, but maybe she should get one to-go for later.

The Starbucks employees were zipping around the coffee shop, most likely doing their pre-closing responsibilities, and ignoring Kendall and Drew. He laid one big hand on the table between them and leaned back in his chair as he looked into her eyes.

"To answer your question, I have to say that I am happy with what I've attained so far, but there's always more." He inched his hand a bit closer to hers. She had an almost overwhelming urge to lace her fingers through his. "There are plenty of things I'd still like to achieve."

What was she doing? They'd met a couple of hours ago. She didn't know anything but his first name. The spark of attraction between them was almost overpowering. She remembered how his big, warm hand felt when he shook hers. She wanted more.

She snapped out of her reverie as he said, "The book sounds interesting. Maybe I should grab a copy before they close up for the night next door."

At that moment, one of the coffee shop employees clicked the locks shut on the glass doors that separated the coffee shop from the bookstore. The bookstore lights dimmed too. "Last call," one of the baristas joked. "Can we get anything else for either of you?"

"I guess this means I'm not buying that book right now," Drew murmured to Kendall.

"Would you like to borrow my copy? It's in my hotel room. I'd be happy to get it for you," she said.

"I would love that," he said. "Plus, I can walk you home." He glanced out of the panoramic coffee shop windows into the parking lot. "Is there anything else you'd like to drink or eat before we leave?"

Kendall caught the eye of one of the employees behind the counter. "Are there any more of those chocolate caramel bars at all?"

The employee smiled at her. "Welcome to your new worst habit. I'm in love with them too. How many would you like?"

"How about two more?" Drew responded, and he had his wallet out before Kendall could object.

"I can get it," she said.

"You're letting me borrow your book," he said. "Don't worry about it." He handed the barista some cash and handed the two small paper bags to Kendall to stow in her handbag. "A midnight snack," he said.

"Thank you." She pulled up the hood on her jacket and indicated the still-trashed umbrella outside the front door. "That's mine. I don't know if it's going to work," she said.

He glanced out of the window toward the parking lot. "The rain isn't letting up, Kendall. I think it's actually getting worse. Where are you staying?"

"I'm at the Westin. It's only a block or so. I'll be fine."

She was going to be soaked by the time she got there, but she was glad she'd forced herself out of the room for a while.

"Let me see if I can fix that umbrella for you." They stepped outside, and she handed the shell of her formerly intact black umbrella to him. A path ran directly to the hotel from here, but there was going to be a drenching on the way. He didn't seem alarmed by this. He managed to reconstruct most of the umbrella and handed it to her before he re-zipped his jacket. "We're going to have to run, but we'll make it," he said. He re-opened the door and stuck his head inside.

"Good night," he called out to the employees still working.

"Good night," the barista shouted back. "Go Sharks."

He smiled. Maybe this was an unusually team-oriented coffee shop.

She opened the umbrella as much as she could while looping the plastic bookstore bag and her handbag around her other arm. He reached out for the umbrella, holding it over her head, and took her hand with his free one.

"Ready?"

"Always."

THEY ARRIVED AT Kendall's hotel soaked to the skin. The rain was falling in sheets, the wind was blowing, and she'd never been so thankful to see a hotel lobby. She hadn't let go of Drew's hand, either. He left the umbrella outside the hotel doors to dry. The doorman ushered them inside, and a hotel employee approached them promising to send more dry towels up to her room.

Drew pulled her toward the elevator banks. She was already shivering. He must be freezing too. He didn't have a hood on his jacket, and the rain must have been pelting the back of his neck. They dripped all over the elevator while the car carried them to Kendall's room on the twelfth floor.

He still held her hand, but now he rubbed it in both of his. She knew she should feel the cold, but at the moment, the sizzle she felt at his nearness was a pretty major distraction. He moved a little closer to her. She inched closer to him. The elevator stopped, and she pulled him through the open doors. "I'm in 1230," she told him and they hurried down the hallway to her room as she yanked her card key out of her coat pocket. She was shivering so hard she missed the card slot the first time. He reached out for the credit-card sized key, slid it into the reader, and heard the lock click open.

She'd already made the decision while they ran through sheets of rain: She was inviting him in. She was a little nervous about it, but the fact she wanted to spend a little more time with an unimaginably hot guy won out over her hesitation. There was a coffee maker in the room stocked with tea and hot chocolate. If he didn't want coffee, there were other options available. They could dry off with the extra towels at least.

"Come on in," she said.

The room was dim. The only illumination spilled through sheers-covered windows from a streetlight floors below. Kendall heard the door click closed behind them, and she tossed her handbag toward the luggage stand in one corner of the room. She ran one hand over the wall-paper searching for the light switch. She felt Drew's big hand over hers.

"Wait," he said.

He reached out to pull her into his arms, and his mouth found hers, warm and gentle. She tasted rain. She also tasted the spicy-sweet of chai tea on his tongue as it slipped into her mouth. Water dripped off of his knit cap onto her nose, but she didn't care. She wrapped her arms around his midsection. He backed her up against the wall she imagined the light switches were on, but she made no move to pull away from him or turn on a light. His body surrounded her. He pressed himself into her and leaned his forehead against hers.

"I had to kiss you," he murmured.

She leaned her cheek against his wet coat, slid her hands up his chest, and wrapped her arms around his neck while she tried to catch her breath. Right now, breathing was overrated.

"Do you want to kiss me again?" she whispered.

"More than my next breath."

It was dark, but his hands were sure on her. His mouth slanted over hers. Her tongue slipped into his mouth, moved around his, and she felt his hands unbuttoning her coat. "Good idea," she tried to tell him, but she couldn't talk right now. She was too busy kissing him. Plus, she was now searching for the zipper pull that would get his jacket off him in the shortest amount of time. Their wet clothes weren't exactly comfortable, but even more, she wanted to touch him. Her shivering turned into trembling as he managed to pull her coat off and drop it onto the carpeting. His sweet, gentle kisses turned long and hungry. She was still trying to get the zipper on his jacket down as his hand moved over her abdomen and up her ribcage until he cupped her breast over the thin sweater she wore. His thumb did a slow back-and-forth across her nipple. She arched into his hand and temporarily forgot getting his jacket off as she reached out to drag her palm over his erection.

He let out a groan.

"I can't get your coat off," she said. "I have to touch you."

He let go of her for a moment and pulled both the jacket and his long sleeved shirt off over his head. He reached out for her again, and he pulled her sweater off over her head\. Her bra was soaking wet. Her panties were wet too, but that had nothing to do with the rain. He unbuttoned her jeans, slid the zipper down, and shoved them off of her in one smooth movement.

She tried to get the pants off over her shoes. It wasn't going to happen. He reached out to pick her up, stepped on the pants, and pulled both pants and shoes off as she wrapped her arms and legs around him.

The front placket of his jeans rubbed against her as he moved through the darkened room, sending jolts of sensation through her. This was a new record for her; a couple of hours between "Hi, my name is Kendall" and ending up in her underwear in a hotel room (crazed with lust) didn't usually happen. She wasn't into one-night stands, but she wanted Drew. He wanted her as well, if the erection straining against the zipper on his jeans was any indicator. They had to get warm anyway. Stripping to the skin was sounding better and better, especially when she remembered there were condoms in her handbag.

"I don't do this without protection," she said.

"I don't either, Kendall." He laid her down on the bed, reached into his pocket, and pulled out his wallet. She heard the soft sound of a wrapper hitting the nightstand. "I have a condom too." He grabbed it off the nightstand and put it into her palm. "Would you like to put it on me?"

Would she? That would be a *hell, yes*. She tried to maintain some dignity. It wasn't working. "I want you so badly."

"That's good, because I want you too," he said.

The room was dim, but she heard two thuds as he kicked his shoes off. Next, she heard the zipper sliding on his jeans. She might not be able to see him clearly, but she couldn't wait to run her hands all over those bulging muscles and that gorgeous golden skin.

"Hurry," she said.

His laugh was low and sensual.

Seconds later, they both heard a loud knock at the door.

"Shit. Must be the towels," he muttered. "We'll be right with you," he said.

She resisted the impulse to blurt out a particularly descriptive four-letter word and scrambled out of the bed.

"I'll get it," he said. "You lie down and warm up."

He must have had the vision of a bat; he didn't fall over anything on his way to the door. She heard the door open and an unfamiliar voice.

"Here are the items Ms. Tracy asked us for. I also took the liberty of adding a robe as well. There is another robe hanging in the coat closet to your right."

"Thanks so much," Drew said.

She felt slightly embarrassed that the hotel staff knew she was in here with a man she hadn't checked in with. Hotel staffs were probably used to this kind of thing.

"If you'd like us to dry your clothing, please dial zero and we'll send someone up from housekeeping to get it."

"Please add a tip to my bill for this," Kendall called out.

"That's not necessary," the employee said. "If there's anything else we can do, let us know."

"Thank you. Good night," Drew said.

The door closed, and she heard the sounds of Drew locking the deadbolt. His shadowy form moved through the room again as he dropped the bundle in his arms on top of what must have been the computer desk in the corner. He shoved his pants off. Seconds later, he climbed into the bed and back underneath the blankets.

"It's so cold," she said.

"I think I'd better kiss you again."

Drew made quick work of ridding them both of underwear, soaking wet socks, and she watched him tug the knit cap off his head and send it sailing across the room. She reached up to take his face in her hands, and soft, slightly damp hair slid through her fingers. *Long, soft, slightly damp hair.*

The blond stubble on his face, the piercing cornflower-blue eyes, the brilliant smile, the amazing muscles, *Go Sharks*—all coalesced in a split second in Kendall's memory. She *knew* where she'd seen him before.

Despite the fact the hormones coursing through her screamed in anguish, there was no way she could sleep with this man.

Chapter Two

KENDALL JERKED AWAY from Drew like she'd stuck both of her hands in an open flame. She flung herself out of the cocoon of blankets and Drew's body, fumbling around until her fingers found the switch to the bedside light. The room was lit seconds later, and so was the face she couldn't believe she hadn't recognized immediately.

"You're Drew McCoy," she cried out.

She scooted to the edge of the bed, clutching the sheet around her torso as she went. It was a little late now for modesty. Retaining some shred of dignity might be a good thing.

She'd watched Drew's game film with the coaching staff. She'd seen his commercials for hair products and sports drinks and soup a hundred times before. His contract with the Sharks was done as of the end of football season, and the Miners wanted him to play for them. Drew was San Francisco's number one target in next season's free agency. She'd planned on asking the team's owner to write a big check to Drew and his agent next March. If all that wasn't enough, Drew was eight years younger than she was.

What the hell was wrong with her? It must have been the knit hat covering his famous hair, or finding him in a non-jock hangout like a bookstore. Maybe it was the temporary insanity brought on by an overwhelming surge of hormones.

"Is there a problem?" he said.

"I can't have anything to do with you. I have to go."

He shook his head in adorable confusion. She couldn't think of anything she wanted more right now than to run her fingers through his gorgeous hair.

"This is your hotel room. Where do you think you're going?"

She yanked as much of the sheet off the bed as possible, attempting to wrap it around herself and stand up at the same time. He was simultaneously grabbing at the comforter to shield himself. It didn't work.

She twisted her foot into the bedding while she hurled herself away from him and ended up on the carpet seconds later in a tangle of sheet and limbs, still naked. Her butt hit the floor so hard she almost expected to bounce.

The number-one reason why Kendall didn't engage in one-night stands as a habit hauled himself up on all fours in the middle of the bed. Out of all the guys in the world available for a short-term fling, of all the times in her life she thought that might be an acceptable option, of *course* she'd pick the man that could get her fired or sued.

He grabbed the robe he'd slung over the foot of the bed, scrambled off the mattress, and jammed his arms into it as he advanced on her.

"Are you okay? You went down pretty hard." His eyes skimmed over her. "That's going to leave a mark."

He crouched next to her as he reached out to help her up. She resisted the impulse to stare at golden skin, an eight pack, and a sizable erection. She'd heard Drew didn't lack for dates. He had other things to offer besides the balance in his bank accounts.

"I'm okay," she told him.

She felt a little shaky. She'd probably have a nice bruise later. She was going down all right, and it had nothing to do with sex. It had everything to do with the fact that if anyone from the Miners organization saw him emerging from her room in the next seventy-two hours, she was in the kind of trouble with her employer there was no recovering from. The interim general manager of a NFL team did not sleep with anyone from the opposing team, especially archrivals that hated each other with the heat of a thousand suns. Especially a star player her own organization was more than a little interested in acquiring. *Especially* before a game that would mean the inside track to the playoffs for both teams.

Drew and Kendall would be the Romeo and Juliet of the NFL. Well, without all the dying. Death by 24/7 sports media embarrassment didn't count.

He reached out, grabbed her beneath her armpits and hoisted her off the floor like she weighed nothing.

"I've got you. Let's see if you can stand up," he said.

His warm, gentle hands moved over her, looking for injuries. "Why don't you lean on me for a second here?"

She tried re-wrapping the sheet around her so she could walk away from him while preserving her dignity. It wasn't going to happen. She couldn't stop staring at him. If she let him take her in his arms, she'd be lost. She teetered as she leaned against the hotel room wall.

"I'm . . . I'm fine. I—"

"Hold still," he said. She heard his bare feet slap against the carpeting as he grabbed the second robe out of the coat closet and brought it back to her. "If you don't want to do this, that's your decision, but I don't understand what's wrong."

She struggled into the thick terry robe as she tried to think of a response. He was staring at her as she retrieved the fabric belt and swathed herself in yards of fabric. Judging by his continuing erection, he liked what he saw, even if it was covered up from her neck to below her knees. He licked his bottom lip. Her mouth went dry. Damn it.

Of *course* the most attractive guy she'd been anywhere near a bed with in the past year was completely off-limits.

"You don't recognize me," she said.

"No, I don't," he said. "Is there a problem?"

"You might say that." She finally succeeded in knotting the belt of the robe around her waist, dropped the sheet at her feet and stuck out one hand. "Hi. I'm Kendall Tracy. I'm the interim GM of the San Francisco Miners." His eyes widened in shock. "Nice to meet you."

"You . . . you can't be," he blurted out. "Their GM is one of the owners—"

"He had to step down two weeks ago due to a Securities and Exchange Commission investigation."

The past two weeks in the Miners' front office had been as fun as a root canal without Novocain\ but she wasn't discussing that with anyone outside of the team ownership.

She knew he must have been somewhat smart if he wanted to spend his evening listening to Carl Sagan's biographer in a bookstore, but right now, he was having trouble verbalizing his thoughts.

It took a few seconds, but she saw a smirk spread over his face.

"You . . . you run the Miners? You couldn't get a job with a better team?" The arch rivalry had reared its ugly head.

"A better team, huh? We beat you how many times last season?" she said, but she smiled at him.

He laughed out loud.

"We'll be handing your team their asses on Sunday, Kendall. You're in our house now."

Drew was still holding her hand. She snatched it away. She couldn't believe he didn't recognize her. She'd got an avalanche of press over her new job in the past month. Right now, though, getting Drew out of her room (and hopefully, out of the hotel and undetected) was first on her agenda.

"I'm guessing this means our night is over," he said.

DREW CONSIDERED HIMSELF a pretty easygoing, uncomplicated guy. He wasn't a slave to fashion. He wore what felt good. When he had an attraction as strong as the one he was currently experiencing toward the robe-clad woman two feet from him (and he knew the feeling was mutual), he acted on it.

He'd like to hurl himself back into Kendall's warm and dry bed for a while, preferably with her. He understood the word "no." He also understood he wasn't going to be able to go outside and grab a cab to get home while commando beneath a stolen Westin Hotels bathrobe. He could call one of his teammates to haul his ass out of here, but again, buck naked in a hotel bathrobe in the middle of a windstorm: The resulting cell phone photos would be trending on Twitter before he made it out of the parking lot.

He tried pulling his jeans on; they were so wet he couldn't get them over his thighs. She'd vanished into the bathroom.

"Hey, Kendall," he called out.

She emerged from the bathroom a few seconds later. God, she was beautiful. Her cheeks were pink with lust, embarrassment, or both. She'd brushed her hair. The faint scent of green apples drifted toward him again. Her mouth was a little swollen from his kisses too. If he started thinking about what she was or was not wearing underneath that bathrobe, he'd have to go stand in a cold shower for a while.

She glanced at the jeans stuck halfway up his thighs. She was having a tough time tearing her eyes away from him.

"I'm guessing you might need something dry to wear," she said.

He kicked the jeans off and sat down on the couch, tucking the robe around him so he didn't flash her.

"Maybe you have a pair of sweat pants and a T-shirt I could borrow in that suitcase."

"I have yoga pants and—"

"I'll take them," he said.

"They might not fit."

She was probably half his size. They weren't going to fit at all, but beggars couldn't be choosers.

"I'll make it work. Don't they stretch?"

She turned to the soft-sided suitcase on a rack by the dresser. "Let's see here." She pulled out a pair of black, short-ish yoga pants and a bright orange racing bra thing. "I'm going to have to find you a T-shirt of some kind. I don't wear them for yoga. I—"

He reached out to take the yoga pants out of her hand. "I'll try these first."

He'd had more than one girlfriend who wore these. The brand fit like a second skin, and whatever it was they were constructed out of clung to a woman's ass. His ex-girlfriend hadn't made it to a single yoga class when she'd worn them in front of him. He'd removed them as quickly as possible.

He stuck one foot into the pants. He could at least pull them over his thighs. They covered him to just above his kneecap. He was used to wearing short pants on a football field, so this wasn't a problem. He'd look like an idiot, but he'd be covered.

A grin crossed Kendall's face. "Maybe they will fit after all."

He stuck his other foot in and slowly drew the fabric over his thighs and up to his waist. Surprisingly, there was a limit to spandex. He heard Kendall let out a gasp and glanced up to see even more color spreading over her cheekbones. She swallowed hard.

His package looked massive as he looked down. The fabric outlined every ridge and every contour. The entire city of Bellevue was about to learn he was circumcised. His dick wasn't calming down anytime soon with soft fabric rubbing against it—soft fabric that held Kendall's green apple scent. Those tights-wearing ballet guys had nothing on him. Holy shit. The shorter pants were the least of his problems. If he went out like this, he'd get arrested for indecent exposure. He wrapped the robe around himself again.

"This may not work," he said.

She still regarded him warily, but he saw her lips curve into a reluctant smile. "It seems to be working just fine."

"So, let me get this straight," he said. The yoga pants were cutting off his circulation. He wrestled them off himself and shook them out. Suffice it to say he was buying Kendall another pair; he'd stretched them out. She watched him fold them and put the soft bundle on the computer table next to the couch he sat down on. He turned to face her again and took a step in her direction. He stared into her silvery-gray eyes. "You want me. I want you."

"We can't do this—"

"We're consenting adults stuck in a hotel room together."

"That doesn't mean we have to act on our every impulse," she said, but she wouldn't look him in the eye. He would never force any woman to be with him, but her body language told him she was wavering. She swayed toward him. He moved a little closer. She still wouldn't look into his eyes. He reached out for her hand. She didn't yank it away.

His voice was soft and beguiling. "How are we going to resolve this?" He rubbed the back of her hand with his thumb. She still wouldn't look up at him, and she bit her lower lip.

Her voice was low and unsteady. "We're not stuck," she said. "All we have to do is find you some dry clothes. I don't have a rental car this time, so I'll ask the front desk to call you a cab." She dropped his hand, hurried over to the bedside table, and picked up the phone's handset to make a call.

"Hello. May I talk to housekeeping, please?" she said.

Drew spent the next few minutes listening to Kendall's side of the conversation, which was increasingly comical. She was polite but persistent. Even a luxury hotel had a problem coming up with clothing that would fit a six foot four, 250-pound linebacker at almost midnight.

"Is it possible to wash and dry his clothing? How long will that take?" She listened to the answer, and the only indicator Drew had that Kendall didn't like the answer she got was her folded lips. "There has to be some clothing he could wear to get home in. Is there a lost and found? How about an extra employee uniform?" She listened for a moment. "Got it. We'll take whatever you have, and thank you for the extra effort." She hung up the phone and turned to Drew again. "They're sending the manager up with clothes for you, and they're calling you a cab."

"Thanks."

The hotel had superior soundproofing, but he could hear the storm raging outside. The lights flickered. He knew there were generators, so power outage wasn't really a concern. The power might be out at his house, though.

Kendall gave him a nod. She picked up the abandoned sheet on the floor, shoved the comforter off the bed, and tried to re-spread the sheet. "I can never get these on the first try," she muttered.

Drew covered the room in a few strides to the opposite side of the bed, grabbing the sheet in both hands and spreading it across again more evenly. "How's that?"

"Better. Thank you."

She continued smoothing wrinkles out of the bedding, tucking the sheet in as she went. Drew spread the downy comforter over the top of the smooth sheets and fluffed the pillows. He didn't typically perform domestic chores on what could still be considered a date, but he liked watching Kendall's attention to detail. Her brows knit as she straightened the pillows and made sure the comforter was even. She'd be sleeping in the bed alone, but she wanted to make sure she was comfortable.

She glanced up from her painstaking attention to bedding perfection and said, "We need to talk."

He straightened to his full height and forced himself to smile. There wasn't an adult anywhere who enjoyed hearing the words "We need to talk," but he would take whatever was coming like a man.

She brushed hair out of her eyes and shoved her hands inside the pockets of the robe. Kendall's poised and sophisticated veneer melted away as he saw hesitation and a flash of sadness in her expression.

"You're right. I am attracted to you," she said. "You're interesting, funny, and I want to keep talking with you. I don't think I've ever met anyone like you, and I've wanted to for a long time now. At the same time, getting involved with you is professional suicide." She let out a long sigh and looked into his eyes at last. "It won't help your career, either, and maybe that should be a sign to both of us."

"I feel the same way about you," he said. "Why is it anyone else's business but ours?"

"You know it would be," she said. Her voice dropped again. "I wish it could be different."

They stared at each other for a few seconds. She was right. The pull of attraction was almost overpowering, and this never happened to him so fast after meeting a woman. He shouldn't take the chance that they wouldn't be found out if they tried to meet each other in secret. "I understand," he said.

He gathered his wet clothes off the hotel room floor, folding them enough to cram them into the plastic bag the hotel typically collected laundry in. They heard a knock at the door.

"I'll get it," he told her. She'd wrapped her arms around herself.

The hotel manager handed him another plastic bag. "It's not stylish, but it will work. If you could return these at your convenience, we'd appreciate it." Drew reached out to shake his hand. "Are you sure you want to go out in the storm tonight? We have a room available and I can offer you the walk-in rate."

"I need to get home," he told the guy. "Thanks for the offer and for the clothes."

"If there's anything else I can do, please let me know."

Drew hurried into the bathroom, shut the door behind him, and started pulling items out of the bag. A doorman's uniform and a worn but clean Dallas T-shirt that must have been left behind by another guest. He'd still have to go commando, but if he could get downstairs and into a cab, he'd be home in fifteen minutes. The guy had been nice enough to include a small bag of hotel toiletries, including a comb. He used the covered black elastic he always wore on one wrist to pull his hair into a ponytail.

He yanked the polyester pants on, jammed his feet back into his soaking wet cross trainers, and pulled the T-shirt on over his head. He wondered if the team fine would be bigger for the obscene fit of Kendall's yoga pants or the fact he might be photographed in another team's merchandise. He left the uniform's tunic unbuttoned. It didn't fit well across his chest.

He stared at himself in the mirror. He looked ridiculous. He didn't want to leave, but he had no choice. It was best for them both if they stayed away from each other.

KENDALL STOOD UP from the couch when Drew emerged from the men's room. A mismatched hotel bellman's uniform and ratty old T-shirt looked spectacular on him. He grabbed his wet jacket off of the couch and shrugged into it.

She handed him the plastic bag with the new book he'd bought in it. His fingers brushed hers. It felt like she'd stuck her wet fingers in a power socket. The shock of attraction and lust forced her to struggle for words.

"I . . . I put the Malcolm Gladwell book in there too. Don't worry about getting it back to me. I hope you'll enjoy it."

"I think I will." He moved a little closer. There was an invisible force field pulling her into his warmth. "How about a hug?"

She knew any further physical contact with him was a stupid, stupid move, but she did it anyway. His hold on her was gentle. The jacket was damp, but she didn't care. He laid his stubbly cheek against hers and said into her ear, "I hope we'll see each other again soon."

She relished the feeling of her arms around his neck, the cool brush of his hair against her skin, and the powerful muscles beneath her hands.

"Sunday afternoon," she whispered.

"I'll be the one in the Sharks uniform."

"I'll be the one in the Miners' suite." She hauled in a breath. "Good luck."

"You too." His mouth touched hers in a sweet and fleeting kiss. She wanted more. "Should I call you when I retire from the league?"

She should let go of him. She should push him out of the hotel room, lock the door, and pretend like she never wanted to see him again. She couldn't. Instead, she nodded.

"Don't say goodbye," he murmured. He stroked her cheek with one big hand. He turned to walk away.

She watched the hotel room door shut behind him.

Chapter Three

DREW ENDURED THE equivalent of Mr. Toad's Wild Ride through the streets of Bellevue on his way home. The cab driver was skilled, but he was having a tough time navigating standing water, streets strewn with tree branches, and random debris that had blown out of people's yards. Drew heard his phone chirping with e-mails and text messages a few times during the trip home, but he ignored it. He was too busy willing the towering evergreens bent almost double in the wind to stay standing and not hit the car he was traveling in if and when they fell.

He reached into his pocket when the cab driver pulled up in front of his house and handed the guy the two fifty-dollar bills he had in his wallet for a fifteen-dollar trip.

"If I had any idea it was this bad, I would have stayed at the hotel. I'm sorry you had to be out in this. Thank you for driving me home," he told the guy. "I hope you'll get back there safely."

"I'll be fine." The guy stared at the money for a moment. "Would you like your change?"

"No. It's all yours." He unsnapped his seatbelt. "Thank you again."

The guy gestured at Drew's front door. "Get inside where you're safe, sir. Have a nice evening."

Drew spotted his teammate Derrick's car in the driveway as he got out of the cab. The wind blew him sideways up the front walk of his house. He'd been in Seattle for a couple of years now; he'd never seen weather like this before. The wind howled, rain sluiced down in sheets, and he jumped at the rumble of unexpected thunder: It was all he could do to put one foot in front of the other right now.

He grabbed his house keys out of the uniform pants pocket and promptly dropped them onto the mat. "Shit." He heard thunder rolling again, and the sizzle of lightning lit up the night. He jammed the key in the lock, turned it, and shoved against the door with all his might. It swung open. He managed to get inside the front door of his house, shoved it closed, and checked the alarm system keypad to his left by reflex. It was disabled.

Relief washed over him. He was home, he was safe, and despite his stupidity in driving over in the first place, Derrick (the knucklehead) was safe as well. He could hear the sound of someone (actually, *someones*) playing video games from his family room.

He laid the bag with the books on the hallway table and dropped the bag with his wet clothing next to it. He'd deal with all of it later.

He grabbed his phone out of his pocket as he padded on almost silent rubber soles toward his family room. Seven texts, four of which were from Derrick. Maybe he'd let Derrick live. He heard his teammate Seth Taylor's voice.

"Where the hell do you think McCoy is, anyway?"

Drew heard Derrick answering Seth. "Damned if I know. His car's still in the garage. I talked to him at four o'clock. I *told* him it was double-points weekend on Xbox Live. Of course it's the weekend the fucking power goes out."

"Nice to see you could both stop by," Drew said as he rounded the corner. The two men sitting on his family room couch were staring intently at his flat-screen TV and working their game controllers. Good. If they remained focused on the game, they wouldn't notice his ridiculous outfit. His coffee table was festooned with the remains of two large Pagliacci pizzas, dirty paper plates, and empty beer bottles. They'd been here a while. Of course there were no leftovers for him.

"Shit, McCoy, where the hell you been? I told you my mama and grandma are staying in my condo right now. Can't game while they're there," Derrick said.

Seth shook his head. "I love his grandma, but she was reading Bible verses out loud while we were trying to get to the next level on *Titanfall*."

"Grandma's worried about our spiritual lives," Derrick said. "My mama wanted me to take her to some church revival thing tonight. I love her, but it wasn't going to happen."

There were two grocery bags on Drew's kitchen island. Maybe there was something edible in there. One of the bags contained two six-packs of microbrew. He glanced into the other bag, moving aside two bags of Juanita's tortilla chips to spot four large bags of Skittles, a bag of mini Reese's Peanut Butter Cups and the biggest bag of plain M&M's he'd ever seen. It was carb-loading at its finest. He was going to have to look through his own refrigerator for sustenance, it seemed.

The guys still hadn't glanced over at him. They might put the game controllers down if some young, beautiful women walked into his family room. Then again, probably not.

"How'd you get out of that?" Drew said.

Derrick stabbed at one of the buttons on the game controller while Seth let out a groan.

"I gave five thousand dollars to the church's building fund this afternoon. My mama acted like I gave her some diamonds. I also ordered them dinner from Lot No. 3 and told them they could watch whatever they wanted on pay-per-view," Derrick said.

"Doesn't your grandma like watching MMA?" Seth said.

A smile that could only be called calculating spread over Derrick's mouth. "Why, yes. She does."

"She seems like such a harmless, sweet little old lady," Seth muttered. Derrick laughed out loud.

The Sharks had acquired middle linebacker Seth Taylor in a blockbuster trade with San Diego just before the start of the regular season, unloading a rookie who wasn't cutting it at the same time. The defense kept improving, which Drew loved. Great defenses equaled championships. Seth wasn't a bad guy, either. He'd been quickly accepted into the group of single Sharks that spent most of their free time gaming, clubbing, or both.

Derrick's comments were punctuated by the chirping of an incoming text. Derrick grabbed it off of the coffee table and stabbed at the phone's screen with one finger while continuing to play. "It's my mama. She wants to know if we're safe." He tapped in a short message and put his phone back down on the table.

"It's late. Don't they sleep?" Seth said.

"Does your mama sleep when she thinks you're up to no good?" Derrick said.

"I'm guessing all the pizza's gone," Drew said.

"There's an entire extra pepperoni and sausage in the fridge," Seth said.

Drew grabbed a cookie sheet, shoved a few slices of pizza on it to reheat them, and turned on the oven.

The TV set went blank. Drew heard groans and some choice obscenities from Seth and Derrick as they worked the game controllers.

"Goddammit, did Xbox Live crash?"

"What the fuck. I had the high score!"

Seth jumped up from the couch and tried rebooting the gaming system. It wasn't coming back on. Drew could get upstairs, change, and rejoin them before they noticed what he was wearing. Maybe the late night, the storm (and three beers each) made them less observant.

He was wrong.

Derrick dropped the game controller onto the coffee table and whipped around on the couch to face the kitchen. Derrick looked, and then he stared at Drew.

"Hey, big guy. Did you go shopping in a dumpster earlier? What the hell is THAT?" He indicated Drew's outfit with a nod in his direction and let out a booming laugh. "Does Coach know you're wearing another team's merchandise?"

Seth turned to look at Drew. "Dallas. You're joking, aren't you?" Seth said.

"My clothes were wet. I needed something to change into."

"How wet were they, and what the hell were you doing earlier?" Derrick got up from the couch and moved closer. The grin bloomed over his face like a flower filmed in slow motion. "Nice logo. You were at the Westin, you dawg."

"I was not—"

"Our boy got laid, Derrick," Seth said.

"Doing the walk of shame, were you? This calls for a beer." Derrick vaulted off of the couch and invaded the kitchen. "Do we know her?"

Telling them nothing happened would do no good. It was also a lie, but he knew they wouldn't believe it. He tried it anyway. "I told you. My clothes were drenched. I borrowed these."

"Borrowed, huh? Is that what it's called now? I'm surprised you're not in a better mood, McCoy," Derrick said.

"What's her name?" Seth said. "Are you going to see her again?"

Derrick strolled back into the family room gripping three cold and already opened beers. He handed them around. "Let's drink to Drew's love life."

"Let's not," Seth said. "He gets more than the rest of us do."

"Come on. Don't you have a girlfriend?" Drew said to Seth.

"Bad topic," Derrick warned.

"Yeah, I have a girlfriend." Seth didn't elaborate.

"And she's why you're here playing video games with two of your teammates on a Friday night," Drew said.

"Uh huh. And I'm about to beat your ass at *Madden* again if we can find the game DVD."

DREW TRUDGED INTO his bedroom after one AM. He'd made sure the guys were settled in guest rooms before hitting the sack himself. He should have been in bed hours ago. The storm raged on, though, and he couldn't send Derrick and Seth out in it. Luckily, he had plenty of room for the guys at his place until things calmed down a bit outside. He pulled on clean, dry pajama pants and a T-shirt.

His teammates gave him shit on the regular for buying a 5800-square foot, five bedroom family house as a single guy. Whatever. They seemed to end up at his place a lot. He liked doing the yard work, and there was somewhere for his parents, three siblings, and their spouses and kids to stay when they visited. Truthfully, he bought the house because he could see his future wife and kids here. He'd like to think he could be lucky (and persuasive) enough to end up with a woman like Kendall.

She was beautiful, but that wasn't the most attractive thing about her. She was sophisticated, intelligent, interesting, had a sense of humor, and she loved books. He also had to admit he wanted to spend some time in her bed; she pulled him toward her like metal to a magnet. Unfortunately, it didn't look like he'd be spending any time at all with the lovely Ms. Tracy anytime soon.

He wanted to find someone he could spend the rest of his life getting to know, just like his parents had. His mom and dad had been happily married for thirty-five years now. His mom had dinner on the table every night at six. Her whole world was his dad and Drew's brother and sisters, and he wanted the same thing: a woman who wanted to make his house a home.

If that made him old-fashioned, so be it. He loved the idea of coming home every day to a beaming woman, dinner on the table, and a few little rug rats to liven the place up.

He was used to hearing the house settle at night while he lay in bed, or the gentle patter of raindrops on the roof. The storm's fury wasn't letting up. Water slammed into the windows and broken tree branches thumped onto his house. He wondered if sleeping in a room with a gigantic clerestory window facing those trees was such a great idea tonight. Maybe he should move to another room, at least temporarily.

He wondered if Kendall was asleep yet. He needed to stop thinking about her, but he couldn't think of anything (or anyone) else. He couldn't stop remembering how she felt in his arms.

KENDALL PULLED ON a nightshirt a few minutes after Drew left and crawled into the bed. Normally, she didn't mind sleeping alone, but tonight, she didn't want to. She knew he couldn't stay with her, but she wished he had. Even if they didn't make love, she would have had someone to talk to while she tried to fall asleep. His house was only a couple of miles away, he'd said. He was probably already there, safe and warm in his own bed. She wondered if he slept with his hair in a ponytail, or did he let it fan out over the pillows? She sat up, adjusted her pillows once more, and sank into them. She heaved a long sigh.

He was incredibly sexy. Even more than that, he was interesting, funny, smart, and caring. And she'd kicked him out of her hotel room. She meant what she'd said to him about any involvement between them being career suicide for her, but she couldn't believe she'd met a guy that had every possible quality she'd ever wanted and he was off-limits.

Again.

Maybe she'd get sleepy if she read a little. She reached out for the Kindle on her bedside table and reconsidered. She'd better check her e-mail one more time tonight. Who was she kidding—she wasn't settling down any time soon. She was still thinking about Drew and how different her evening would have been if she'd asked him to stay. The wrapped condom he'd had in his wallet was still on the nightstand. He'd forgotten his slouchy knit hat; it was still lying on the floor in the corner of the room. It probably smelled like him too. At least she'd sent the books home with him . . .

"Oh, shit," she said to herself. "My dad's book—and my phone!"

She remembered slipping the phone into the plastic bag with the new book she was giving to her dad and rolling up the top to seal the contents before they'd set out for the hotel from the coffee shop. She'd thought putting the phone in a plastic bag was better than carrying it in her pocket, and it was raining so hard she was afraid the things in her handbag would get wet. She jumped out of bed, hurried across the hotel room, and dug through her handbag.

The small paper bags containing the salted caramel bars were a little smashed, but the bars were still edible. Everything *but* her iPhone was in her handbag. Maybe she left the phone in her coat pocket after all. She grabbed the still-damp coat off the corner of the couch and went through the pockets. No phone.

She flipped on every light in her hotel room and looked everywhere. No phone. It wasn't worth calling the front desk to ask if she'd dropped the phone outside or in the lobby on the way up to her room. She knew where it was, and she also knew she had no way of getting it back: It wasn't like she could walk across the field on Sunday afternoon and ask Drew McCoy if he'd seen it.

She'd have to make do until she could get another

one. She couldn't imagine how she was going to explain this to the Miners' front office, either.

THIRTY-SEVEN HOURS LATER, the Sharks were playing the Miners in Sharks Stadium. Sharks players and fans had been anticipating this game since the season started. The winner would have first place in the division and an easy path to the postseason, which was always a great place to be in early October. It was a perfect day for football: Cotton-candy quality clouds dotted an impossibly blue sky while the sun warmed the sold-out stadium.

Drew spotted Kendall standing on the sidelines. She'd evidently abandoned the team suite to enjoy the crisp fall day with her colleagues and was having an animated discussion with a few of them while the teams lined up on the field for the kickoff.

He saw her laugh at something someone said to her. The guys standing with her were in suits and ties. She wore black pants, a team logo jacket, and a silver-colored silky-looking scarf tucked into her neckline. The rain-washed air put color into her cheeks. She brushed the bangs out of her eyes with one gloved hand. She was gorgeous, and it took everything he had to not run across the field and kiss her again.

There were a hundred women in the stadium right now that would love to have a cup of coffee with him, see a movie, have dinner, or anything else he could possibly dream up. He couldn't stop staring at Kendall on the opposite side of the field, though. If he didn't knock it off, one of his teammates or the coach was going to notice, and he'd be in deep shit.

She'd told him "no," and he should accept that. She wasn't the first woman he'd ever met, and she wouldn't be the last. His eyeballs didn't seem to get that memo, though. He kept glancing over to stare at her. He forced himself to pay attention to the game instead.

The first two quarters of the game went faster than usual. The Sharks' defense wasn't allowing the Miners to advance the ball, which was always a plus. He'd sacked the Miners' quarterback twice. He wanted their unprotected quarterback to remember his name as the kid limped off of the field. Maybe the Miners should have spent some of the money they forked out for his overpaid ass on some decent offensive linemen instead. The Sharks' defense was manhandling them; the score was 14–3. The halftime whistle blew, and he joined his teammates and coaches for the jog into the Sharks' locker room.

He snagged a few orange sections and a cold bottle of Gatorade off of the cart that sat on one side of the room. If he could manage to get a few calories down while he listened to the coach, he was always better off during the second half.

Seth plunked himself down on the bench next to Drew and elbowed him in the side. "Trying to burn a hole through the Miners' GM with your eyes or something, McCoy?"

Drew had crammed an orange section into his mouth. "Mhmm?" *Shit.* This would teach him.

Seth leaned closer. "You stared at her after every play. She's staring at you too. Is there something you'd like to share with the class?"

"Fuck, no."

"At least you have something to look at. Damn, this game's boring. I could be jerking off out there and they still wouldn't get a first down," Seth said.

Derrick choked on what looked like half a bottle of Gatorade. Drew pounded him on the back until he quit coughing.

Seth shook his head.

"The Miners will make second half adjustments," Derrick warned Drew. "We both might have something to do. Stick with us, will ya?"

Drew was saved from a response by the coach's beginning his typical halftime instructions and two minute motivational speech. Twenty minutes later, he'd managed to down a few more orange sections, drink the Gatorade, hit the bathroom, and jog back out onto the field with the team.

Kendall was gone from her spot on the sidelines. Maybe she was getting a bite to eat or taking care of some business. He'd liked the idea she wasn't hiding in the suite, and he was oddly agitated that she wasn't on the sidelines right now. For a woman he was determined to ignore, she was sure taking up a lot of space in his head. He took his place for the warm-up exercises and put himself through the stretching routines he could do in his sleep. He glanced over at the Miners' sideline again just before the second half kickoff. She wasn't there.

He glanced up at the visiting team's suite a few times during the second half as well. He didn't see her.

Derrick sidled up next to him while the second-string

offense was schooling the Miners' defense in the fourth quarter. Coach wasn't going to play his starters when the score was 28–3 and the Miners hadn't succeeded in getting a first down since the second quarter.

"So, you've been looking for someone the entire game. Want to tell me about it?"

"No." Drew concentrated on the field once more.

"I *will* find out who she is, dawg," Derrick said.

Drew continued to ignore him. Derrick chuckled and moved away.

The final score remained Sharks 28, Miners 3. Drew had showered and dressed in his street clothes. He'd made a short appearance in front of the media to address the two sacks and eight tackles he'd made during the game, and he signed some Sharks merchandise that would be taken to the Miners' locker room by request. Someone's son, daughter, niece, or nephew would end up with a team-autographed T-shirt or football. All teams did it; the Sharks had already received the bag of autographed Miners merchandise for distribution a few minutes ago.

Typically, Drew would be joining the group of players making their way to a local restaurant for dinner after a win. He enjoyed celebrating as much as the next guy, but right now, he wasn't in the mood. He was happy about the win. He was always happy after a win. He was frustrated over his inability to be a little less obvious with the staring at Kendall for starters. No matter how intrigued he was by her, nothing was happening between them until he was out of the league.

Maybe he'd feel better after a good night's sleep. After

tomorrow morning's post-game medical checks for injuries, he could burn off some of his frustration by cleaning up the storm damage in his backyard. He had other things to do with his time than moon over an unattainable woman.

Zach Anderson stopped by his locker as Drew picked up the overnight bag he brought to home games.

"Hey, come on out with us. We're going to Jak's Grill in Laurelhurst. Cameron's meeting us there too," Zach said. He grinned at Drew. "You know you want a big, juicy steak and a beer."

"It sounds great, but I think I'm going to have to pass this time."

"Other plans, huh?"

"You could say that. Give your woman a hug from me." Drew got to his feet and gave Zach an elaborate handshake. "I'll see you tomorrow morning."

Drew stopped on the way home and picked up a to-go dinner. He'd watch some mindless TV, have a beer, and go to bed early with the book Kendall had given him.

He pulled into his garage, disabled the alarm system, and walked into his house. He dropped the overnight bag in his laundry room. He'd unpack it later. He moved through the kitchen and turned into the hallway by his front door to scoop up the book he wanted to start reading.

As he picked up the plastic bag with the two books, he heard a phone ringing. He unfurled the top of the bag, pulled the phone out, hit "talk," and said, "Hello?"

"Is this Drew? It's Kendall Tracy. You have my phone."

Chapter Four

DESPITE HIS EARLIER resolve to forget her and move on with his life, Drew's heart skipped a beat as she continued talking.

"I put the phone in the bag before we left the coffee shop. I've tried to call a few times, and I wondered if it maybe fell out or something on your way home the other night." He heard her laugh a little. "It's like losing an appendage, isn't it?"

"I left the bag in the entryway of my house the other night. I didn't hear it ringing before now," he said.

"Don't worry about it. How could *you* know I stupidly stuck my phone in there?"

"It wasn't stupid. You wanted it to stay dry," he assured her. "I hoped I wouldn't have to buy a new phone," she said. "Plus, I was worried about losing my contacts list."

The conversation was polite, between two people

that had met before but weren't planning on a further relationship. He noted that the phone was almost out of charge and turned back toward his kitchen to plug it in before it died.

"Your contacts are safe, but I'd better get this on a charger before it shuts off. Are you still in Seattle?"

"We're at the airport. The players are boarding right now. I'm using my assistant's phone." He heard something read over the PA in the background, and she said, "May I call you back when we arrive?"

"Of course. Would you like me to overnight the phone to the Miners' headquarters? It'll get there on Tuesday."

She sounded a little out of breath, like she was running. "Don't send the phone there. I'll call you with my address. I'd be happy to pay for the overnight shipping."

"It's not a problem—"

"We're boarding now. Thank you so much," she said.

"You're welcome. Have a good flight, Kendall."

"Okay. Thank you. Bye."

He heard the phone she was talking on disconnect, and silence.

KENDALL SETTLED INTO her airplane seat as she handed her assistant's phone back to her.

"Thanks for the loan," she said.

Sydney grinned at her in response. "I could have gone to the Apple store for you before the game started."

"They didn't open until eleven AM, and we were already at Sharks Stadium. My phone will be back on Tuesday."

Kendall tried to pretend like her heart wasn't still racing after a few minutes of conversation with Drew. She kept her voice casual. "It's a good thing the hotel bellman who found it is an honest guy."

"He could have sold your phone and the contacts on eBay for a fortune."

The guy who still had it could spend at least an evening scrolling through those contacts. She hoped he wouldn't. The temptation might be too much to resist, though. He wouldn't care about obtaining the cell phone numbers of the Miners' front office. He might be interested in the contact info of others in the league, or giving her ex-boyfriend a call to chit-chat. The ex could be a problem. She almost groaned out loud.

Drew would know who her ex was. Most pro athletes, especially football players, would know him. Unfortunately, she hadn't at the time she'd met him. Tony Kelly was a sports apparel and shoes manufacturer. He'd picked her up at the ESPYs after-party two years ago. He was handsome, interesting, wealthy, charming, —and she didn't find out until almost six months later—*married*. He'd started his business out of his garage fifteen years ago with two partners, one of whom was a former pro athlete and the public face of the business. Tony handled the behind-the-scenes stuff: dealing with the factories that made their merchandise, suppliers, and the stores that carried them. They were the hottest name in shoes and apparel, and most athletes asked to sign an endorsement deal with them did so quickly. Drew had chosen to sign with Under Armour instead. She wondered why.

Before she met Tony, she'd never had much time to date. She'd started working for the Miners after school and on the weekends at sixteen, and climbing the corporate ladder after she graduated from Wharton Business School took most of her time and energy. She couldn't believe she was lucky enough to meet a guy that was the living personification of her fantasies. She should have known it was too good to be true.

Tony lived in the San Francisco suburbs, like her. She'd been to his place, which looked out over San Francisco Bay. There wasn't a trace in the professionally decorated home of the wife and two under-five kids who lived in Connecticut. He made frequent business trips, but she never dreamed he was going "home" on those flights, supposedly to suppliers and buyers on the East Coast. She found out about his wife and family when Tony's wife called her at work one day and asked if she'd like to be named in their divorce filing. Kendall dumped him minutes later.

She couldn't believe she'd been as stupid as every other mid-thirties single woman who met a guy that was everything she'd ever hoped for and believed his line of BS as a result. She flinched at the memory.

Sydney leaned over the seat across the aisle and said, "I have an extra blanket. Want it?"

The air in the cabin was still somewhat chilly, but Kendall wasn't that cold.

"I'm fine. Thanks." She reached out for the Kindle

she'd stuffed into the seat back and waited for the pilot to announce it was okay to turn on electronic devices. She'd left the work in her briefcase for a change. She'd be home again in ninety minutes, and shortly after she bought a disposable phone at the local grocery store, she'd be talking to Drew.

THREE AND A half hours later, Drew was restlessly prowling his house. He'd tried reading a book. He attempted answering his e-mail. Video games weren't even a distraction. He was always keyed up after a game, but tonight's edginess was unusual for him. He should have gone out with the guys. A good dinner and a drink or two would have gone a long way to helping him settle down a bit.

He jumped a little when he felt Kendall's phone vibrate in his pocket. He pulled it out and stared at a number with a Los Angeles area code. She'd said she would call him; he'd better answer. He hit "talk" and said, "Kendall's phone."

"Hello," the man on the other end said. "Who's this?"

"Kendall has stepped away for a moment. May I take a message?"

"I thought her assistant was a woman." The guy let out a breath. "It's Rick Thomason. I'm Sherman Washington's agent. I understand the Miners are looking to make a change at the strong safety position. Would you ask her to give me a call at her earliest convenience?"

Drew wondered if the Sharks' front office knew

Sherm was doing a little shopping ahead of free agency. He shouldn't be surprised by this; he was used to teammates who were there one season and gone the next. He was a bit surprised at any Shark voluntarily going to the Miners.

"I'll do that. Does she have your number?"

"You must be new. She talked with me last week," the guy said and hung up.

He walked into the kitchen and pulled the refrigerator door open. A piece of fruit might hit the spot before he went to bed. Who was he kidding? He wouldn't sleep until he talked with Kendall again. He hoped for a little more conversation. He was also a bit concerned about Thomason's calling her at ten PM Sunday night on the West Coast. Did he want to talk about his client, or was he about to ask Kendall out on a date?

The cell phone in his other pocket vibrated, and he pulled it out. The display showed his parents were calling from their home in Wisconsin. He knew what time they went to bed. Midnight their time was too damn late for a social call.

He dragged breath into his lungs and hit "talk." "Mom?"

"Son, it's your dad. How are you doing?"

"I'm fine. How are you?" He grabbed an apple out of the crisper. "It's pretty late there. Is everything okay?"

"We're all doing well. Everyone came over for dinner earlier, and your nephew Hunter took his first steps. Your mother is thrilled."

"He'll be running before football season is over,"

Drew said, ignoring the pang he felt every time he heard about the family things he missed during the season. He went home to visit during the offseason, but he didn't get to see the first teeth/first steps/ /first bike ride and the other "firsts" his nieces and nephews experienced. Maybe his sister had taken some pictures with her cell phone camera. He heard his dad's low chuckle.

"Probably. Son, we heard there was a storm in Seattle a couple of days ago. Everything looked normal during the game broadcast. How are you doing?"

"The house has a generator, so I was fine. There's some downed branches and stuff in my yard. Most of the people who lost power are online again." He let out a long breath. "I expect extreme weather in Wisconsin. I don't usually see it in Seattle."

"The newscasters said it was odd."

What was odd was his dad's calling him at close to midnight his time to chat about the weather. His mom was usually where the chatty phone calls originated from. She wanted to tell him all about what his family was doing and how they were looking forward to seeing him soon.

"Hey, Dad, did Mom go to bed already?"

"She was pretty tired after cleaning up after everyone earlier," his dad said. "She sends her love."

"I love her too. Dad, don't you have to get to bed yourself pretty soon? You have to work tomorrow, right?"

"I do. I guess I'd better hit the hay." His dad was quiet for ten seconds or so. "We miss you, son."

"And I miss you, Dad. Give Mom a hug for me."

"I'll do that."

Drew heard his dad's phone click off and stared at his own phone. Something was wrong. His dad was in bed every night by ten. He awoke at five AM each morning, whether it was a workday or not. It was too late to call back tonight. Maybe he should call tomorrow morning, just to make sure nobody was sick or something else happened he should know about.

He rinsed off the apple, grabbing the slicer his ex-girlfriend bought him out of a drawer. He dumped the apple slices onto a napkin so he wouldn't dirty a plate and sat down at his kitchen table. The thought that there was something wrong at his parents' house nagged at him. He took a bite of apple and ran over the last few conversations with his mom in his head. She'd seemed distracted. Even more, she seemed unusually tired. She mentioned the fact his dad complained about a bit more convenience food at dinner now that he and his siblings were out on their own. Drew had laughed it off at the time.

"Mom, you've been spoiling Dad for thirty-five years. I'm sure some grocery store freezer case pasta and jarred spaghetti sauce won't be the worst thing ever."

"Honey, he expects the same kind of dinners we had when you were young. Cooking that amount for two people is ridiculous." She let out a sigh. "I shouldn't complain."

"Tell Dad I keep hoping I'll find someone like you to make *me* some freezer case pasta and jarred spaghetti sauce."

He remembered the little laugh she gave and knew her

cheeks were probably pink with embarrassment. "You're sweet."

"So are you, Mom."

He was so lost in thought that Kendall's phone ringing in his pocket startled him again. He grabbed it out, hit "talk," and said, "Kendall's phone."

"Hi, Drew," she said. "It's nice to talk with you again."

Twenty minutes later, he'd relayed the agent's message, written down her home address and office direct line, and promised to send her phone back by overnight mail to her house. Drew hit "end" on the call and stared into space, lost in thought.

The phone would get to Kendall's house, but if she worked the same hours as the Sharks' GM did, there'd be nobody home to sign for it. He wasn't going to send something so valuable overnight without making sure she got it back safely. She'd asked him twice to *not* send it to the Miners' headquarters. She'd end up going to wherever the delivery facility was located to pick it up, which might be an even bigger problem.

He rubbed his hand over his face and let out a groan. His concern about how he could return her phone in the most convenient way possible wasn't self-serving at all. It had nothing to do with wanting to see her again, or spend a few more minutes chatting and laughing together. He'd go to the same lengths for anyone else.

He shook his head and muttered, "No, I wouldn't."

He got up from the table and put Kendall's phone back on the charger. Maybe he'd figure out a better way to return the phone if he got a good night's sleep.

An hour later, he was still tossing and turning, but he'd made a decision. He sat up in bed and grabbed his smart phone off the bedside table. He pulled up an airline site and bought a ticket to San Jose, the closest airport to Kendall's house.

"Nothing like door-to-door service," he said to himself.

Chapter Five

THE MINERS' GAME in Seattle was a disaster, and it was up to Kendall to get things back on track in her organization. She needed to find a way to accomplish this, as well as to make a dent in the typical workload on a Monday during football season, all without her typical phone. The throwaway phone wasn't cutting it by any stretch of the imagination. Once again, she wished Drew had texted her the tracking number for the overnight delivery. For all she knew, the delivery box was sitting on her front porch right now in full view of passersby who'd want to help themselves to anything important enough to justify overnight delivery.

If she wasn't having enough fun already, she was hungry. And tired. The tired part probably had something to do with the fact that she had lain awake long into the night, thinking about Drew. She went up into the team suite at halftime of Sunday's game because she was staring at him like a twelve-year-old. She'd prefer to keep the drooling over him private.

She needed to wrap things up at the office and go home, but there was too much work still, which wasn't getting done while she continued daydreaming over Drew.

Kendall's assistant, Sydney, skidded into her office with a bakery bag and a paper coffee cup.

"You have to get out of here unless you want to spend the evening waiting at the FedEx place to claim your package," Sydney said. "If you had had it sent to the office, I could have signed for it while you were in the meetings."

"I know." Kendall wasn't sharing with Sydney exactly why that was impossible. She frowned at the updated salary cap numbers on her iPad screen. "There's too much work to do."

Sydney put the bag down on Kendall's desk. "Turkey on whole wheat, thanks to that guy at the deli who has a crush on you. He also made you a triple-shot latte."

"He must have read my mind," Kendall said as she dug her handbag out of her desk drawer. "How much do I owe you?"

"The sandwich was six dollars. The coffee is on the house." Without being asked, Sydney grabbed the soft-sided briefcase Kendall brought to the office each day and started loading it up with Kendall's throwaway cell phone, iPad, and various printed reports to take home. "Eat your lunch while I finish this. You don't want to be sitting on the freeway chowing down."

Sydney was going to graduate from Stanford and rule the world. Right now, Kendall was grateful she'd had the foresight to hire her before some other company snapped her up.

"Is it too soon to give you another raise?" she joked.

"Yeah," Sydney said. They both laughed. "I just paid off my tuition bill for this quarter."

Sydney was in her next-to-last quarter at Stanford. Kendall was hoping that Sydney would choose to stay on with a somewhat reduced work schedule while she went to grad school. She'd need to have a chat with Sydney about her future plans. It was one more thing to add to Kendall's towering to-do list.

Kendall wiped her fingers on a paper napkin and extended her hand across the desk. "Thank you again for saving my life every day."

Sydney's smile was brilliant as she shook Kendall's hand. "It's my pleasure."

Kendall let out a huge sigh of relief an hour later as she drove into the garage of her townhouse. Traffic was a nightmare as usual. Unless the guy had hidden it in the bushes, she didn't see the tell-tale FedEx box leaning up against her front door. Her delivery hadn't arrived yet.

She hurried up the flight of stairs to the main living area of her house, dropped her briefcase on the kitchen table, and kicked off her high heels. She hadn't been home this early on a workday for a while. She could make a big salad for dinner, pour herself a glass of wine, and do some work on the sunny patio in her postage-stamp sized backyard. She'd pulled the refrigerator door open to grab a bottle of pinot grigio when the front doorbell rang.

"Just in time," she said to herself as she crossed the living room to answer the door. She took a quick look through the peephole before answering; the delivery guy was tall and blond. He also wasn't wearing a FedEx uniform.

She was suddenly breathless.

"Drew," she said.

DREW HAD PULLED up in front of Kendall's townhouse development twenty minutes ago after driving through the streets of Santa Clara. He was more of an LA guy after spending four years of his life there, but he glanced around at a tidy, upscale community drenched in sunshine as he drove. He loved playing for the Sharks and he'd almost got used to Seattle's weather over the past couple of years, but the warmth and blue skies lured him again. He wouldn't mind spending some time here again soon.

He knew the chances Kendall was already home from the office were slim to none. He'd brought a book along to keep him company. He could hang out here on the other side of the street for a little while before the neighbors called the cops.

Minutes later, a late-model, latte-colored Lexus crossover turned the corner onto Kendall's street, and he recognized her behind the wheel. He waited until she drove into the garage and the door lowered behind her car before parking his rental car in her driveway. He reached out for the bouquet of flowers he'd bought and patted his front jeans pocket to make sure her phone was still there before opening the car door.

He climbed the flight of stairs to her front door, rang the doorbell, and waited. He heard her voice a minute or so later through the door.

"Drew."

She pulled the door open. Her eyes flew wide. He saw a flush moving over her cheeks. She looked a bit startled, but she smiled at him.

"What are you doing here?"

"Special delivery." He held out the bouquet of flowers. "I have your phone too."

She took a deep, appreciative sniff of the bouquet and said, "You didn't have to do this."

"I wanted to," he said. They stared at each other for a few seconds, or an eternity. He told himself to breathe. "May I come in?"

"Oh! Oh," she said. "Of course. Please."

She moved back, pulling the door open enough for him to step inside. He moved over the threshold into her house. They were still staring at each other, and she licked her lips. He tried and discarded twenty things to say to her in his head. Maybe he should keep things light. He reached into his pocket, pulled out her cell phone, and handed it to her.

"I believe this belongs to you," he joked.

Her fingertips lingered as she took the phone out of his hand. He felt the tingle all the way up his arm.

"It does. Thank you so much," she said. The phone vibrated with an incoming call, and she shook her head a little.

"It was going off the entire time I was walking through the airport," he said. "You're popular."

He glanced around her house while he attempted to come up with something dazzling to say. She liked medium blues and celery green. The somewhat formal furniture in her living room flowed into a more casual dining area, bathed in sunlight. The flowers he'd brought would look perfect in the vase on her table. She bit her lip a little, as if she didn't know what to say. At least she hadn't said, "Go away."

"Nice place," he said.

"Thank you." She sniffed her flowers again. "I . . . I can't believe you're here."

He took a step toward her and bent down to kiss her cheek. "I wanted to see you again."

She moved closer to him and tipped her head back to look into his eyes. "Me too," she said.

If she told him to leave, he would. He wanted a date with this woman more than he'd wanted anything else for a long time now, but he'd really rolled the dice by showing up at her house. The next few minutes were up to her: If she didn't want him here, he'd get in the car, go back to the airport, and call her five minutes after he retired from the league.

The calm, coolly sophisticated Kendall seemed to be struggling to think of something to say at the moment, but she reached out for his hand.

"Would you like to have a glass of wine with me?"

He nodded as he clasped her smaller, softer hand in his.

KENDALL COULDN'T FIND the wine opener. She usually put it in the silverware drawer. For some reason it wasn't there. She rifled through the drawer, looking under the silverware holder and moving the other utensils and odds and ends around to look for it. She found an unopened package of crackers in the pantry and sliced some cheese to arrange on a plate with some fresh raspberries for a snack, but the wine opener was nowhere to be found. Drew was lounging against the counter in her kitchen.

Maybe she should rephrase that. The most attractive thing in her kitchen right now had braced one hip against the counter and was watching her while she hunted around for the wine opener. A heathery pullover sweater and a pair of oft-washed jeans looked like designer fashion on him. His long blond hair was tied back with a piece of leather. His eyes were impossibly blue. He was beautiful on the outside, but she wondered what other enticements she'd find when she talked with him a little more.

"What are you looking for? Is there anything I can do to help?" he said.

"I can't find the corkscrew. I know it was in here. I—"

He held up the corkscrew. "How's this?" The gentle amusement in his eyes made her breath hitch.

"Y-yes. Where was it?"

"You must have left it over here before you answered the door."

She rolled her eyes a little, and he reached out for the plate of food.

"I'll carry that. Would you like me to grab a couple of

glasses?" He pulled a few paper napkins out of the holder she kept on the kitchen counter.

"Sure."

She picked up the now-opened wine bottle and followed him out to the small backyard. Birds were chirping. The heat of late afternoon was softened somewhat by a mild breeze. She could smell the neighbor's orange blossoms. He held the lawn chair she sat down in like it was an antique.

"Maybe I should get a plate or two—"

She started to rise from her chair and he said, "We don't need plates to eat finger food, do we? You had a long day. Relax." He poured her a glass of wine, poured one for himself, and touched the rim of his glass to hers. "Cheers."

Her day hadn't been especially long, but she wasn't going to argue with him about it.

"Cheers," she said.

The wine was tart, fruity, and perfect in the California heat. He put his glass down long enough to put a slice of cheese atop a cracker and held it out to her.

"Aren't I supposed to be serving you?" she said.

"It's good to make myself useful," he said. "What were you planning on doing tonight before I dropped in?"

"I was about to start searching the bushes outside to see if the delivery guy was here earlier and hid my phone. I didn't get the shipment tracking number," she said, but she smiled.

"So, you'll forgive me for delivering the phone myself?"

"I'll consider it," she said. "Haven't you had a long day today also?"

"I got checked out by a trainer and left by noon," he said. "I don't have to be back until Wednesday morning at seven AM or so." He took another sip from his glass. "I'm not typically a wine guy, but I'm enjoying this." He picked up the bottle and noted the label.

"It's not expensive, but it's delicious."

She moved forward in her chair to pour herself another glass of wine, poured a bit more into his glass, and set the bottle down on the table. She reached out for another cracker and a piece of cheese. Silence fell between them as she nibbled on the snack. He helped himself to a few perfectly ripe and juicy raspberries.

She fidgeted a little and took another sip of wine.

"Drew," she said. "We can't do this."

"Do what?"

She twirled the stem of her wineglass in her fingertips.

"I could deal with the fact our teams hate each other. If we dated each other, it would be bad, but survivable." She looked into his eyes. "People would talk about me, they'd talk about you, and it would be embarrassing. That's not the worst, though."

He reached out for her hand. She let him take it. He saw her try to smile, to soften the blow, but her lips trembled. "The Miners are going after you in free agency. If Mr. Curtis doesn't manage to survive the SEC investigation, you'd be working for me until they hire someone else for the GM job. Any romantic involvement between us would be considered sexual harassment. You could sue the team, and I'd lose my job."

"What if I don't want to sue the team?"

"Doesn't matter."

He turned to face her. She was still holding his hand. "My agent's going to do the talking, Kendall, but I want to stay in Seattle."

"We're waving a lot of money around—"

"So it's already being discussed."

"At the highest levels, and I'd appreciate it if you'd keep that confidential," she said.

"I'm not going anywhere unless I'm offered stupid money. My agent will be asking for top five defensive players in the league money."

"By the way, we never had this discussion," she said.

"Got it," he said. Her palm was a little damp. He knew how much she was risking by telling him this, but part of him was just pissed off. He wanted her. He couldn't give up quite so easily, but she'd outlined exactly why he should walk out of her house, get in the car, and fly back to Seattle without a second thought. "Why is your organization spending so much on a defensive free agent when what they should be doing is beefing up the offensive line so your quarterback doesn't get killed out there every Sunday? That's insane."

"Our owner wants to make a huge splash in free agency—"

"So go after New England's left tackle. He's the best in the league. He's going to cost you some money, but you can get three or four very good players for what I'd want to leave Seattle. You can grab some other offensive linemen through the draft, and your offense will look much better within a couple of seasons as a result."

"Don't you care about a huge contract?"

"I make three times as much from endorsements now as I do playing football. I'm getting paid, but I want great guys around me too. If you break the bank on one player and he gets hurt, your season goes to shit." He consciously lowered his voice. "You know this. What the hell's going on in your front office, anyway?"

She took another sip of wine. "You don't want to know."

"Of course I do." He layered a piece of cheese on a cracker, stuffed it into his mouth, and chewed while he thought. "Let me guess. Everyone's freaking out at the idea your owner may end up in prison."

She didn't respond. She seemed lost in thought. Maybe the best thing to do was to change the subject. He brought the back of her hand to his lips and kissed her knuckles. A few seconds later, her mouth curved into a smile.

"How about dinner?" he said.

"Right now?"

"Whenever you're hungry. I haven't been in the neighborhood since college, so I might need a pointer or two about restaurants."

A cute little wrinkle formed between her eyes when she was worried about something. "There's just one problem," she said.

He tried to appear casual while bracing himself.

"Someone's going to recognize you if we leave my house."

His exterior was cool while his innards were doing the

little kid on Christmas morning dance. He'd expected her to ask when he had to be at the airport to fly home, or why he'd persisted when she told him she didn't think they should date at all. Instead, she was accepting his offer.

"It might happen," he said.

He had played for and graduated from UCLA, and a few alumni recognized him in the San Jose airport earlier. People recognized him when he went home to Wisconsin, when he was at the local grocery store picking up a half-gallon of milk and a loaf of bread in Bellevue, and anywhere else people owned a TV that showed commercials for one of the products he endorsed. They were typically nice and he was flattered, but he'd prefer spending some time alone with her tonight. Being seen together in public (and being recognized) would be disastrous for Kendall.

"It *will* happen," she said.

"Maybe we should order a pizza or something, then," he said.

To his surprise, she grinned. "You grew up here, didn't you? I thought you'd suggest In-N-Out. I know a little something about the secret menu."

"I grew up in Wisconsin. You probably already know I went to UCLA."

She gave him a nod and a mischievous smile.

"I went to Wharton in San Francisco, but my brother worked at In-N-Out during high school. He used to bring food home a lot."

"So, you know all about the Double-Double Animal Style," he said.

The sweet sound of her laughter rang out. He had to laugh too. He never dreamed they'd bond over their shared love for a fast-food place Californians revered. Guys who had game didn't take a stylish and sophisticated woman to a burger place on their second date, but he was happy to know she wouldn't object to it.

"And the root beer float. You're not dealing with an amateur here," she said. She took another sip of wine and put her glass back down on the table. "I was planning on a big salad and maybe some garlic bread for dinner tonight. I could go to the store and get some steak—"

"Salad sounds great. What can I do to help?"

"You're going to need more food than that," she protested.

"We'll make it work."

He popped another raspberry into his mouth and almost choked on it when she said, "What time is your flight back to Seattle?"

He managed to swallow the little piece of fruit, gazed into her eyes, and said, "What time would you like it to be?"

Chapter Six

KENDALL COULDN'T SEEM to let go of Drew's bigger, rougher hand. She'd told him they shouldn't date. She was risking public and professional humiliation by even talking with him. Yet she couldn't bring herself to tell him to leave. The guy had dropped everything to get on a plane. Anyone else kind enough to return her iPhone would have taken it to the nearest overnight mailing facility, paid the fee, and sent her the tracking information via e-mail or text instead of buying a last-minute airline ticket.

The phone was a convenient excuse, and they both knew it. She should be worried about the difficult to resist energy between them, but instead, all she could think was *this is the most romantic thing any man has done for me.*

She was in over her head already. She kept telling him this couldn't happen, but she wasn't convincing herself of that fact.

"The last flight to Seattle is at eight this evening." He pulled his phone out of his pocket and consulted the screen. "I could still buy a ticket—"

"I don't want you to," she blurted out, and she barely resisted slapping her hand over her mouth.

If he stayed, they would sleep together, and saying goodbye to him again would be worse. But she couldn't stand the thought of his leaving. He'd just gotten here. The part of her that was so fixated on getting him out of her hotel room was gone, or at the very least, silenced temporarily.

He tried to hide his smile while blotting his mouth with a napkin. "Maybe I should look for a morning flight instead?"

She bit her lip and nodded. Despite her behavior in that hotel room, she wasn't really into one-night stands. She wasn't altogether sure about "friends with benefits," either. She'd prefer someone she could develop a relationship with. That could never be Drew. Despite all of her misgivings, however, she knew she was going to sleep with him tonight.

He glanced at his phone again, but not fast enough to hide the hungry expression in his eyes. He had more on his mind than dinner. He scrolled down the screen of his smart phone with a fingertip. "Here's a flight for six-thirty in the morning."

She tried to focus on the discussion at hand while her cheeks got hot. If the evening went as well as she hoped it would, she wasn't going to want to pull herself out of bed to get him to the airport by four-thirty AM.

"That's too early," she said. She grabbed her phone, hit a few buttons, and said, "How about eight-thirty? It's early enough so that you'll still be able to enjoy your day off."

"I'm enjoying myself right now, Kendall." His eyes caught and held hers.

"I'm enjoying myself too." She knew she was still blushing, and she tried to ignore the rush of excitement in her belly. She also knew she might as well have been wearing a sign saying *you're getting laid tonight*. She hit more buttons on her phone. "Let me buy your plane ticket home. You did me a huge favor—"

"I did it because I wanted to. I'd do it again. Thank you, but it's on me." He touched a few more buttons on his smart phone's screen and said, "I have a confirmation and I'm already checked in for the flight." He got to his feet and helped her up. "Let's see what we can come up with for dinner."

Instead of parking himself on a kitchen stool while she assembled food, he pushed up his sleeves, washed his hands, and asked, "What would you like me to do?"

"You're the guest," she insisted. "Why don't you sit down and take it easy?"

"Later," he said. "It'll get done faster if I help."

"Are you too good to be true?"

"No," he said, but he grinned. "My mom taught me a long time ago that pitching in is always best."

Kendall defrosted a couple of chicken breasts in the microwave and put them into a glass baking pan, drizzling them with olive oil and garlic powder before sliding them into the oven. Maybe she should add some more vegetables or something. Drew probably ate a lot more than a chicken breast and some salad at each meal.

"Is this going to be enough? Maybe I should steam some vegetables or bake a potato for you," she said.

She was enjoying sharing the simple tasks she carried out each day with him—two people making their way around a kitchen, assembling a meal. She knew asking him to stay wasn't the brightest idea she'd ever had. Additional involvement with a guy she shouldn't be involved with in the first place wasn't a terrific plan, but she couldn't seem to help herself right now.

Spending the night with Drew was a one-night guilty pleasure. She'd get him out of her system. Other women did this kind of thing all the time. It was her turn.

"Do you have any food allergies I should know about?" she said.

She hadn't shared her kitchen with anyone else since Tony and felt a twinge of embarrassment at the thought. She reminded herself that according to everything she'd ever read or heard about him, Drew didn't have a wife and a couple of kids in Connecticut.

"No food allergies. Well, I'm not especially fond of wasabi," he said.

"Wasabi?"

"One of my college roommates loved the stuff and put it on everything." He shuddered a little, and she had to smile. "Other than that, I'm easy." She watched him rinse fresh spinach like he'd been doing it his entire life and add it to the salad bowl she'd put out for him. "And this is plenty of food."

"Do you enjoy cooking?"

"Sometimes. I'm more of a fan of eating, but my mom insisted that I learn to make the basics before she turned me loose." He crossed the kitchen to her refrigerator and said, "Mind if I look in here for salad stuff?"

"That would be great," she said.

He opened the door, pulled out ingredients, and stacked them on the kitchen island.

"Let's see here," he said, grabbing a chopping knife out of the block. "I'll put some sliced mushrooms and some other stuff in here, and I can cut up some avocado just before we're ready to eat. How about a few more raspberries?"

"Of course." She handed him the container from the refrigerator. "What else do you know how to make?"

He put the knife down to grin at her. "Meatloaf, spaghetti, toasted cheese sandwiches, and my dad taught me how to grill a steak. I'm also excellent at takeout." She had to laugh at that. "I have a chef five days a week during the season, but the rest of the time, I'm on my own."

"You have a chef?" It wasn't unheard of among league veterans, but she was still a little surprised.

"Let's just say he takes care of the nutritional stuff I need while I'm playing," he said. "I go to the practice facility to eat too."

"What's the last thing you cooked for yourself?"

He chuckled a little. "Does heating up pizza count? A couple of my teammates dropped by the other night and brought me some."

"Did they invite themselves over?"

"There was a little conversation earlier in the day

about them visiting, but I ... I got a better offer. They would have ditched me for coffee with a beautiful and interesting woman."

It wasn't the first time in her life a man had called her beautiful, but his sweet, almost shy delivery of the word made her heart skip a beat. Maybe she should keep things light.

"Does that happen a lot? The blowing them off part, or the getting a better offer part?" she teased.

His cornflower-blue eyes held hers. "Nope. It doesn't." He took a deep breath. "I hope you don't think I'm in the habit of routinely ditching my friends. They tend to drop in often. We didn't have anything formal going, so I walked to the bookstore to get a little exercise. I thought I'd listen to the biographer guy for a few minutes before I went home. Then I met you." He let that hang in the air for thirty seconds or so.

If a six foot four inch, 250-pound man could be called "adorable," Drew was it. He was a fascinating combination of warrior and Boy Scout. She'd seen his game tapes more than once. He'd beat his opponents on the football field to a bloody pulp and walk out of the stadium minutes afterward to tenderly help some little old lady across the street.

She wanted him so much. Too bad she couldn't have him. She'd make the most of tonight, and then she'd throw herself into her work to forget him.

DREW FELT LIKE he was walking barefoot through a minefield. The pull he felt when she was near was almost

irresistible. She was lovely, funny, smart, interesting—
all the things he'd wished for in a woman and more. He
wanted to find out more about her. She was determined
to advance in a cut-throat industry and excel at a high-
powered job, which meant the last thing she'd want to
do with her time was have enough babies to fill up his
huge house and have dinner on the table when he walked
through the door each evening.

He realized his expectations were ridiculous. It wasn't
that he thought the woman of his dreams should spend
her days polishing his Pee-Wee football trophies. He
wasn't too much of a he-man to throw in a load of laundry or do the vacuuming. It took two to make a house a
home. And yet, he really wanted someone who wanted
a family and a home like the one he grew up in. He pic-
tured a bunch of blond-haired kids filling up the silence
in his big house with laughter and fun, a big dog cuddled
up with all of them in the evenings while they watched
TV or read or played games together. He saw Easters and
Thanksgivings and Christmas mornings in his mind's
eye. He'd like to spend his weekends at his children's
soccer or T-ball games and have his and his wife's friends
over for a little barbecuing or a beer on Saturday nights.

He also realized he was probably looking in the wrong
places for the wife of his dreams. Women who wanted
to focus on their families didn't hang out in a corporate
boardroom or the front office of a pro football franchise.
Maybe he should try going to church or something to
meet a potential mate. He wasn't especially religious, and
he was fairly sure his long hair would get him tagged as

a "troublemaker" or worse in a big hurry, though. The imaginary women he might meet in the future paled in comparison to the one he was talking with right now.

Kendall led him to her small backyard again. He spied a five-gallon bucket next to her sliding glass door with trowels, shears, and some well-worn gardening gloves he hadn't noticed previously.

"You must enjoy gardening," he said.

"I do," she said, gesturing toward a small patch of flowers. "It's not much, but it's relaxing. There was nothing but dirt back here when I bought my house. I wanted to make something I'd enjoy seeing when I was doing the dishes."

"My mom did the same thing at our house. She talked my dad into putting in one of those gardening windows so she could grow herbs in the kitchen." He smiled at the memory. "She was so proud of herself when she could use the herbs she grew in family meals."

"Speaking of meals, our scouting department was considering sending you a year's worth of Kringle and brats as an enticement." Racine, Wisconsin, was the home of Kringle—a butter-laden, multi-layered filled pastry as world-famous as New Orleans' King Cake or the cheese-cake of New York City.

"I love 'brats, especially when they're marinated in beer and grilled. I'm also pretty fond of Kringle. Maybe you could come over and help me eat them."

He saw her lips curve into a smile. "I might take you up on the Kringle. I had some the last time we were in Green Bay. It's delicious." The sun was setting, and she sat down on a glider in a small patch of shade. "Didn't you want to play for Green Bay?"

He sat down next to her, close enough to hold her hand. She didn't resist.

"I was drafted by Minnesota," he said.

"You could have asked for a trade."

"Yes, I could have, but I was happy there, and after the Sharks made me an offer I couldn't refuse, I've been happy there too."

"Do you miss your family?"

"Does a bear poop in the woods?" He laughed as he said it. "Yeah, I miss them. I go home for a few weeks when the season's over each year, and they come and visit me when they can't take the ice and snow anymore." He watched the setting sun turn her pale skin to gold. "Is your family in the area?"

"You might say that. My parents are in Southern California. My brother and sister and their families live on the East Coast."

"It must be tough at the holidays."

"We all meet up at my parents' house for a week." He was a little surprised she didn't seem like she wanted to elaborate. He'd like to know something about her family. In the meantime, he wanted to keep the conversation light.

"Well, that sounds fun. I usually have Christmas these days with some of the guys. It's too hard for my family to all get out to the Seattle area."

"What do you all do instead?"

"Zach Anderson and his wife, Cameron, invited us all over last year for Christmas lunch. We had to play three days before and she had to work, so we paid the chef that cooks for several of the guys during the season a little extra to make the holiday feast."

"I think I read about that."

"Her network brought cameras and filmed a story about it that was broadcast at halftime the Sunday after Christmas." The memory of Cameron's excitement at hosting the holiday gathering (and the obvious love and pride in her husband's expression as he looked on) still made Drew smile.

"You all went to Children's Hospital later that day as well."

"Now THAT was fun. A few of the guys made a toy run the night before Christmas Eve, and we handed the stuff out. They made sure to get low-tech stuff like board games and Jenga so we could play with the kids for a little while. The boy I was playing Uno with has cancer, but I made him laugh. I made sure he got a few extra cookies too. I think it was the best Christmas I've had so far," he said.

The boy's name was Nolan and he was Drew's favorite Tuesday afternoon appointment these days. If Drew moved his ass tomorrow, he'd make it back to Seattle in time to stop at the hospital with a frosty Dick's chocolate shake and maybe some French fries he smuggled in. Every time he went to visit now, Nolan wore the team logo hoodie Drew peeled off himself on Christmas Day and put on Nolan. It hung to the kid's knees. They'd had to cut the sleeves to accommodate the IVs, but Nolan would be getting a brand-new one when he left the hospital.

Drew found out Nolan's mom was a single parent. She was having a tough time paying the rent while her son was in the fight of his life. Drew did a little scouting around and pre-paid her rent for a year—confidentially, of course.

Kendall's voice was gentle. "I've heard several of the Sharks go there every Tuesday afternoon."

He blinked a few times and cleared his throat. He wasn't Mr. Emotional as a rule, but he saw his own nieces and nephews in every kid in those hospital beds. If spending a few hours every Tuesday afternoon visiting brightened their day, he was happy to do it.

"Yeah. Our QB takes one for the team every week. The media takes pictures of him, and a bunch of us sneak in through another entrance."

She leaned a little closer to him. "My parents thought I'd be a nurse."

"Why is that?"

"I kept bandaging up my dolls. Being a nurse went out the window, though, when I figured out I couldn't stand the sight of blood."

"That might be a problem." He leaned closer to her. "I'll save you from it."

"You will?"

"Of course," he said. "I specialize in rescuing women."

He wrapped one arm around her shoulders and dropped her hand to cup her cheek in his palm. She reached up to touch the tendrils of hair that escaped the elastic band he'd pulled it into to keep it out of his face.

"It's so soft," she whispered.

Her lips were trembling a bit with emotion. She moved a little closer to him\ and looked into his eyes as she touched and explored. Growing his hair out was now the best decision ever. He pulled in a breath and savored the tart, clean scent of green apples.

"I want to run my fingers through it. Is that weird?" she said.

He reached back and pulled the elastic band out of his ponytail. His hair spilled down his back and over his shoulder. He looped the elastic over his wrist.

"Hell, no," he said. "It's all yours."

She bit her lower lip and reached out for him with both hands. Her fingers stroked his sun-warmed hair. It was thick, fine, and the length slid through her hands like liquid silk. His response was to pull her closer. By now, she was settled in his lap, and she laid her head on his shoulder.

"Has everyone you've dated wanted to play with your hair?"

"My ex-girlfriend didn't like it when it wasn't tied back. It got in her lip gloss."

"Maybe she should stop wearing lip gloss," Kendall blurted out.

He grinned at her. "I like how you think."

"No offense, but she's crazy." The laughter rolled out of him. She twirled a thick lock around her finger. "I can't stop touching it."

He passed one big, gentle hand over her hair. "Your hair's soft, and it smells like green apples."

"Long hair looks terrible on me."

"I don't believe that," he said. "Has anyone ever told you you look like Snow White?"

"I tried out to be Snow White at Disneyland one summer. I couldn't make it work with my current job," she joked. She ran her fingertips over the stubble on his cheeks and chin. "Maybe another time."

"You know, the same thing happened when I auditioned for that movie—what was it? Thor?" he said. "They told me I worked out too much and they were going to have to pick some actor instead." He pretended to let out a sigh, and she had to laugh. "Their loss. I guess I'll just have to play football instead."

"Thor probably wants *your* job," she said.

"He has stunt people. I don't."

HE MOVED CLOSER. He was going to kiss her, and she was going to let him. She was going to take him upstairs too. She was going to spend all night touching his hair because she couldn't get enough. Tomorrow morning, she was going to watch him walk out of her house, and she was going to spend the next few years counting the minutes until he retired from the league.

Talk about playing with fire. This was all kinds of stupid, but she couldn't let go of him right now. She couldn't have stopped if she tried. She was going to have to keep tonight a secret. And do her best to forget it when it was over to protect her heart.

Chapter Seven

DREW CUPPED KENDALL'S face in his hands. Every time he looked at her, he was struck anew by the changeable gray of her eyes. Right now, they were the silver-gray of a winter's dawn in Seattle. She'd probably laugh if he told her that, but he couldn't think of anything else he'd ever seen that compared to the color.

She was still holding strands of his hair and rubbing them between her fingertips. He'd grown his hair out for the hell of it when he was in college, and it was now part of his identity—that guy with the long hair that wasn't the other guy in the dandruff shampoo commercials. He'd never met a woman who wanted to touch his hair like Kendall did, though, or run her fingers through it.

"I want to kiss you," he said.

She looked up at him from beneath her eyelashes. She said she didn't want to date him, they couldn't get involved, but she was currently sitting in his lap with her fingers in his hair. He'd better ask a few more questions before they got physically involved. They were a little carried away already, but he wanted to make sure this was what she wanted to happen.

"I want you to kiss me too," she said.

"You still don't want to date me."

"Aren't we on a date right now?"

"There could be an argument made for that."

"Let's kiss now and argue about it later."

"I love the way you think," he said, and he brushed her mouth with his.

She wrapped her arms around his neck, fused her lips to his, and he felt her tongue slide into his mouth. She tasted like the wine, with a little tang from the raspberries. She'd tangled her fingers in his hair again. He slid his hand over her lower back and under the waistband of her pants. She was soft everywhere, and he was harder than nails right now.

He'd always liked kissing. He wanted to take his time, tasting, touching, and discovering what a woman enjoyed. Every woman he'd ever kissed was like a treasure map; he sought out her secrets one at a time as he made his way. This one was currently rubbing up against him while she devoured him. He wasn't objecting. Maybe they could try it his way in a little while. Right now, he was all for her doing whatever she'd like to him.

"I think it's a date now," she murmured when they finally came up for air a while later. She was breathing heavily and flushed, with sparkling eyes and a big grin. "How hungry are you?"

"For food, or for you?"

"You've answered my question." She hopped off of his lap. He saw her smile when she glanced down at him. "How do you feel about cold chicken sliced into the salad?"

"What salad?" he joked, and she held out her hand to him.

The beeping oven timer told them the food was done when they re-entered the kitchen. The baked chicken was put into an appropriate container and into the refrigerator for later.

"It's all set," she told him.

"I'm sure it's delicious, but I have other things on my mind right now," he said, pulling her into his arms again. "Where would you like to go?"

"My room. It's at the top of the stairs."

One of the better things about his job was that he could carry a woman up a flight of stairs without even breaking a sweat. After shoving tackling dummies and offensive linemen around a football field, a warm, sweet-smelling woman wasn't a chore at all. She wrapped her arms around his neck again and laid her cheek against his.

He walked through the doorway and halted in shock.

"Is something wrong?" she asked.

"No. Not at all." He couldn't stop staring.

Kendall's room was nothing like the rest of her house. The only thing in common was sunshine streaming through windows covered with crisp cotton curtains and the feeling of comfort. Her living room furniture was formal. This room was vintage. Her bed was an old-fashioned four poster painted with turquoise blue enamel. The sheets were blinding white. Multiple pillows rested against the headboard. A framed close-up photograph of a riotously-colored bouquet of flowers hung above the headboard. A raspberry-colored patterned throw rug covered most of the hardwood floor.

"It's a little girly," she said.

"It looks comfortable, though," he said.

"I know you don't sleep in a bed like this at home."

"Maybe I do," he joked.

"I'm betting you have a huge bed, the color scheme is dark blue or earth tones, and you'd rather be run over than spend one minute of your time making sure fifteen decorative pillows are perfectly arranged every morning."

He walked over to the bed, lowered her onto it, and said, "We'd have to get out of it long enough to fix the pillows. I'm sure you can appreciate my dilemma right now."

"I don't understand."

He nodded at the headboard. "Do I put them on the bench at the foot of your bed like a good guest, or do I fling them all over the room and try to make it up to you later?"

Her smile dazzled him as she arched her back and reached toward the headboard. The decorative pillows were off the bed seconds later and scattered all over her room.

"How's that?" she said.

"Perfect," he said. She pulled him down next to her, and he went willingly. The thuds of four shoes hitting the floor followed. "Come here." He wrapped his arms around her. They wriggled until they were both comfortable.

"I'm so glad you're here," she said, smoothing the hair out of his eyes.

The heat and the urgency of their kisses on the glider outside had transformed into a much slower seduction. His hands slid down her sides to cup her hips. She tucked the curtain of her dark hair behind one ear as she leaned forward to rub noses with him.

"I'm happy too, Kendall, but I'm a little confused."

"Why?"

"What you've said is true. We really can't date. Someone's going to find out, and it's going to be hell to pay for both of us—"

"You told me you're not interested in the Miners."

"No, I'm not."

"No matter how much money we offered you, what incentives are in your contract or that year's worth of brats and Kringles I suggested—"

"They might get a little further if they offered dinner with their interim GM."

"So in other words, I'm what you want," she said.

"Yes," he said.

"Then let's make a deal," she said. "A side offer, if you will."

"I'm all ears." She rubbed against him a little. God, she felt good.

"One night," she said. "One night, and we'll both go back to our lives." Her voice dropped. "It'll be our little secret."

"That's a pretty big secret," he teased. "You might want more."

"I might, but we can't. Not right now." Her eyes held his. "Deal?"

"Are we shaking on this?"

"Of course we are."

"Well, then, I accept."

She gave him a fist bump in response. She pulled herself up on his chest, straddled him, and he told himself to breathe. The late afternoon illuminated her skin in sunbeams. She was the beautiful conquering warrior home from the executive suite, and he was her willing servant/ pool cleaner/lawn maintenance professional. He'd be anything she wanted him to be as long as she kept rubbing herself against his hard-on. She was driving him out of his mind, and they hadn't taken off one stitch of clothing yet.

"I'll remember that," she teased. Her fingers moved over his chest, streaking fire as they went. "Back to our negotiation. What kind of contract concessions would you be willing to negotiate if I took off my clothes?"

She slowly licked her lower lip and gave him the same saucy, enticing, confident smile he imagined women had been giving the men in their beds since the beginning of time. She fingered the hem of her sweater, pulling it off over her head and letting it dangle from her fingertips before it hit the floor.

"I'd play for a dollar a year with those terms," he said. A *dollar*? He'd pay *them*.

"A dollar?" She unbuttoned the top button of her

slacks. "I don't know about that. This might require more discussion."

He brushed her fingers aside and made short work of the zipper. "I'm guessing sexual favors might work better." With one quick movement, he shoved the pants over her waist and halfway down her hips. "Better?"

"You're still dressed."

"We'll work on me in a minute here. Let's make sure you're comfortable first."

He reached to pop open the back hooks on her bra; the lace and satin confection fell away to reveal breasts that fit perfectly in the palms of his hands, tipped with small brown nipples. Her eyes gleamed as he braced her against himself and rolled over so she was beneath him.

He stripped away her slacks and peeled off the panties that matched her bra, dropping them on the floor. He felt her hands skimming up his back, pulling the sweater and T-shirt he wore off with one quick movement over his head. She unbuckled his belt, unfastened the jeans, and tried to shove them off. She couldn't budge his weight.

"Let me help," he teased. He was out of the jeans and his boxer briefs less than a minute later. A few seconds afterward, he held a naked and trembling Kendall in his arms again. He couldn't think of an endearment he hadn't used before, and this occasion seemed to call for something special. He'd think about it right after he figured out why she was shaking. Maybe she wasn't sure about what they were about to do, and he needed to back off.

"What's wrong, Kendall?"

"Nothing." She let out a sigh and reached out to pull his face closer to hers.

"You're shaking all over. Are you scared?" He traced the tendon in her neck with the tip of his tongue. "If you don't want to do this, we don't have to."

Her head tossed on the pillows that didn't hit the floor earlier.

"Not scared. Maybe nervous."

"Tell me all about it."

She drew one finger down his chest. "You're the first guy I've been with who didn't wax off his chest hair."

"I'm not into pain." He kissed her brow. "Are you into pain?"

"Not especially."

"Well, that works well for both of us, doesn't it?"

She grinned at him, and she let out a breath. "How long has it been since you—well, since you slept with someone?"

"Six months," he said.

He'd had plenty of volunteers, but he'd rather jerk off in the shower than have another meaningless fuck. Most guys would give their left nut to have scores of women at their beck and call, or better yet, women who came right out and propositioned him on a regular basis. He was ready for something more, a relationship that *meant* something. They both knew this couldn't last, but he wanted her anyway.

"It's been a year for me." She rolled onto her back and looked up into his face. "Bad breakup."

"Do you want to talk about it?"

She looked a little surprised. "I'm naked, you're naked—isn't this usually not a great time for a detailed conversation about previous relationships?"

He moved the bangs out of her eyes with one hand. He rolled onto his back and pulled her into his side, wrapping one big arm around her.

KENDALL RESTED AGAINST a chest that looked like it was carved from granite. Warm, clean-smelling, golden-toned granite with springy, coarse dark blond chest hair and light-brown, flat nipples. He reached one hand behind his head, twirled his long hair into a low coil of sorts to get it out of the way, and wrapped his other arm around her.

"Before we talk about the stupidest man in the universe, there's a few things I'd like to say to you. I don't have sex without using a condom. I'm tested for STDs yearly. I stopped screwing as a recreational pursuit when I was in college. In other words, I don't have sex unless there's feelings involved."

She had to smile while her fingertips explored his chest. She wanted to trail her hands over every inch of him. She moved one thigh over his leg and brushed his erection; he must have been ready to explode, but he was waiting for her. Showing up at her front door with her lost cell phone and a bouquet of flowers had just been eclipsed as the most romantic thing any man had ever done for her.

He wanted to talk *first*. Most guys didn't want to talk at all, before *or* after. She hauled in a breath.

"I get tested with my physical every year now for the team's insurance policy. I don't have sex without protection, either. I didn't lose my virginity until I was in grad school, so my number's relatively low," Kendall said. "I prefer sex with feelings too."

"But you're nervous."

"Please tell me you're not secretly married and have two kids and a wife in Connecticut."

"No, I'm not and no, I don't. I've never been married. I'd like to marry just once."

She was going to rock Drew's world, as many times as he'd like her to, and then she was going to tell him about Tony.

Kendall took a deep breath, and the clean scents of soap and the outdoors filled her lungs. That distinctive scent would always mean *Drew* to her. Even though he'd mentioned a subject that usually left her feeling betrayed and sad, her body was ready for what they both knew was going to happen. She'd never wanted like this before, and the only thing she was afraid of right now is that one night wouldn't be enough to lose herself in his big, strong body.

She grabbed his face with both hands and looked into the bluest eyes she'd ever seen.

"Drew McCoy, I'm going to make you the happiest man in Santa Clara right now."

"Done," he said. He covered her mouth with his seconds later.

She skimmed her hands over bulging biceps, an abdomen so cut she could grate cheese on it, the smoothness of his back. She wrapped her legs around his thighs, which didn't quite fit, but seemed to make him happy. She couldn't resist cupping his butt in both of her hands. She felt him hard against her abdomen, but he didn't seem in any hurry to penetrate her. Mostly, she luxuriated in his long, slow, tender kisses that started a different kind of trembling. He was touching her with big, gentle hands, but she was hotter than the surface of the sun from his deep, unhurried exploration of her mouth. She wondered what was going to happen when he got around to the rest of her.

"Drew," she finally murmured.

"Yes?" He'd moved down and taken one of her nipples in his mouth. She gasped. "I'm guessing you like that."

"Uh huh. Oh, God. Please don't stop."

She heard a low chuckle. "Let's see if I can figure out something else you might like."

"You must be really into kissing. Oh!"

"I am, but I like this even more." He took her nipple back into his mouth and reached between her legs. He stroked her, wetting his fingers with her moisture. She let out a moan and arched toward him. "Easy," he said. "Let's take our time."

He suckled and stroked, moving his fingers agonizingly slowly over her, close to her clitoris but not enough direct stimulation that she'd come quickly. Her heart was pounding. Heat rolled over her in waves. She spread her legs more to encourage him; he'd get close, but not quite close enough.

He took his mouth off of her nipple long enough to murmur into her ear, "I'll bet you want me to touch you there, don't you?"

"God, yes. I want to come! Why aren't you letting me?"

He captured her mouth with his again, plunging his tongue into hers, and finally sliding his fingers into her, stroking in and out. Maddeningly slowly. He bumped the palm of his hand against her clitoris, sending shocks of sensation throughout her body. She writhed beneath him, tore her mouth away from his, and cried out in desperate need when he finally picked up the pace. She wrapped her legs around him as best she could to offer even more access.

He stroked as quickly as possible as he rubbed and rotated the heel of his palm over the most sensitive nerves in her body. His voice was low and dark in her ear.

"I can't wait to watch you come, Kendall."

She felt the pull of sensation, the skittering prickling over her skin, the first contractions of a massive orgasm. She let out a shriek as stars burst behind her eyelids. Her heart was pounding, her body felt like fire, and she tried to catch her breath.

His fingers were still moving, but his touch now was tender, soothing. She could still feel the ripples of the orgasm throughout her body, and she heaved a sigh.

"That was unbelievable."

His lips curved into a smile.

"Where did you learn that?" she said.

"What do you mean?"

"I . . . I . . . are you always . . . how did you DO that? I usually have to use a *vibrator* to get anywhere close, and . . . oh, God."

His eyes locked onto hers. He looked happy. Even more, he looked a little bit proud of himself. "Did you enjoy that?"

"Other than the part in which you made me *beg*—"

"You're not mad at me, are you?" He kissed the middle of her forehead. "Delayed gratification can be a good thing."

"I thought my head was going to explode." She grabbed his wrist and placed his hand flat on her abdomen so he could feel the continuing waves of sensation. "Feel that?"

He was quiet for a moment.

"I've never had a woman demonstrate what I did to her before," he said. He gazed into her eyes. "It's hot."

She rolled onto her other side, scrabbled in the bedside table drawer, and pulled out a strip of condoms. She turned back to him, waving it teasingly in front of his eyes.

"I'll show you some delayed gratification, Mr. McCoy."

"Is that so? What did you have in mind?"

She pushed him onto his back, ripped one of the condoms off of the strip, opened it, and rolled it over his still-erect penis.

"Watch and learn," she joked. She straddled him, balancing herself with flattened palms on his abdomen. He grabbed her hips. She bent over him, capturing his mouth with hers. She stroked his tongue with hers while grinding herself against his penis. She played with his nipples, and she was rewarded with a groan of pleasure.

She tore her mouth off of his for a few seconds. He sat up, gripping her upper arms in both hands. He tried to push her onto her back. She wasn't having any of it. It was his turn to beg, and she was going to make it happen. His eyes were almost black with arousal. His breathing was ragged. His erection was inches from where they both wanted it. She wondered how much more he could take before his superior strength won out, he flipped her onto her back, and plunged inside.

"You want me?" she whispered.

"Jesus, yes. I'll do anything."

"Anything? What are you willing to do?"

"You thought that orgasm was big. Wait until you find out what I've got for you now."

"You are such a sweet talker," she said as she wrapped her arms around his shoulders.

"Kendall. Let me in, for God's sake. I have to have you."

"How badly?" she said.

He groaned again. She felt his fingertips biting into her hips as he pulled her up to her knees.

"Ride me," he hissed. "Fuck my brains out."

Oh, she would. She reached to position him, and she sank half an inch onto him. He let out a long, harsh breath. "Want more?"

He said something unintelligible, and she sank another half an inch onto him. She could feel the head of his penis sliding into her, and she raised up and down on her knees a couple of times for the hell of it. He pulled her down a little more onto him. She wasn't sure how long it took while she teased him and moved down a fraction of an inch at a time but finally, he was seated inside her, and his hands guided her into a rhythm that worked for both of them.

Up and down, up and down, and she gasped for breath. She felt his fingers stroke through her wetness again, and he applied his thumbs to the opening between their bodies. He tried some direct pressure this time, and she couldn't control her gasps.

"Ride me. Harder," he said. She increased the tempo, and his groans increased too. "Shit, that feels good. More."

She heard their bodies slapping against each other, and the bed moving with his thrusts. She could feel the tell-tale rushing in her head of an oncoming orgasm. Her body gripped him, and sweat poured off of her in the cool room. She was gasping, her body was shuddering around him, and fireworks burst behind her eyelids.

He let out a shout, and she felt him thrust up into her even faster. They were racing to the end. It didn't matter who got there first; they were both going to the same place. Her world burst into unbearably intense sensation as the orgasm took her over. She forced herself to open her eyes and watched his face convulse as he came.

Sweaty and sated, she slumped onto his chest. He was sweating too. He was trembling. His arms surrounded her as his lips brushed her hair. They were both silent while she tried to catch her breath.

A few minutes later, Drew's breathing was deep and regular. He'd fallen asleep. She wasn't sure why she was disappointed by this. He still held her close and didn't seem to mind the fact she was lying on top of him, so it wasn't all bad. She shifted a little.

"Sweet dreams," she whispered.

She felt the rumble of his voice. "I'm not asleep. I'm very, very relaxed, though." He stretched a little. "That was incredible."

Her momentary unhappiness dissolved into a starburst of elation. "I enjoyed it." She could lie on him all night, but he might like to take a deep breath. "Maybe I should move off of you so you're more comfortable."

He let out a snort. "I'm fine if you are, Kendall." He pulled her into his side and reached over her head for the mini-carafe of filtered water and clean drinking glass she kept on her nightstand. "Want some water?"

They took turns sipping out of the water glass. He propped himself up on one elbow.

"Are you hungry yet?"

"Nope," he said. "I believe I promised you a little chat, and I'm too comfortable right now to leave your bed."

"Ahhh. That's right." Kendall was sated and happy in her post-orgasmic haze. She really didn't want to spoil a wonderful evening with any discussion about her ex, but it was time to come clean. "Once upon a time, there was a woman who chose the wrong guy to date."

He tipped her chin up with one finger. "Weren't you dating Tony Kelly?"

Her mouth dropped open. She felt the surge of embarrassment all over her body. *Oh, God.* "How did you know that?"

"My agent was negotiating with his company for an endorsement for me at that time. You made quite an impression on Lance. He said, and I quote, 'It's too bad San Francisco's director of football operations is dating such a shit. I'll bet she has no idea about the wife and two kids he already has.'"

"And you didn't sign with them."

"Again, a better offer. I'm no choir boy, but I don't want to associate myself and my brand with any guy who thinks he's only married and a father when it's convenient for him."

"You must think I'm really gullible," she said. "I still can't believe I fell for him."

"I think you were attracted to him and you didn't know."

"His wife called me at the office one day."

"I'm sorry." He shook his head and gave her another squeeze.

"It was the worst fifteen minute conversation of my life. I apologized to her. I'm always going to feel guilty. He was too good to be true, and I should have known that." She let out a sigh. "When we played in New Jersey last season, I met her for a drink. She'd like to leave him, but she needs a job first. We've been working on it ever since."

In other words, his first impression of her was correct. Instead of being so embarrassed at finding herself caught in a situation that any other single woman would do almost anything to distance herself from and shift the blame, she apologized and did her best to make some kind of amends. It was impressive.

"How's that going?"

"Miami's front office needs an executive assistant. She's not going to live in a five thousand square foot house and drive a Cadillac Escalade anymore on the salary, but I don't think that matters to her. There's also a place for her in Atlanta if she wants it. Mostly, she's getting her ducks in a row before she makes the move."

"That's pretty nice of you."

"Thank you for saying that, but it was the only way I could live with the guilt. I could help her and the kids get out and make sure they were on a better path." She let out a sigh. "If anything good came out of this, I made a new friend. And I learned."

"We all learn," he said. "I'd like to learn some more about you."

He rolled atop her again. His fingertips brushed the ticklish skin under her arm, and she let out a laugh as she reached up to kiss him.

One night was not going to be enough. She was crazy to think it ever would be.

Chapter Eight

DREW AWOKE IN Kendall's bed at the soft light of dawn. He glanced over at the clock on her bedside table. Five AM. He'd have to be at the airport in the next hour or so to have any chance at all of being on the eight-thirty flight to Seattle. He didn't want to go.

Kendall was lying on her side, the sheet wrapped around her hips, breathing deeply. She'd tucked one hand beneath her pillow sometime during the night. She was still naked, and he was hard.

He knew continuing to see her was out of the question. She was right: Even if their relationship was consensual, it would cause more of a furor than the league's attempts to eliminate kickoffs. She'd be the one that would suffer. The guys he spent nine months a year with would give him a ration of shit, but he cringed to think of what they'd say about her.

He knew what was waiting for her too. She'd told him

that she enjoyed being the director of football operations; managing the team's salary cap made sure she mostly stayed off the radar of men in the league who thought women had no business in a pro football team's front office. Being an interim GM left a huge target painted on her back, especially if she decided she wanted the job for real. Even more than the job title, the proof she was intimately involved with one of the Sharks might be enough to cause the owner of the Miners to fire her on the spot, SEC investigation or not.

He shouldn't have slept with her. She shouldn't have slept with *him*. He knew seeing her again was asking for trouble and he was the worst kind of stupid. It made him a real candy ass to admit it to himself, but he was lonely. There were always women around. They weren't the right ones, and it had nothing to do with whether or not they shared his ideas about a home and family. They weren't what he really wanted, and the list had got shorter the longer he'd dated: smart, funny, thoughtful, compassionate, and beautiful. Even beautiful was negotiable; he wasn't the guy that went for the bleached blondes with gigantic foobs, and he never had been. He'd appreciate someone with good health habits and someone who could keep up with him, but mostly, he wanted someone he could see making a home and raising a family with.

Walking into his parents' house was still something he relished—the scent of food cooking, the hugs and sometimes, a few tears from his mom, who was always his and his siblings' greatest cheerleader. Shaking hands with his dad and being wrapped in a huge bear hug.

Since his career didn't allow him to live in Wisconsin, he wanted those things in Seattle. It was why he didn't bitch too much when he came home to find yet more of his teammates lounging in the family room, and why he enjoyed getting invited over to Zach's house.

He'd been in Seattle two seasons now. The team was his family, his home away from home. They weren't there during the wee hours of the morning, though. He needed a wife.

He watched Kendall sleep. She must have been having a great dream; he saw her smiling a little. He'd love to know what (or who) she was dreaming about. He hoped it was him. He could moon over her like a lovesick middle school student all he wanted, but she was on a different path in life.

She wasn't going to leave the Miners. He'd retire from football in a few years, he'd find something else to do with his time, and she would still want to live in California. Did he want to as well? Would she enjoy weekend soccer games and inviting friends over for a meal, or would she be required to go to the high-profile events any franchise's front office personnel attended? They weren't important to him at all.

Maybe he should take it down a notch before he planned his entire future in the next ten minutes. He was interested, but he didn't know enough about her to give her the starring role in his fantasies of domestic bliss. It would take many more dates to do so. The best course of action was to get his ass back to Seattle, stop in to see his young friend Nolan at Children's, and figure out if they both were interested enough to pay the price for getting involved with each other. She'd said she wasn't into one-night stands. He wasn't into them, either, but right now, this felt a lot like one.

There was also the consideration that his actions could get her fired, which he didn't want either.

He swung his legs over the side of the bed and surveyed her bedroom floor, which was littered with their clothing. He bent over to snag his stuff, and he heard her sleep-thickened voice.

"That's quite a view."

He turned toward her. "I could say the same."

He saw the flash of her smile, and she pulled up the sheet to her neck. She blushed a little. He returned to the bed, leaned over her, and kissed her forehead. "Good morning."

"Good morning," she said. They stared at each other. There was so much to say, and he wasn't sure where to start.

"It's a little after five. I didn't mean to wake you."

He saw her frown for a split-second. He could see the moment she told herself to act like it wasn't a big deal in her face too.

"Sneaking out?"

She was trying to play it cool. He took her cue. His voice was casual.

"Nope. It's early. I wasn't going to leave without saying goodbye."

"I wish you didn't have to leave at all," she said, and she clapped one hand over her mouth. She shook her head. "Maybe we could chalk that last comment up to still being half-asleep."

He crawled back into the bed with his phone. "Is it going to be a crisis if you get to the office at nine this morning instead of eight? Maybe we could grab a cup of coffee on the way."

Sadness flitted over her features before she pasted on another smile. "My meetings start at eight. I can't do it."

"Well, then," he said. He put his phone back on the nightstand and reached out for her. "A hug, and I'll go get in the shower."

He smelled her green apple scent one more time and tried to memorize what she felt like in his arms. He rested his cheek against her much softer one. She cuddled against him. He'd hold her for a few more minutes.

The silence grew. He heard the chirp of an incoming text. Judging by the time, it must be a member of his family.

"I don't know what to say," she said.

"I don't, either."

He gave her one last squeeze, crawled out of bed, and headed toward the shower.

Half an hour later, he was dressed and ready to go. His backpack was over one shoulder. He patted his front pocket; the key fob to his rental car was there along with his phone. He checked for his wallet.

"I had a great time," he said as they walked to the front door of her house arm-in-arm.

"Me too," she said. He saw the tell-tale glimmer of rising tears in her eyes. He opened his mouth to say something before he kissed her goodbye, and she laid her fingers over his lips. "Don't say goodbye."

He kissed her fingertips, and then he kissed her mouth. She wrapped her arms around his waist. They stood in silence as they both fought for something to say besides the usual clichés two people spouted when their feelings went far beyond a casual encounter. She pulled herself out of his arms and opened the front door of her house.

He squeezed her hand one last time as he walked out the door. He heard the click of the door shutting behind him seconds later. He felt it in his gut.

She was gone.

KENDALL WENT THROUGH her morning routine numbly. She dried her hair into a perfect shiny bob that framed her face, applied her makeup, dressed, and made sure she was wearing matching shoes. Her phone was already chirping with incoming texts and e-mails. She rooted through the bag Sydney sent home with her last night; everything was still there. She hadn't done thirty seconds of the work she was now behind on, and she wasn't sure how she could BS her way through this morning's meetings.

She picked up her laptop bag and glanced at her smart phone's screen before she put it into her handbag. She had an e-mail from Drew.

> *Kendall, I'll never forget last night. Since I*
> *have your cell number and home address,*
> *it's only fair you have mine. Drew*

She clicked on the attachment. A map to his house from Santa Clara, CA, opened on the phone's screen, and a Google street view of the front of his house.

He'd issued the challenge. It was up to her to accept or decline.

DREW'S TRIP TO Seattle was mostly uneventful. He got searched at the airport for being in San Jose less than twenty-four hours and carrying nothing but a backpack. He was used to this by now. Big dudes with long hair were obviously up to no good. The flight attendant recognized him and offered him a complimentary Bloody Mary. When he politely refused, she made the rounds of the other passengers and returned to him about an hour later. She asked if he'd like something else instead.

"It's very nice of you to ask, but no, thank you."

"Are you sure?" she asked. Her voice dropped an octave. "I have lots more to offer."

He gave her a nod. "Thank you, but no thank you."

She swished away from him. He was still thinking about a certain dark-haired, gray-eyed woman who was probably well into her first meeting of the day. The flight attendant reminded him of the Paul Newman quote he'd read years before, the one in which Mr. Newman was asked how he managed to resist the women who cast themselves into his path, despite the fact he was married: "Why eat hamburger when you have steak waiting at home?"

The older guy sitting next to him waited a grand total

of thirty seconds before he said, "Does that happen to you often?"

If he said "yeah," he'd be an egotistical ass. If he said "no," he'd be a liar. He smiled and shrugged one shoulder.

"I'd be happy to help her out," the guy said.

Drew gave him another nod and went back to reading the book he'd stowed in his backpack before he went to Kendall's house. He'd seen the economist who wrote it on *The Daily Show*. The pilot was flying over South Seattle, descending into Sea-Tac Airport. He'd be through the airport, in his car, and on his way in half an hour or less.

DREW WALKED THROUGH the front doors of Children's Hospital with a couple of poorly-concealed Dick's Drive-In bags an hour later. The nurses behind the desk on Nolan's floor pretended like they couldn't see what he was carrying.

"He's in the room," one of them called out. "He's about to have a treatment." She glanced at the bags and glanced up at him. "A few bites, okay? Don't let him go crazy."

"Okay." He moved closer to the desk. "How about I bring enough for you ladies next time?"

"Sure," she grinned. Her colleagues shook their heads, wagged fingers at him, and laughed. Even health care professionals couldn't resist Dick's food.

Nolan was sitting up at the rolling table in his room with an older-model computer tablet playing a game. He was so deep in concentration that he didn't glance up when Drew walked into his room.

"Hey, buddy. How ya doing?"

Nolan's face lit up. "Drew! You're here!"

He put down the tablet and tried to scramble off the bed like any other ten-year-old boy, but his movements were slow. Drew knew Nolan would be feeling even worse in a couple of hours due to the chemo treatment he'd just been warned about. He crossed the room for a fist bump and wondered if he should help the kid back into his bed.

Nolan wouldn't want Drew to treat him like he was sick.

"Of course I'm here. It's Tuesday." He put the Dick's bags down on another rolling table. "Listen, dude, the nurses are onto me."

Nolan's brow furrowed. "Did they tell you I can't have any of that?"

"Nawww. They told me to take it easy, though. I'll tell you what." He pulled the chair that sat next to the bed closer to Nolan. "You can have some, and I'll put the rest into the mini-fridge for you later."

"My mom can heat it up?"

"Sure." Drew grabbed the bag with two chocolate shakes. "Let me get you set up here." He spread a paper napkin over the rest of the rolling table, pulled one of the shakes out of the bag, and put a straw in the lid. He handed it to Nolan. He shook a few still-hot French fries out onto the napkin, unwrapped a cheeseburger with ketchup for him, and uncapped a small plastic cup of ketchup for the fries. He pulled a cheeseburger out of the bag for himself.

"Can I have more fries?"

"In a while. I have plenty, you know. And another cheeseburger, but we'll save that one for later. What were you doing with the tablet over there?"

"My mom got me some games," Nolan said. "I wanted the really bloody one, but she got me *Fruit Ninjas* and a tower game. They're okay."

"You can't play *Madden* on a tablet, can you?"

"I don't think so." Nolan was stuffing French fries in his mouth. He already had ketchup on one cheek. He sat up on his knees and took another sip of chocolate shake. "Do you play *Madden*?"

"Sure. We play when we're done with practice and sometimes on the weekends."

Nolan fell silent while he chewed more of his cheeseburger. Drew polished off a cheeseburger and ate a few fries. He could hear his phone vibrating in his pocket; his teammates were most likely on their way over here for an hour or two and texting to see if he'd join them.

"So, N-man, got a question for you."

Nolan grinned at him. For all of his protests about wanting more food, he'd taken a few bites of the burger and was having a tough time polishing off the fifteen or so fries Drew shook out of the little paper sack. He'd taken more sips of the shake. Maybe it was easier on his stomach.

"Would you like me to stay while you have your treatment? If it will help, I'll do it. If you want to spend time alone with your mom, I understand and I won't be mad."

Nolan's brows knitted together. "You can stay if you want. My mom tries to get me to sleep sometimes."

"Does sleeping make it easier?"

"A little. Sometimes I throw up, so I have to sleep sitting up."

"That's not fun."

"No." Nolan took another pull on the straw.

"Okay, then. If you don't mind, I'll ask your mom."

Nolan nibbled at his cheeseburger and played a little with the food still on the napkin. Drew took a sip of his own shake. He was musing on whether or not he wanted another cheeseburger when he heard Nolan's voice again.

"Drew, am I going to die?"

Drew felt that like a fist to the gut. Any Shark that visited kids in the hospital braced himself for the unexpected, but he hadn't faced this question before. He sat up in his chair and leaned forward.

There were a million things he could have told Nolan at that moment, but the truth was always best.

"I hope not, Nolan. You have great doctors and nurses who care about you, and they're doing everything they can to help you get well."

"My mom cries sometimes."

"I know she does, buddy. She's just scared."

"Are you scared?"

He looked into Nolan's eyes. "No. Do you know why?"

Nolan shook his head.

"You can do this. You're brave, and you're tough." Drew took a deep breath. "Do you know what we do every day before we go out on the field to practice?"

"No."

"There's a sign over the door that leads onto the practice field. Every day, I pass that sign. It reads 'Always Win.' I tap it before I go outside, because I'm in. I'm on the team, and I want my teammates to know that. I'm on your team. The other Sharks that visit here are on your team too. Your mom is on your team. So are all the doctors and nurses. We all want you to get better."

Nolan's eyes were huge. Drew was up off of the chair, looking for paper and markers in the small stack of items Nolan's mom must have brought for him to do while he was in the hospital. He found a big piece of blank white paper and a black felt-tip marker, found an old magazine to blot the ink, and wrote in block letters: NOLAN WINS.

"Nolan, ring the nurse, will you?"

Nolan looked on in amazement.

"I'm going to hang this up by the door and every time someone goes in or out, you ask them if they'll tap it. I'll tap it. We're your team. We want you to win. Will you do that for me, buddy?"

Nolan's face lit up. His fist shot up in the air. "Yeah!"

The nurse arrived on the run. "Is something wrong?"

"No. Do you have a couple of pieces of tape we could use?"

She glanced at the sign. She started to shake her head, but she smiled. "I think I can find some. I'll be right back."

Nolan's mom arrived twenty minutes later, and Nolan asked her to tap the new sign. She stared at Drew in amazement. Several of Drew's teammates stopped in for a few minutes while Nolan had his treatment. They tapped the sign.

Derrick bumped fists with him and said, "You're part of the team, Nolan. Don't let us down."

Nolan was a little drowsy, but managed to say, "I won't."

Derrick and Seth tapped the sign as they went out the door.

Nolan was falling asleep due to the medications and exhaustion. It had been a big day for him. Drew reached out to squeeze his hand.

"I'll be back next Tuesday."

"See you then," Nolan said. "Tap the sign."

"You know I will."

Drew ran into Seth and Derrick in the hallway outside of Nolan's room. The three men were silent until they got outside the hospital doors.

Seth turned to face them. "I need a beer."

Twenty minutes later, they grabbed a table in a local pub. Seth held up his pint glass. "To Nolan."

They toasted. Drew took a sip of his beer. "He asked me today if he was going to die," he said.

Three men looked down at the table as they struggled for words. The kids they met at Children's grabbed their hearts and didn't let go. Most recovered and went home with their parents. Some would never leave. Visiting every week was a double-edged sword. They got to know the kids. They also grieved the kids that lost the fight.

Seth slapped Drew on the back. "He's going to make it."

Derrick's voice was fierce. "That kid's running out on the field with us," he said. "Just you wait."

DREW PULLED INTO his garage at home an hour or so later. He yanked his backpack out of the car and headed toward the security system to disable it before he went inside. It was off. He knew he'd set it before he left for California. The teammates who would drop in on him had all been at Children's earlier. Who the hell was in his house?

He opened the door to the laundry room and grabbed the baseball bat that sat in one corner. He needed to investigate before he called the cops. Considering the fact it was an open secret among the people who knew him well where the key to his front door was (atop the doorframe) and his security system's combination was his parents' wedding anniversary, at least thirty people knew how to gain access. If and when he finally found a serious girlfriend he was going to have to change the policy, but for the most part, it worked for him. He padded around the corner to his family room.

His dad was asleep on the couch.

Drew stared at him for a minute or so. This was even weirder than the late-night phone call from the other night. His parents visited; it was arranged in advance and they usually came to see him around national holidays so it wouldn't interrupt his dad's work schedule.

He reached behind him to lean the bat against the low cabinet his Xbox and other TV-related paraphernalia rested on.

"Dad?" he said. "What the hell are you doing here?"

Chapter Nine

DREW'S DAD PULLED himself into a sitting position on the couch.

"It's good to see you, Son. I wondered where you were last night."

"Is Mom here? When did you get in? I didn't know you were coming. Did you try to call my phone?"

His dad didn't just show up at his house. Ever. Plus, he could hardly wait to explain to his dad where he'd been last night. It wasn't like his parents thought he was a virgin. Well, maybe his mom did. She probably didn't want to think about that stuff.

His dad didn't answer his questions. He got up off the couch and hugged Drew. "How are you doing?" he said.

"I'm fine, Dad. Where's Mom?"

"She's at work."

Drew pulled away from his dad's bear hug and stared at him with disbelief. "She's at *work*? She got a job? She hasn't had a job besides all of us since you got married. What is going on?"

His dad rubbed a hand over his face. "Maybe we should get a beer and talk about this."

Drew knew he might need to calm down a little, but he couldn't seem to stop asking questions. "What about your job? Dad, I don't understand."

Drew's dad was a plumber. After his kids were grown and gone, he'd opened his own shop with a couple of other guys he'd worked with for a while. They had more work than they could handle.

"I told the guys I needed a few personal days."

"Personal days?" Drew realized he was starting to sound like his parents after he came home past curfew. He was still so dumbfounded at his dad's uncharacteristic behavior he hardly knew what to say. He heard his cell phone ringing in his pocket. "Let me see who this is."

He grabbed the phone to see his mom's smiling face on the screen.

He hit the "talk" button and said, "Mom?" His dad started shaking his head and making the "hang up" gesture.

"Hi honey, how are you?" She sounded a little stressed, he thought. "Is your dad there?"

His dad was waving his arms in the "no" gesture and mouthing, "Don't tell her." He loved his dad, but this was getting weirder and weirder.

"I'm fine, and yeah, he's here. Mom, what's going on?"

"Your father and I had a little disagreement, and I came home to a note. I'm relieved to know he is fine. I'll talk with you later. I love you."

"I love you too, Mom." She'd clicked off halfway through his words, and Drew stared at his father in shock. "Why don't you want Mom to know where you are?"

"Now she'll be calling me every day and wanting to know when I'm coming home." His father heaved a sigh. "This is why I didn't go to your brother's house. She can sit and think for a few days. It'll be good for her."

"Excuse me? Dad, what is up with you? You *left* Mom because you had an argument? This isn't happening." Drew rubbed one hand over his face.

"It's personal. And I didn't leave her. I'm just staying here for a few days." Drew realized that men his dad's age were uncomfortable talking about their feelings, but this was ridiculous.

"Okay. That's it." Drew said. He flung one arm out and pointed toward his kitchen table. "Go in there and sit down. I'll get us a couple of beers and you can tell me what the hell is going on."

His dad parked it at the table, and Drew pulled a couple of Elysian Brewing's Men's Room Original Reds out of the refrigerator. Owen, the chef, would be here in a couple of hours to start dinner; maybe he should text Owen and let him know he'd be making twice as much of whatever was on the menu tonight. His dad regarded the beer with a skeptical eye.

"What the hell is that?"

"It's good, Dad. Try it. I also have some Arrogant Bastard Ale if you'd like some of that."

"Doesn't this town have some Bud or maybe a Coors Light?"

"Dad. You're in Seattle. Everyone drinks microbrews here." Drew grabbed his phone out and texted while he talked. "You and Mom are fighting?"

"She's mad at me because she served me takeout Chinese food for dinner the night before last, and I told her I wanted a home-cooked meal instead."

Drew hit "send" on his text and regarded his father with disbelief.

"You said that to *Mom?* You love Chinese takeout."

"Not right now I don't. Your mother made me a sandwich for dinner. A *sandwich.* She used to make a big dinner every night with sides and salad, and now it's a sandwich and takeout." He pounded a little on the table. "I don't work all day to come home to a sandwich—"

"Maybe she was tired or she didn't feel good. Dad, I know damn well it wasn't only a sandwich. She probably made potato salad or some other thing, and she made sure it was your favorite, didn't she?"

"It was pulled pork," he mumbled.

"And?"

"She used to cook for me. She used to make sure everything was the way I liked it. Now I'm lucky if the laundry makes it into the laundry room, let alone my shirts have that starch in them I like. She's too busy for me." His dad wrapped a ham-like fist around his beer and took a swallow. He didn't meet Drew's eyes.

"Dad. She's never too busy for you. What is causing this? You and Mom don't fight."

"Oh, we fight. Just not in front of you kids."

His dad was acting like a recalcitrant teenager. Or, he

was acting just like Drew did when his parents told him there was a curfew, and he was expected to keep up his grade point average or he couldn't play football, or one of a hundred other things he tried to get away with as a teen. The bowed shoulders and sadness in his dad's face told him this wasn't something minor, but Drew was fighting the impulse to drag his dad out to the car, take him to the airport, and shove his butt onto a plane home.

He wasn't going to be able to solve this. His parents needed to fix it. Plus, he couldn't figure out why his mom had suddenly decided she wasn't cooking and cleaning for his dad anymore. The last time he was home for a visit, she couldn't do enough for them. Things seemed normal. How could a thirty-five year marriage fall apart in less than five months?

Drew heaved a sigh. "Dad, maybe you should start at the beginning and explain what happened."

His dad took another swig of beer. He claimed he didn't care for Drew's taste in beer when he visited Seattle, but he managed to drink a few. Maybe Owen, the chef, might pick up a six-pack or two along with the ingredients for tomorrow night's dinner if Drew gave him a few extra bucks to do so. Grocery stores were yet another place Drew stayed out of during the season; a beer run might take two hours after signing autographs. He knew it was part of his job. He enjoyed meeting Sharks fans. Sometimes, though, he longed for the same quick, anonymous errands people in his family or his non-football friends enjoyed.

Drew settled back in his chair and waited. His dad put

the bottle back down on the kitchen table with a slight thump and let out a long breath.

"Your mother went out and got a job."

"Why?"

"She said she hardly knew what to do with herself. You all are out on your own, it's just us, and it didn't take her eight hours a day to wash my shorts and figure out what was for dinner. She also said something about wanting her own money, which is ridiculous. I told her thirty-five years ago that it wasn't "mine" or "hers," it was ours. She said she feels weird about buying me a present with my money. I told her I didn't give a shit about that." His dad passed one hand over his face again. "She works during the daytime. Sometimes she works on the weekends. I want to sit and watch the game with my best girl, and she's taking clothes orders or working in the returns department instead."

"What's she doing, Dad?"

"She got a job with that big mail-order clothes company in Dodgeville. All their operators are women your mom's age that help people buy things, and then they chat a little about their grandchildren or the Green Bay team or whatever the customer wants to talk about. She's all excited because one of her cookie recipes is included in this year's holiday catalog. I think she likes being there more than she likes me right now."

"That can't be true."

"She . . . Son, maybe she doesn't love me anymore." His dad rested his face in both hands.

Drew's dad was as big as he was. He remembered

thinking his dad was the biggest man in the world next to his grandfather when he was younger. He'd never seen his dad cry. The biggest show of emotion from him was when his mom had to have an emergency gallbladder removal a few years back. He told the surgeon that Drew's mom was his everything and to make sure she came back to him. He wasn't a lovey-dovey kind of a guy, but he bought Drew's mother flowers and told her she was the love of his life when she woke up from the anesthesia.

"If she didn't love you, she wouldn't have called around looking for you," Drew said. "She's not doing this to hurt you. She might want something to occupy her time while you're working, Dad." He awkwardly patted his dad on the back. "Do you want me to talk to her?"

"I can handle it."

"Then why are you here?"

His father let out a long breath. "You're not happy I came to visit."

"I'm always happy to see you. I'm a little confused, though."

"If she wants a break, maybe she should have one," his dad said. "I'll stay for a few days, let her think about it, and then I'll go home."

Drew loved his family and missed them a lot, but he couldn't imagine what his dad was going to do with himself when Drew was at the Sharks practice facility for twelve hours a day. If this kept up all week, he was also staying overnight in the team hotel before the game on Sunday; it wasn't like his dad had any poker buddies or golf cronies in the area to hang around with.

"Dad. I love visiting with you, but I'm worried there won't be a lot for you to do over the next few days. I have to be at the facility."

His dad pulled a handful of colorful brochures out of his back pocket. "I got these at the airport. I'll have plenty to do." He dropped them on the table in front of Drew. "There's a Museum of Flight, which has the Concorde and the space shuttle simulator. I've never been to the Space Needle or Pike Place Market. There's a candy factory in some place called Issaquah. I've never been on a tour of the stadium you play in, and see, here's a brochure for it."

"Dad, I can get you a VIP tour—"

"Don't worry about me. I have a rental car and some money. We can get together for dinner or something in the evenings. How about that?"

"Sure. I'd enjoy it."

Drew heard the insertion of a key in the front door lock. Owen was here to start his prep for dinner. He worked for several of the Sharks during the season. Luckily for him, his other clients lived within a two-mile radius of Drew's house.

Owen walked into the kitchen and bumped fists with Drew.

"Got your text. There's plenty of food for both of you tonight."

"Great." Drew indicated his dad with a nod. "Owen, this is my dad, Neil. Dad, Owen."

Owen extended his hand to shake Drew's dad's. "Nice to meet you. Are there any food sensitivities I should know about before I start?"

Neil McCoy shook his head. "Nope." He folded his lips a little.

"My dad's not going to ask you this, but I know he's hoping there's no chick food on the menu tonight."

Owen hefted the refrigerated bags he'd brought and his knife case onto Drew's kitchen island. "How does cilantro-lime fish tacos served with mango salsa and avocado crème sound to you? I've got some Mexican rice and beans to go with them. I have some dulce de leche ice cream for dessert as well."

"Sounds great, Owen. Dad, you'll enjoy it." His dad looked a bit befuddled, but Drew knew his idea of cuisine was a piece of meat and a potato. He'd be okay. "Do you need anything else right now?"

"Nope." Owen glanced over at the beers on Drew's table. "I tried to get some of that when I was at the store last week. It sells out."

"I had to carry the last six-pack out in my teeth," Drew assured him. Owen let out a snort and arrayed pots and pans on Drew's cooktop. "Want one?"

"Hell, yeah, and thanks. I'll crack it open later. Will Neil be here the rest of the week?"

"Yes," Drew's dad said.

"I'll make sure there's plenty of food, then. How do you feel about quinoa and kale casserole?" It was obvious by Owen's grin he was teasing a little, but Neil looked horrified.

"Dad. He's joking," Drew said. "If you'd make some stuff that's friendly for a guy who likes entrees like spaghetti and meat and potatoes, I'll eat the chickified stuff.

I'm going to need a little extra bulk on Sunday, that's for sure."

"Dallas?" Owen said.

"Shit, yeah, and their offensive line is a nightmare these days."

"You'll kick their asses," Owen said. "Watching their QB sit on the turf and cry at Sharks Stadium is one of my favorite memories."

"That was excellent, wasn't it?" Drew got up from the table and crossed to the island, feeling around for his wallet. "If you're making more stuff for Dad, I need to spot you some cash for the ingredients."

"I'll bill you. Don't worry about it." Owen grinned at Neil. "By the time I get done with you, you'll be eating ceviche and Thai coconut curry."

"Ceviche," his dad said in a low voice. The food alone might scare him right back to Wisconsin.

"Would you also be willing to bill me for a couple of decent six-packs when you make a store run?" Drew said.

"I can do that." Owen poured a slick of extra-virgin olive oil into his frying pan. "You must have gotten ambushed in the grocery store again."

"Yeah. It was two hours before I made it out of there, especially since Tom Reed was one aisle over loading up a cart with ice cream and avocados for his pregnant wife. I'm ordering stuff from Amazon Fresh now, but I have to sign for the beer myself—"

"I can handle it, D. Don't worry about it."

Owen gently laid two pieces of tilapia in the frying pan and turned the heat down a bit as he stirred the beans and the rice. He'd already put the tortillas in the oven to warm and was pulling more items out of his bag to construct the mango salsa and the additional taco filling. Drew could assemble a few dishes and feed himself, but nothing like this.

"Hey, Dad, why don't you go relax? Dinner will be ready in twenty minutes or so. Your stuff's in one of the rooms upstairs, right?"

His dad shoved himself out of the dining room chair and got to his feet. "Good idea. I took the room next door to yours, by the way." He walked into the family room, sat down on the couch, and clicked the TV on.

Drew patted his pocket to make sure his phone was still in there, and he said to Owen in a low voice, "I'll be back in fifteen minutes or so."

"Great." Owen went back to making their delicious looking and smelling dinner, and Drew ducked into the small office he kept in the little bonus room off of the kitchen, shutting the door behind him. He punched in the contact for his parents' number.

His mom answered on the second ring. "Hi, honey."

"Mom, are you going to be up later? I'm about to have dinner with Dad, and I'd like to hear your side of what's going on."

His mother sighed. "There isn't a lot to tell. I've wanted to go back to work for a while. You kids are all grown and gone. The grandkids are only here on the weekends. It's not like I had a lot to do, and your dad's gone all day. I wanted something for myself," she said. "Your dad is acting like I've run off with another man. I don't get what his problem is. He doesn't talk to me before he works overtime or on the weekends."

"He's hurt because he thinks he's not getting the same dinners and attention these days."

"That's not true. I'm just not hovering over him twenty-four hours a day anymore. It's good for him. I keep encouraging him to go fishing, or take those buddies of his up on their poker invites every Friday night. I'd like to go see my friends too, but he doesn't like 'chick flicks' and book clubs. Plus, his doctor told me if he doesn't cool it on the red meat and fried stuff, he's going to have to go on cholesterol drugs. I don't want that to happen." She let out another sigh. "I love him more than anyone else in the world. I've loved him for thirty-six years, and I'll love him until I die, but honey, he needs to realize that I need a life."

"He said you made pulled pork for him."

"And coleslaw, and made sure the buns were toasted the way he likes them, and I made a peach pie too."

"Will you marry me, Mom?"

His mother burst out laughing. "I'll make sure your future wife has all of my recipes, honey." She was quiet for a few seconds. "How's that going?"

"I met someone, but it's not going to work."

"Why not?"

"I'll tell you, but you have to keep it between us."

"Of course."

"She runs another team. She doesn't live here. I'd get traded or benched and she'd probably be in a lot of trouble if we keep seeing each other."

"That's crazy. They can't tell you who you can fall in love with. Are you sure it won't work?"

"Yeah. I'm sure." He heard Owen call out, "Soup's on!"

"I have to go. Could we talk again later?"

"How about tomorrow morning, honey?"

"Okay then. It's a date. I'll call you when I wake up. I love you, Mom."

He heard her blow a kiss through the receiver. "I love you too, honey. Take care of your dad for me."

"Will do."

Owen was loading the dishwasher when he emerged from his office, and his dad was already sitting at the kitchen table. Drew was a little surprised to note the table was already set.

"Did you do this, Dad?"

"Gotta earn my keep."

Two hours later, his dad was asleep in the guest room upstairs, and Drew was relaxing on the couch in the family room and watching a little TV before he went to bed. It was a jam-packed day, but he wasn't sleepy yet. He couldn't stop thinking about Kendall, and how she'd looked when he awoke this morning in her bed. He wondered if she thought of him too, and if she felt as frustrated as he did about the fact that any romance between them couldn't last.

He heard the chirp of an incoming text.

I can't stop thinking about you. Good night.

Chapter Ten

KENDALL SHUT THE conference room door behind her. She'd been up to her ass in alligators since yesterday, when she showed up at the first meeting of the day having done exactly zero research and even less preparation. The only reason she managed to get through it at all was the fact she over-prepared every other day and she had a great memory.

She'd had to play catch-up all day yesterday and most of last night. She was ready for them this morning. Unfortunately for her, the front office group decided to dispense with the original meeting agenda and embark on a fun new one.

"Is Drew McCoy of the Sharks dating someone who lives in San Jose?" The Miners' owner, Donald Curtis, took a sip of coffee and set his mug back down on the table.

She almost spit her mouthful of triple-shot latte across the conference room table. She managed to recover her composure in milliseconds and glanced around the table to make sure her reaction wasn't detected. None of the guys noticed anything wrong. Sydney gave her a raised eyebrow, though. Damn it. She'd be asked about it later. She dabbed at her mouth with a paper napkin and attempted to look unconcerned with the topic.

"How the hell should we know or care who McCoy's dating? He's still with Seattle," the head coach said. Jack Phillips hated these meetings and never passed up a chance to let everyone in the room know it.

"There were photos of him in the San Jose airport with some UCLA alumni on Twitter the day before yesterday, according to a sports website. If he's involved with someone in the area, it might be easier to persuade him he'd like to live in California and play for us," the director of scouting for the team chimed in. He was looking for any possible angle (that didn't cost money) to pry Drew McCoy away from the Sharks.

Rod Carpenter, the director of player personnel, steepled his fingers as he listened.

"You know, it's not the worst idea I've ever heard to follow up on that information. Why else would a player fly anywhere for twenty-four hours during the season? That's odd, especially since it's not like he can't afford to have a woman meet him in Seattle instead."

"Must have been a hot date," the head coach said and snickered. The other guys at the table laughed out loud.

"Maybe he couldn't find anyone he'd rather have in Seattle."

"Those Sharks aren't hard on the eyes."

"He'd be laughed out of the locker room if he dated a cheerleader," Jerry Berggren, the director of scouting, said.

Kendall needed to get this meeting back on track.

"Maybe he has a family member in the area, or maybe he wanted a good look at the Golden Gate Bridge. Let's get back to the agenda," she said, glancing down at her iPad screen. "We lost Tarvaris Walters to a hamstring injury for the rest of the season Sunday. His backup will play, but we're now looking for another starting cornerback in free agency. What's the progress been since this morning? Did you talk with Chase Adams' agent?"

Tarvaris would have surgery and be assigned to injured reserve for the rest of the season. His replacement would be offered a one-season contract, most likely with a small signing bonus for the alleged inconvenience of living in San Francisco for another two to four months. Kendall knew Seattle had cut Chase Adams, a starter-quality cornerback, due to the impact of his veteran's salary on their cap when a rookie low-round draft pick ran rings around the guy. He'd be expensive, but he'd also be a quarterback's nightmare.

If the Miners had any hopes of making the postseason, they weren't doing it with just one cornerback. They needed at least another guy on the depth chart in case of injury.

"We talked with the agent. Adams is motivated to come here and will sign for less than market value in hopes of catching on for more than one season," Rod Carpenter said.

"What's the holdup?" Kendall said.

"You'll authorize his salary and a hundred thousand dollar signing bonus," Rod said.

"Yes. Call the agent right now before Adams signs with another team," Kendall said.

This was the most frustrating thing about Kendall's current position: The guys she worked with were cordial to her face, but she knew every male in the Miners' front office was rooting for her to fail. They all wanted her job, and they weren't afraid to make that clear.

They'd appointed her because she'd been with the organization the longest, she was very good at her job, and she had enough football knowledge to not embarrass herself in public or at a meeting. It looked good to the league that the Miners appointed a woman too. In other words, she'd probably hold this job for a few weeks, they'd appoint one of their cronies as GM, and she'd (hopefully) go back to her former job.

Frankly, the GM job was a nightmare. She preferred being the director of football operations. She still had to go to meetings and listen to a bunch of guys pontificate on topics that could be solved much more rapidly without listening to their high school/college football exploits and the usual shit talking about women or wives. Her days used to consist of managing the team's salary cap, dealing with player contracts and agents, ensuring the team's financial health, and making sure the heads of other departments were doing their jobs. She listened to other people tell her why the ticket prices should go up or how much it was going to cost to serve organic food in the team's cafeteria instead of what they were currently serving.

She spent a lot of her day now signing off on other people's research and decisions. She couldn't make an effective decision without doing her own research, though, and the system she'd had in place in her former job wasn't working so far in the GM's job. It was like trying to drink from a fire hose, and every guy in the room right now knew it.

She stifled a sigh as Rod Carpenter came back into the room and told the group, "We got him. He'll be here tomorrow morning for a physical and contract signing."

The team was damn lucky Chase Adams was still available during the period of time since they'd made the initial call, and someone who should have known to pick up the phone and ask her for the authorization didn't do so.

One more emergency solved. Of course, that left a few more, including the fact the Miners' head coach had become even more difficult to deal with in the past three weeks. Team personnel tiptoed around him. Another assistant coach had been ordered by his doctor to take a leave of absence due to stress-related health issues last week. Jack Phillips' reaction to this was to call the assistant coach a "pansy" in front of the players and tell him if he didn't show up he was fired. HR had since gotten involved. She was waiting for a hostile work environment lawsuit filing to land on her desk any minute.

She was also dealing with Rocky Hill, an All-Pro offensive lineman with two previous DV arrests. Hill had violated a protective order two days before the team played in Seattle and spent the night in jail. She wanted to cut Hill from the team. Her colleagues (vociferously) disagreed. He was on the agenda, and her stomach churned in anticipation of what was going to happen when she told them she'd made a decision. She was cutting him and starting the backup, and if they disagreed, she was going to let the local press know exactly why he was benched for Sunday's game.

She wished she could go back to her office, shut the door, and construct spreadsheets for the rest of the day, but it wasn't going to happen.

Kendall had started working for the Miners in their mail room at sixteen years old. Her family's next door neighbor was the team's former GM, and she'd needed a part-time job for a few hours a week after school and on Saturdays. She enjoyed watching her high school's team play football, but the more she was around the Miners and the headquarters, it grew into a passion. She wanted to keep working for the Miners. The former GM told her that the only way she'd get a front office job was to focus on business education, so she earned a Bachelor's first and her Master's at Wharton in San Francisco. She kept working for the Miners all through college and grad school, and she was rewarded with a promotion to the assistant to the director of football operations job the Monday morning after she graduated with an MBA.

Two years ago the director retired, and she landed his job.

She knew other women doubted their career paths or took time off to get married and have babies. She wanted children and a husband, but she also wanted her career. She couldn't see any reason why it wouldn't work. She'd have to hire a very reliable nanny and marry someone who was willing to pitch in, but it could be done.

Three hours of mind-numbing discussion about the minutiae of running a professional football franchise later, Kendall was able to escape to her office. She'd been taking notes the entire meeting. There was research to be done and decisions to be made, but first of all, she needed some lunch. She stuffed her tablet into her handbag and glanced up as Sydney walked into her office.

"I'm going to grab a sandwich. Do you want me to get you one too?" Kendall said.

Sydney shut the office door behind her and leaned against it. She raised one eyebrow.

"You know why Drew McCoy was in San Jose, don't you?"

"Want one of those Izze things? I know you really like the clementine. It sounds refreshing. Maybe I'll get one for myself too." Kendall heard her phone chirp. She grabbed it out of her pants pocket.

"Were you talking to him?" Sydney said. There was no doubt who Sydney meant. Damn it.

"I can't officially *talk to him*. It's considered tampering," Kendall said.

Sydney let out a gasp. "You talked to him."

"It wasn't that big of a deal . . ."

Actually, it was a huge deal, up to and including the fact they'd had sex, but she wasn't going to share that with her assistant. Kendall had tried to keep the friendly, engaging Sydney at arm's length and be professional for the first few months or so they worked together. Her detachment had collapsed in a heap one afternoon when Kendall discovered her usually unflappable assistant in tears in the ladies' room because the boyfriend she'd been dating since high school dumped her via text message.

Six months later, Kendall was the one falling apart in the ladies' room during a workday. Sydney had cancelled all of her meetings, gotten her a fresh box of tissues, and bought her a two and a half pound bag of M&M's.

"If it wasn't a big deal, you would have told those guys about it." Sydney crossed to Kendall's desk, grabbed a clean sticky note and a pen, and said, "I'll order lunch. What do you want?"

"Turkey on wheat."

"And provolone, I know. I'll get you an Izze. Anything else?"

"Do they have M&M's?"

Sydney grinned at her. "I want the whole story when I come back."

HALF AN HOUR later, Sydney returned to Kendall's office with a couple of bakery bags and spread the booty over her desk. "Okay. Two sandwiches. Yours is marked. Here's your drink, and here's your M&M's. I got some too." She pulled one of the chairs that sat in front of Kendall's desk to the edge and sat down. "So, start at the beginning."

"Do we need to talk about the circle of trust?" Kendall joked. "This has to remain a secret."

"Of course it does, because I'd like to keep working here. What happened?" Sydney pulled a veggie wrap out of butcher paper and uncapped her Izze. "Don't leave anything out."

Kendall would be leaving plenty out, but she wasn't going to admit that. "Two nights before the Miners played the Sharks, I left my hotel room to go buy a book."

"You read books on your e-reader."

"Yes, I know. I needed to get out and stretch my legs."

"In a *rainstorm?*"

"I didn't know it was that bad before I went out there."

"Kendall, I would have called the bookstore and asked them to send something over—"

"I know you would have. I just needed a walk."

"Wasn't that the same day Jack Phillips went absolutely ape shit over the fact that you changed the free agents marketing brochure?"

"Yes, it was." Kendall shook her head. "There was a bookstore about a block and a half from the hotel. I needed to get out for a few minutes, and there was a presentation by the author of Carl Sagan's latest biography."

Sydney looked a bit confused.

"Very famous astrophysicist. My dad used to watch his show when I was younger. I knew Dad would love the book, so I sat down to hear what the guy had to say. He didn't show up, but I grabbed a book anyway for my dad. Drew McCoy was the only other person in the audience."

"Did you recognize him?"

"He had this big slouchy knit hat over his hair and he was dressed in casual clothes—"

"He's on TV ten times a day!"

"I don't watch much TV," Kendall said. Sydney grinned at her and shook her head. "He asked me if I wanted to have a cup of coffee with him, and I said yes. We went to the coffee shop next door, we had something to drink, and he decided he wanted to walk me back to the hotel."

Sydney's eyes narrowed. "How did he get back home?"

"Took a cab."

"So the whole time you were talking with him, you didn't recognize him, and then he was nice enough to walk you back to the hotel in a driving rain and seventy mile an hour winds?"

"It didn't really get bad until we were back at the hotel—" Kendall blurted out, and then she wished she could bite her own tongue off.

"Back at the hotel, hmm?" Sydney was giving her the raised eyebrow again. Kendall would give her own story the raised eyebrow if someone else was telling it to her.

"He walked me back there. He had to dry off before he could go home."

Sydney stared at her. She reached out for the M&M's bag, ripped it open, and held it out to Kendall. "I should have gotten a bottle of tequila, a lime, and a couple of shot glasses." She tossed a handful of candies into her mouth, chewed, swallowed, and said, "He had your phone, didn't he?"

"Yeah."

"And he flew to San Jose to bring it back to you."

Kendall reached out for another handful of M&M's.

"I take it that's a yes," Sydney said. "I'm guessing he didn't bring the phone to your house and run back to the airport the same night, either." She picked up her Izze and took a swig. "Are you going to see him again?"

"No. Yes. I don't know." Kendall pushed her half sandwich around with one fingertip on the butcher paper it came in.

Sydney picked up her wrap, took a bite, and chewed. Kendall had lost her appetite. Well, she'd lost her appetite for anything besides chocolate. She grabbed a few more from the bag and popped them into her mouth.

"He's interested, isn't he?"

Kendall's voice dropped. She leaned forward. "Yes. I already told him that being involved with him couldn't happen. He'd get cut or traded if anyone found out, and I'd be in serious trouble as well around here."

"The team wants to go after him in free agency."

"Yes."

"Does he want to play for the Miners?"

"You have to promise me you will not tell anyone this—"

"I promise," Sydney said.

Kendall shook her head. Sydney's eyes got huge again.

"Jack Phillips is going to lose it completely when he finds this out," Sydney said. "He wants him BAD."

"I know."

"Are you going to tell them?"

"No. If I did, I'd be in trouble I couldn't get out of. He said the only way he'd consider it is if the team threw what he calls 'stupid money' at him."

"Do you plan on doing that?"

"No. He identified several issues the team's already having that could be fixed with the money we'd have to pay him to leave Seattle."

Sydney stared at her. "I think that's crazier than the fact you had the discussion."

"He's fair," Kendall said.

Actually, Drew was generous. She knew the problems with the current team. They'd been over it multiple times already with Jack Phillips, who insisted the players in question were simply "lazy" and "unmotivated." She knew from talking with those players' agents that they'd had it with the head coach and were looking for a way out of San Francisco as quickly as possible.

"So eat something. You're meeting with the equipment guys a little later, and then we'll be prepping for tomorrow morning's agenda," Sydney said.

More meetings. More decisions. The guys who were gunning for her job were probably rubbing their hands together with glee. She had never wanted the GM job to begin with, but she'd do her best while she had it.

The next several days were a whirlwind. The Miners were playing at home, which meant she wasn't required to travel to an away game with the team. Kendall also did her best to stop thinking about Drew. It wasn't working. She'd sent him some junior-high quality text the other day about missing him, and he didn't text in response. In other words, she needed to get over it and keep her mind on her work.

She was finishing up some e-mails at seven PM on Friday evening when Sydney walked into her office.

"What are you doing here?" Kendall said. "You were out of here an hour ago. You have homework."

"It's Friday night, and I can do the homework tomorrow or Sunday. You should have been out of here an hour ago too. It will all wait until Monday morning." Sydney reached out to shove Kendall's office door closed. "Have you heard from him?"

They both knew who "him" was.

"No. Maybe it's better that way."

"Your meetings on Monday don't start until noon."

"I thought there was some kind of breakfast thing."

"No," Sydney said. She handed Kendall her tablet; flight times between San Francisco and Seattle were already on it. "Throw a few things in a bag and I'll tell everyone you have an appointment."

"Why are you doing this for me?"

Sydney grinned at her. "You and this job are getting me through undergrad. It's the least I can do."

Chapter Eleven

THERE WAS A reason for that old cliché about houseguests and fish starting to stink after three days. Neil McCoy wasn't exactly a houseguest, but he'd been slowly driving Drew insane for the past several days while camping out at his house. Drew would be staying overnight at the team hotel this evening in preparation for tomorrow's game. He could pack his garment bag in his sleep, but he was worried about what mischief his dad could get into while he was gone. He'd already asked Owen, to make something meat-and-potatoey for his dad's dinner tonight. If Drew was lucky (and Neil wasn't bored) he would stay home and order an action-adventure movie on pay-per-view or something.

Drew wanted to send his dad to his room without his dinner. Neil had been sullen and irritable since he arrived in Seattle.

"Dad, this is not a competition. You love her. She loves

you. Go home and work it out," Drew pleaded for the hundredth time since he found his dad napping on his family room couch. His older brother and both of his sisters had tried to convince their father to return to Wisconsin via long distance phone calls and Skyping. "What's going on with you? You're acting like a child, Dad. What would you say to *me?*"

"No, I am not acting like a child, and I am not calling your mother. She can apologize to me. I'm not the one who's ignoring my household duties, and I'm not crawling back to her, either," Neil said. "You . . . you wouldn't be happy if your wife wasn't cooking dinner for *you* and making sure things were nice at home, either."

Neil put his hands on his hips and tried to look angry, but Drew could see the sadness in his dad's expression. Instead of talking with Drew's mom and telling her he felt worried he was losing her, he blew his stack and stomped around. Drew's mom didn't take that from her kids, and she sure wasn't taking it from her husband, either.

"Crawling back to her, Dad? Really? That's not the point. You're being stubborn. Mom's not doing this to hurt you. It's a part-time job. She's happy. Why can't you accept the fact she wanted something else to occupy her time besides all of us, something she enjoys doing?" Drew heaved a huge sigh and grabbed the suit and tie he'd need tomorrow out of his closet. He'd already grabbed a freshly laundered dress shirt, appropriate underwear, dress socks, and shoes. "You remember how to set the security system when you leave for my game tomorrow, right?"

"Yes, I do."

Drew reached into the closet again. "You'll need something to wear," he told his dad and handed him one of his game-worn jerseys. "I think I might have a brand-new Sharks hat in here. The weather tomorrow is supposed to be overcast and chilly. Do you need a turtleneck or something to wear under that?"

"I brought my heavy jacket. I'll be fine." Neil told him. "Thanks for the jersey. Your mom wears hers every Sunday when we're watching your game at home."

Thank God for pay-per-view. He'd fly his parents in each week, but they preferred being at home surrounded by Drew's siblings and the grandkids. He made a point of finding a TV camera during the third quarter each game, giving his mom a little wave, and mouthing, "Hi Mom. I love you." Needless to say, the Sharks fans (and the team's PR department) ate it up, but he wasn't doing it for them. He knew his mom got a kick out of waiting and watching for it.

"Okay, then. Let me get the hat, and I'm almost ready to go." Drew grabbed his shaving kit out of the bathroom and made sure he had a couple more of the black covered elastic bands he pulled his hair back with. His fingers closed over the brim of a brand-new Sharks logo hat, which he handed to his dad. "Dad, Owen will be here in about an hour. He's making you some steak and potatoes for dinner, and he's bringing you a few snacks and maybe a Bud or two. If you want to stand on the sidelines for the game, you'll need to be there a couple of hours early. The guy at Will Call gets a team employee to make sure you get where you're going."

"Thanks, Son." His dad held out both arms. "Good luck tomorrow. We are so proud of you." Drew was folded into the huge bear hug his dad had been giving him since he was a little boy. They slapped each other on the back.

"I'm proud of you too, Dad, and I'll be prouder still when you go home and make up with Mom." He backed away a little and grabbed his dad by the biceps. "I'll be driving you to the airport Monday morning, so if you want to get Mom some of that candy you talked about, you might want to stop by there tomorrow before the game."

"Yeah, yeah, yeah," his dad said, but he smiled. "Kicking your old man out?"

"Sending my old man home where he belongs. Bring Mom next time."

"I might."

The doorbell rang downstairs. Drew wasn't expecting anyone; it wasn't Girl Scout cookie time, so he was tempted to not answer. Owen knew how to let himself in, so it couldn't be him. A minute or so later, the doorbell rang again.

"I'd better see who that is," Drew said to his dad and headed downstairs. He didn't see anyone when he looked through the peephole in the door, but he opened it anyway. He saw her sweet smile when she poked her head around the doorframe.

"Surprise," his mother said.

"Mom! What are you doing here?"

Drew's mom, Bonnie, threw her arms around him. "It's so good to see you, honey. I have missed you so much."

"Why didn't you tell me you were on your way? I

would have picked you up at the airport." He gave her a huge squeeze. "I've missed you too."

"The plane landed an hour or so ago. I took a shuttle here." Drew glanced up to see the driver wave as he got back into the van. "It's so easy, and the flight was nice. I brought one bag." She kissed his cheek. "I won't be here long. I'm picking up your father, and we're going home."

He heard his dad's heavy footsteps on the hardwood floor of the entryway.

"I'll go home when I want to," his father said. Drew almost let out a groan. In other words, he was back to acting like a child.

Drew's mom reached back to grab the handle of a small rolling suitcase, stepped around him, and faced her husband.

"No, you're coming home with me. Our son has enough on his plate without acting as a referee between us," his mother scolded. "I'll stay in the other guest room, and we'll be going home tomorrow."

"Don't you want to see my game, Mom? I can get you a suite ticket. You'll have fun, and I'd love it if you were there."

"Oh, yes, honey, but not if I'm intruding." She glanced up at Drew. "Aren't you supposed to be at the team hotel tonight?"

"You could never intrude, Mom. Let me get this set up." He pulled his phone out of his pocket, scrolled to find the Sharks' PR director's number, and hit "dial."

Drew's parents were still glaring at each other. He had to be at the hotel in less than an hour, but he wasn't sure he wanted to leave at the moment. His dad would never put hands on his mom, but they were sure as hell still angry with each other. He hated to think of them spending the evening fighting and unhappy, but there was little he could do about the situation right now. His little mom looked like a housecat that was defending her turf, and his dad was the neighborhood German shepherd. This wasn't going to end well.

He heard a "hello," and he put the phone up to his ear. "Hi Colleen, it's Drew McCoy. I'm wondering if I could ask you for a favor."

"Of course, Drew. How can I help?"

"My mom, Bonnie, just arrived in town. Both of my parents will be at the game tomorrow, if they can get into the team suite."

"Absolutely. I'll take care of it. Would they like sideline passes?"

"I think so."

"I'll make that happen," Colleen said. "Leave it up to me."

Easiest phone call he'd made all week. He thanked her, said goodbye, and ended the call. Maybe he was imagining it, but his dad had sidled over to his mother a little. He had to get his ass in gear and go to the hotel. He couldn't leave them like this, though.

"Mom, my chef will be here in a little while to make dinner for you lovebirds," he said. He had no idea if Owen would have enough ingredients, but he always seemed to cope admirably with whatever food situation he found himself in. "I need to go, but I'm not leaving until you at least kiss each other and say hello."

"I can make myself a sandwich," his mother said.

"No, Mom, let Owen cook for you." He put his hands on his hips. "Do I need to send you to your rooms? Nice greeting. I need to see it."

His dad folded his lips and raised an eyebrow. His mother put her bag back down on the hallway floor.

"I can be an adult even if you're having problems with that right now, Neil," she said. He scowled in response. She moved closer to his father, slipped her arms around his waist, and stood on her tiptoes to kiss his cheek. "Hello," she said.

Neil's arms surrounded her. "Hello," he said, and he gave her a peck on the mouth.

"That's not a kiss," Drew said.

"This is private—"

"When you dragged me into it, Dad, it stopped being private."

Father and son stared at each other over Bonnie's head. "Fine," Neil said. He stroked his wife's cheek with one big hand. "I missed you, baby."

"I missed you too."

His dad kissed his mother—a real kiss, not that pecking at her stuff. She wrapped her arms around his neck. His parents were ignoring him, and he was happy about that. It was time for Drew to make himself scarce.

THE NEXT DAY, the Sharks beat Dallas 30–6. Drew had a pair of sacks, several tackles, and had batted down a pass. His parents were holding hands on the sidelines. He knew he was going to have to spend a little more time making sure things were fine between them when he got home, but it was great to see them at one of his games.

Instead of finding a TV camera in the third quarter and delivering his message to his mom, he crossed the tape line the grounds guys made each week on either side of where the team set up on the fifty yard line to keep spectators out of their area. She wasn't hard to pick out of the sidelines crowd. He hugged and kissed her and rejoined the team.

Coach Stewart caught up with him a few minutes later. "I'm going to have to fine you for that, McCoy."

"I realize that. Had to say hi to my mom."

The coach gave him a slap on the back. "It's good to see your parents here." He tugged on the mouthpiece of his headset and moved off to another part of the sidelines as the offense took the field again.

Two hours later, Drew walked out of the Sharks locker room and met up with his parents.

"How about I take you out for dinner tonight? You loved John Howie Steak the last time we went there." Drew grinned at his mom. "I'll get you one of those caramel ganache tarts for dessert."

"Thank you, honey, but you don't have to do that. Your dad took me to the store this morning, and I have a roast cooking at your house. I'll make the potatoes when I get to your place. There's a salad, and I baked a chocolate cake." His mom's eyes sparkled. "I can't leave you here without a good dinner and some leftovers for this week."

"Mom, I'll help you with the dishes."

"Your dad actually loaded the dishwasher, honey." His mom was blushing. His dad did a lot more than "load the dishwasher," if Drew was reading the situation correctly. He did his best not to flinch.

Neil slipped his arm around Bonnie's shoulders. "Come on, Son. Let's go home."

Derrick walked out of the locker room and came to a screeching halt. "Mama McCoy," he said.

She let out a squeal and threw her arms around him. "Derrick, it's so good to see you!"

His dad let out a grunt, but he reached out a hand to Derrick. "Nice to see you."

"Nice to see you too, Mr. McCoy." Derrick shook his hand and turned to Drew. "Are you meeting us at Ruth Chris's for dinner tonight?"

"My mom made dinner for us at my house," Drew said.

"Why don't you come over for dinner, Derrick? We'd love to see you, and there's plenty to eat," his mom said.

"Yeah, D," Drew said. "Go get Taylor and ask him if he'd like to come over. We'll grab a drink or something afterward."

The Sharks had won, so the players would visit the facility to verify they were healthy on Monday morning and not be expected back to work until Wednesday morning. Many of the single Sharks could be found at some of the nightclubs in the Seattle area on home game Sunday nights as a result. Drew took it easy on the alcohol during the season, but he liked to socialize with his teammates.

Seth must have heard his name. He emerged from the locker room a minute or so later and headed toward Derrick and Drew.

"What's up? Are we going to the steakhouse? I'm starving."

"We're going to Drew's house instead," Derrick said. "His mom is cooking, and you're invited."

Drew's mom gave Seth a hug. "I baked a chocolate cake," she said.

"I'll be there," Seth said. "Thank you for the invite."

Drew's mom was beaming. "Why don't you invite some more of your teammates, honey?"

"I'm not sharing your chocolate cake with anyone else, Mom. Let's get out of here," Drew said. His dad took Bonnie's arm and propelled her toward the parking lot.

"We'll see you at home in about half an hour or so," Drew called after them.

DREW, SETH, AND Derrick headed toward the team bus. They'd pick up their cars at the Sharks' training facility. Drew hoped his mom had made a side of beef or something. She was used to how much he could eat, but she hadn't fed these knuckleheads for a couple of years. Maybe she forgot what it was like. Maybe he should pick up some more food at the store or something.

Derrick must have read his mind.

"We'd better stop on the way to your place and get

some flowers and wine or something, man. My mama would kick my ass if I showed up empty-handed," Derrick said.

"You know what's going to happen if we walk into a grocery store together," Drew said.

"It won't be that bad," Seth said to Drew. "The wine department is right by the flowers at that store near your house. We're in, we're out, no problemo."

"Oh, sure," Drew said. "Like you know what to buy there."

"Your mom's serving red meat," Seth said. "I'll be buying red wine."

"Where the fuck did you learn that one?" Derrick said.

"My mom told me."

"Well, then," Derrick said. "You're just a goddamn somi ... soma ... what the hell are they called? Wine guys who tell you what to get?"

"Sommelier," Drew said. "Plus, there are tags on the wine displays giving hints on what might be best to buy and drink with the food you're having."

"Oooh. Aren't we fancy?" Derrick said. "Did your mom tell you that too? She's a nice lady, so I'm not going to kick your ass for that."

Seth rolled his eyes, and Drew laughed. Derrick had meted out some punishment on the field today, but he'd be in a much better mood after he had something to eat.

The three men were back in their vehicles and speeding down 405 to Drew's house minutes later. They pulled into the lot outside of the neighborhood grocery store, and Drew gestured for them to gather around.

"Listen. We're asking for it," he said. "Derrick, you grab the flowers. They have those pre-made bouquets, and my mom likes pretty much everything. Seth, you get a couple of bottles of wine. I'll keep us moving. Remember, get what we need and head to the nearest checkstand."

"Got it." They all did a fist bump and half-jogged into the store.

Seth's optimism wasn't rewarded. Three Sharks in one grocery store less than two hours after a team victory was a recipe for bedlam, and this was no exception. Seth darted into the wine section, Derrick headed toward the flowers, and Drew heard the first shouted "Go Sharks!" less than thirty seconds later as he tried to head to the ice cream section. He was surrounded by fifteen autograph seekers almost immediately.

"Great game!"

"Will you sign this, 'To the hottest woman I've ever met'?"

"My son's school is having a fundraising auction. Would you donate a game-worn jersey to it?"

A little girl was tugging on his pants leg. "Would you sign this for my daddy?" She held up an issue of *Sports Illustrated* with the Miners' QB on the cover.

The grocery store manager arrived on the run. Drew glanced up from signing autographs and said to him, "Would you please grab a couple of pints of Ben & Jerry's for me? Something that goes with chocolate cake would be nice."

"Sure," the guy said. Seconds later he heard an announcement over the store's intercom. "Customers, please allow our special guests to get in line at a check-stand. Thank you for shopping at the North Bellevue QFC, and Go Sharks."

Derrick and Seth had emerged from the floral and wine departments and were attempting to steer a cartful through other Sharks fans who also wanted autographs. Drew managed to pull his phone out of his pocket, punched in his home number, and waited until his mom answered the phone.

"Mom, we're at the store. We'll be there in a few minutes."

"What's going on there, honey? It sounds like a mob scene."

"It's fine. I'll be there soon," he said and ended the call.

The store manager was now attempting to disperse the crowd. "They have places to go too. C'mon. Let's let them by." He was also kind enough to open a checkstand just for them, and he walked them out to the parking lot to make sure they got in their cars and away safely.

They pulled into Drew's driveway less than five minutes later. Drew got out of the driver's seat and regarded his teammates. "That was interesting."

"I'll say." Derrick waved the register tape at Seth. "We'll settle up later. Let's go eat Drew's mama out of house and home."

DREW NOTED THINGS seemed a little less tense between his parents than they had been before he'd left for the team hotel last night, but going out with his teammates later was probably out. His dad was back to calling his mother "babe," and she let him have the spatula to lick after she frosted the chocolate cake. Drew managed to distract Derrick and Seth from this fact. He didn't need the two of them in the kitchen badgering his mom to let them lick the mixer bowl. He really needed to make sure his mom and dad at least talked about their differences before he took them to the airport tomorrow. He loved his parents, but he needed a few freaking days of peace and quiet.

Drew's mom took a look at the label on the wine Seth bought and called out, "Honey, are you sure about this? This stuff's pretty expensive."

"I bought it, Mrs. McCoy," Seth said. "It had a ninety-nine from *Wine Spectator*. I hope you'll enjoy it."

Bonnie shook her head. "You boys need to learn the words *table wine*," but she laughed as she said it.

It seemed like an eternity since he'd awoken in Kendall's bed, and it had been less than a week. He'd sent her a text the other day:

I can't stop thinking about you, either.

She hadn't answered. Maybe she'd counted the cost of continuing involvement with him. He knew he was out of his mind to persist at all; his career would go on, but he worried about hers. What kind of shit would he be if he got her in serious trouble at the office over the party in his pants?

Derrick and Seth were attempting to teach his dad how to play *Call of Duty*. Drew walked into the kitchen and sat down on one of the bar stools in front of his kitchen island.

"Mom, is there anything I can do to help you out?"

"Why don't you carry a few of these things to the table for me?"

She indicated a napkin-wrapped basket of bread, the big bowl of salad, and the bowl of mashed potatoes crowned with a big pat of melting butter on top. His stomach rumbled. He missed his mom's home cooking, and the laughter and teasing between himself and his brother and sisters when they got together for Sunday dinner in Wisconsin when he was on the offseason. She was transferring a gigantic roast from the pan she'd cooked it in to a platter when she glanced up and grinned at him. "It's a good thing I got the big piece of meat, honey. I'm afraid there won't be a lot of leftovers."

"That's okay, Mom. I'll have to fly home on the bye week so we can have dinner again."

He carried the bowls and the bread basket to the dining room table. The wine was already opened and waiting for them. If he offered to pay their plane fare, he wondered if his family would be willing to visit over Thanksgiving weekend this year. He had to play on Thanksgiving, but he would be happy to make himself a turkey sandwich with the dinner leftovers when he came home to a house full of his family members.

One of the few drawbacks to playing in the NFL was the fact holidays weren't celebrated on the day they happened for most players, who were far from family and friends six months a year. It was a price to pay, but after retirement, he'd make up for all the Thanksgivings and Christmas mornings he missed with his family.

The four men ate until they couldn't hold any more. Drew's mom beamed as Derrick shoved his chair back, patted his belly, and said, "Thank you so much, Miss Bonnie. I can't eat another bite."

"There's chocolate cake for dessert," his mother enticed.

"Well, maybe one more bite," Derrick said. Drew's mom reached out to pat him on the cheek. To Drew's amazement, Derrick blushed and smiled at her like he was five years old or so.

"Where's your mama and grandma tonight?"

"They're having dinner at their pastor's house."

Seth let out a snort.

"You didn't want to go?" Bonnie asked.

Derrick glanced down at the table. "This is much more enjoyable," he said.

Drew's dad hid his grin behind a napkin.

"Mrs. McCoy, thank you so much for the delicious dinner. Would you like some help with the dishes?" Seth said.

"You boys are so sweet, but I can handle it," his mother said. Four men stood up from their chairs when she got to her feet.

"No, Mom," Drew said. "You go relax. We'll handle the dishes, and then we can have some dessert."

The guys stacked the dirty dishes, cleared off leftovers, and loaded the dishwasher while Drew's mom perched on a bar stool at the kitchen island and directed traffic. Even Drew's dad got in on the action, which he was pleased to see. A few minutes after the last leftovers went into the refrigerator and the dishwasher came on, Bonnie started a pot of coffee, brought out the cake, and sliced large portions for her husband, her son, and his friends.

"Does anyone want some ice cream?" she asked, wielding a big spoon.

"Yes, please."

"Yes, babe."

"Yes, Mom."

Derrick grinned at her. "Will you adopt me?"

"You have a mama and a grandma. I know they spoil you."

"I can always use more spoiling," Derrick said.

She handed the cake and ice cream around, cut a much smaller piece of cake for herself, and sat down on the big sectional couch in Drew's family room.

Seth put his plate down on the coffee table in front of him and pulled the chirping phone out of his pocket. He handed the phone to Derrick.

"They're all at Element Lounge," Seth said.

"There's a gigantic piece of home-baked chocolate cake with my name on it," Derrick told him. "They can wait."

Drew knew Derrick and Seth weren't going to want to hang out with his parents all night no matter how much food his mom made for them. Sure enough, half an hour later, Derrick carried his plate and coffee cup to the kitchen sink.

"We hate to eat and run, but we're going to eat and run," he told Drew's mom. "Thank you so much for a wonderful dinner."

Seth wrapped his arms around Bonnie. "It's the best dinner I've had since my mom made me dinner last week," he assured her. She laughed out loud.

"That's a pretty big compliment, Seth," she said.

"You'll take me in when my mom gets sick of me, right?" Seth said.

"Of course. You're both welcome."

"D. Want to go with us tonight?"

Typically, he would. He'd have a drink or two, dance with some beautiful women, and goof around with his teammates, but tonight, he needed to find out if his mom and dad had officially made up before they went back to Wisconsin in the morning.

"Sorry, guys. I think I'll hang out here."

"Honey, you can go. We're going to pack and get some sleep. Really."

His mom made the "shoo" hand motions, but he wasn't caving.

"I don't get to spend that much time with you in the first place. I can spend some time with these guys next week on that flight to Dallas," Drew said.

"Oh, that'll be a fun time, won't it?" Derrick said.

"Hell, yeah. The flight attendants make sure there are freshly baked chocolate chip cookies on the way home," Seth said. He got up from the couch, hugged Drew's mom, and shook Drew's dad's hand. "I'll look forward to hopefully seeing you soon."

"He just wants more of that cake," Derrick said. "So do I."

A few minutes later, Seth and Derrick were on their way to the nightclub, and his mom was puttering around in the kitchen again.

"Mom, Dad," he said. "Would you like another cup of coffee?"

"No, honey. I won't sleep as it is," his mother said.

"Thanks, Son, but no thank you."

"Why don't we sit down again for a little while?" He gestured to the kitchen table. "We can chat a bit more before you need to get some shut-eye."

"That's really not necessary—" his mom said. She was interrupted by his dad.

"We're fine, Son. Don't worry about us."

"Mom. Dad. C'mon." He sat down at the table. His parents slid into chairs across from him. "What can I do to help?"

His dad let out a sigh. "We don't need help. This is a disagreement. When your mom quits that job of hers, it'll be over."

"I'm not quitting my job, Neil. I'm enjoying it. It doesn't affect your life at all, so I can't figure out why you are reacting this way to it," his mom said.

"You're not home when I want you to be there—"

"Dad, maybe Mom doesn't like it when you work overtime or weekends, either. Did you ever ask her?"

"I'm providing for the family. That's different."

"Dad, it's not different."

"Why are you taking her side?"

"There's no side. We're a family. We team up and work together. Isn't that what you've been teaching me my whole life? Did you forget?" Drew said.

His dad's shoulders were hunched over again, and he didn't look up from the table. "No, I didn't forget."

"Well, then. How can we work this out so everyone will be happy?"

"I'm not sure what you mean, honey," his mom said.

He put his hand on his dad's shoulder. "Maybe you should let your partners do some of the overtime and weekends."

"I'm getting close to retirement. I need to bank that money."

"Dad. Come on. Work with me here. I know there's plenty of money for you and Mom, and if you ever needed help, I'm here."

"We're not taking money from you."

"Well, it's there if you need it," Drew said. "Mom, will you agree to ask your boss if you can work Monday through Friday unless you've made an arrangement with Dad?"

"Honey, the only people who get to work exclusively Monday through Friday during the day are people who've been there a lot longer than I have."

"Ask them. The worst thing they can say is no. Dad, if Mom is making adjustments in her working hours, you'll need to do that too."

His dad's mouth dropped open and shut. No sound came out.

"I mean it, Dad. It's time to compromise."

His father's mouth formed a flat white line, but he nodded.

"In the meantime, Mom, Dad says he misses your special dinners. Can I help with that?"

"I don't understand," she said.

"I can pay for a chef a couple of nights a week so you can relax and enjoy yourselves, or I can get you some gift cards for restaurants you like. Which would you prefer?" Drew said.

"No, thank you," Bonnie said. "We don't need a chef. It's just the two of us, and cooking a big dinner can be a challenge on weeknights. I tried making some ahead and freezing them, but he didn't like that, either."

"Dad—"

"I want to know she thinks of me when I'm not around," his father burst out. "She always made things nice for me. She's busy now."

His mother reached across the table and took her dad's big meaty hand in both of hers. "I'm always thinking about you, Neil. Why would you believe I don't?"

"You have other things to do. You don't cook unless the grandkids come over now. I don't want to sit and watch TV without you."

If Drew had ever gotten a hint that maybe he should make himself scarce, that was the time. He'd gotten his parents talking. They needed to sort out their differences on their own. Maybe they needed to make an appointment with their pastor or something, to talk with a trained professional.

"I'll be right back," he said.

He got up from the kitchen table and headed toward the stairs to his room, grabbing his overnight bag on the way. His parents barely nodded in his direction. His dad was holding his mom's hand and they were still talking. Hopefully, they'd keep talking.

Drew unpacked his bag and changed into some warm-ups and a long-sleeved T-shirt. He couldn't hear what was going on downstairs, but maybe that was best. He grabbed his phone out of his pocket and sent Kendall a text.

I can't stop thinking about you.

Twenty minutes or so later, he heard footsteps in the hallway outside of his bedroom, and he opened the door a crack to see what was going on. His parents were holding hands and turned into the guest room next door. He heard the door shut behind them. This might be an even better time for him to go downstairs for a while. He loved his parents, but they needed some privacy.

He sat down on the couch in the family room, pulled out the book Kendall had lent him, and kept reading the same page over and over before he finally gave up and threw his forearm over his eyes. Maybe he should watch a little TV; it might relax him. He clicked through the channels until he found a rerun of *Treehouse Masters*. Maybe he'd hire the guy to build a treehouse in the greenbelt that ringed his backyard.

Drew was interested in watching the TV program, but he couldn't stay awake. It had been a long day. He usually was in bed by ten on game days. He held up his phone to see what time it was: ten forty-four. Hopefully, his mom and dad were sleeping now. He shoved his phone back into his pocket and heard someone knocking on his front door.

It was pretty freaking late for the guys to drop by and see if the cake was all gone. Maybe one of them left their phone at his house. He hurried to the front door and looked through the peephole.

Kendall looked back at him.

Chapter Twelve

DREW THREW HIS front door open and reached out for Kendall. He pulled her inside his house, nudged the door shut with one elbow, and wrapped his arms around her. He took a deep breath of her green apple scent. She slid her arms around his waist and snuggled against him. He laid his scratchy cheek against her softer one.

"When did you decide you were coming to visit?" he said.

"Last Tuesday morning," she said.

"How long can you stay?"

"My flight leaves at ten AM tomorrow," she said. "Quick trip."

"It's a good thing I didn't go out with the guys tonight."

"Yes, it is."

Their mouths met in a sweet, fleeting kiss. He nibbled at her bottom lip and heard her soft snort of laughter. He had ten hours with her at most. He was exhausted from today's game, his parents were upstairs, and he was going to be sore as hell later from getting knocked on his ass for three hours by guys who outweighed him, but he'd cherish any time at all with her.

"Would you like the good news or the bad news?" he said. He smoothed the hair out of her eyes.

"I'll live dangerously and take the bad news."

"My parents are here. They're in the bedroom next door to mine."

"Aren't they asleep?"

"I don't think so. That's why I'm downstairs."

He felt her laugh. "Oh, no."

"I understand it's the twenty-first century, but I do not want to think about my parents having sex, let alone overhear it." He let out a breath. "Maybe they're reading the Bible to each other or something."

"The last time I visited my parents, I found out they can get pretty loud," she said.

"Reading the Bible?"

"Yeah, that's it," she said. "Let's say I'm happy for them, but I don't want to know, either." She looked up at him. "What's the good news?"

"You're here, and my mom baked a cake earlier. There are leftovers."

"If you'll point me toward your kitchen, I'll race you there," she said.

A FEW MINUTES later, Drew shut off the television and dimmed the lights in his family room. He also flipped the switch to turn on the gas fireplace. He and Kendall sat down on the family room couch with a piece of cake and a glass of wine for her. He slid his arm around her shoulders. Kendall took a bite of the cake and let out a little moan.

"Does your mom visit often? I might have to move in here. This is unbelievably good."

"My mom will be thrilled you liked it. Move in anytime," he joked.

"Maybe I could telecommute." She let out a sigh and balanced the cake plate on her lap as she laid her head on his shoulder. "You can't stop thinking about me and I can't stop thinking about you. I don't want you to get in trouble because you're seeing me, but I miss you. Do we meet up in an airport once a week or something?"

She fed him a bite of cake. It tasted even better than it had earlier. He wondered if she would object if he swiped his finger through the frosting, touched it to the tip of her nose, and licked it off. She'd asked him a question, though. He needed to come up with a substantive answer. The blood had left his brain and rushed to another part of his anatomy, which was currently hard. Verbal communication wasn't his strong suit right now.

He'd met Kendall a little over a week ago. She worked twelve to fifteen hours a day during football season for the Sharks' most hated rival. She'd cut back to ten hours a day or so during the offseason. She lived two states away. She couldn't move, and he had to live in the Seattle area during the six months a year he played for the Sharks. He didn't want her to become the punchline of late-night comedians' jokes or endless discussions on sports radio about a powerful female executive getting romantically involved with what could potentially be a team employee, but he couldn't stand the thought of her with another man, either. He reached out for the plate she balanced on her lap. Setting the plate down on the coffee table in front of them, he wrapped his arms around her.

"I don't know," he said. "I do know, however, that I want to spend more time with you."

He saw her eyes sparkle as she smiled. "I want to spend more time with you too."

"So we're in agreement on this," he said.

"Yes." She moved a little closer to him.

If his parents hadn't decided to visit, they could have had this conversation with a whole lot less clothing on. He wasn't about to entertain in his room with his mom (who had hearing like a bat) one wall away from them. He thought he'd left the worries behind regarding what his parents were going to think or say about his having a female guest over after he qualified for a jumbo mortgage loan. Evidently not.

"Speaking of airports, how do you feel about Portland, Oregon? Nobody knows us there." She laughed out loud, and he had to laugh. "You didn't recognize me when I wore my knit cap," he said.

"I must have been under the influence of those chocolate caramel ganache bars. I knew I'd seen you somewhere before. I just couldn't figure out where."

"What was the giveaway?"

"You took off the cap."

"See? It's foolproof. I'll buy another one of those knit caps—"

"I'll get some dark glasses and a wig or something."

"That's the spirit. I like where this is going."

He touched his mouth to hers. She tasted like cake, and he couldn't resist going back for more. Her lips parted in invitation as she wrapped her arms around his neck. He stroked her tongue with his. She half-rolled onto his chest.

"And your mom and dad are still upstairs," she whispered.

"My mom has been known to get up in the middle of the night for a glass of water or to check on the kids. She has a tough time sleeping."

He slid one hand under the hem of her sweater. Her office clothes concealed her curves, which was a crime against nature in his opinion. He breathed in another wave of green apple scent too. He was going to have a hell of a time visiting the produce section of any grocery store from now on. He had no idea before he met Kendall that the scent of green apples added to her clean, warm skin was going to be the most powerful aphrodisiac he'd encountered yet.

"She caught my brother and his wife red-handed on their living room couch a couple of years ago," Drew said.

She let out a little gasp when his hand cupped her breast. He moved his thumb over her nipple, stroking slowly until he felt her arch into his hand.

"My parents went to their house for dinner, there was a storm, and my sister-in-law didn't want them driving in such bad weather. Dad has a bad back. Sleeping on the couch is tough for him." He was still slowly stroking her nipple, and he was losing his train of thought. Maybe the explanation wasn't all that important after all.

He pushed the sweater up, scooped her breast out of her bra, and took her nipple into his mouth. "So your mom and dad slept in their room . . . oh, God, Drew," she said. He suckled her, moving his tongue over the hardened flesh, and she let out another moan.

He reached up to unhook the bra. He blew softly on her nipple as he made short work of the lingerie. He lifted the bra and sweater off over her head, dropping them onto the family room floor. To his surprise, she reached out, took his ponytail in one hand, and slid the elastic band out of his hair. Her fingers moved through his hair seconds later.

"We're probably getting interrupted, aren't we?" she whispered as he took her nipple in his mouth again.

"Mmm hmm," he said.

"I know I should care about that, but I'm not sure I do right now."

Her breathing accelerated. She was still running her hands through his hair. A few seconds later, she pulled up the back of his sweater and whispered, "This needs to go." He let go of her long enough to yank it off over his head. He unbuttoned and unzipped her jeans while he was at it, and slid them down her hips as he moved down the couch, trailing his mouth over her abdomen. He could spend all day on her gently rounded belly.

"Your hair is . . . oh, God. It's ticklish." She squirmed a little. He shook his head a few more times over her as he licked and kissed his way to where he wanted to go as he pulled her pants off. "Drew!"

He wasn't doing this well enough if she still made sense when she spoke. He wasn't going to stop until there was nothing but heavy breathing and a little begging. Moans or screams would be acceptable too. The screaming would probably work out better for them if it happened behind a locked bedroom door. Noise would definitely bring his mom on the run.

The threat of discovery turned a fun little make-out session into something sexier than he'd experienced in years. He pushed her underwear aside, decided it wasn't enough, looped one finger around the underwear and yanked them down her legs. She slipped one foot out and left them dangling off of the other.

"We'll wreck your couch," she gasped. "We need a blanket."

He reached behind him and pulled the cotton throw he'd been using earlier off the back of the couch, rolled her onto him, and spread it over where she'd lay. It wasn't perfect, but it would work. She settled onto the couch again and reached out for him.

"You're still dressed," she whispered as she sank her hands into his hair again. She wrapped her legs around him, grinding against his erection.

"Not for long," he told her. He supported his weight on both hands as he moved over her in a crouch, kissing and licking his way down her abdomen. He could smell the heavy perfume of her arousal, feel the little tremors as she responded to him, the surprisingly strong grip of her thighs around his hips. He balanced himself enough to flip her legs over his shoulders with both hands as he grabbed her hips and pulled her closer. She let out another moan as his tongue lapped her.

He used one hand to spread her legs a little more, and the other to slide one long, crooked finger inside her as he teased her clit with his tongue. He tried two fingers instead, thrusting slowly, continuing his torment of the small bundle of nerve endings at the notch of her sex with his mouth. He felt her body tensing beneath him, listened to breathing that was now panting, and heard her gasp out, "Oh, God!" He increased the speed of his fingers, gently massaging the spot inside while he licked and sucked the nub between her legs. She pushed into his mouth.

A sudden motion made him open his eyes. She'd let go of his hair and slapped both hands over her mouth. She was trying to say something, but he couldn't make out the words. Seconds later, she gave a muffled scream and he felt the intense waves of her orgasm clench around his fingers. He gently withdrew his hand as she tried to catch her breath, moved over her once more, and pulled her into his embrace as he lay down next to her.

Her body was still vibrating. There was nothing better in life than holding a woman seconds after orgasm, unless he counted the fact he'd helped her get there in the first place.

"It's your turn now," she murmured.

"There's plenty of time. Just rest," he said. He stroked the soft skin of her back as her breathing returned to normal.

"So far, so good with your parents," she joked.

"Maybe they wore themselves out."

"Reading the Bible?"

She turned her face into his shoulder, and he had to laugh. They rested against each other for a few minutes. He noticed they breathed in sync. He could fall asleep right now. Well, he could fall asleep after his hard-on subsided somewhat, which wasn't happening as long as he was holding a beautiful naked woman.

That beautiful naked woman pulled him into a sitting position and knelt between his legs. "Speaking of wearing ourselves out," she teased, "let's try something else." She unbuckled his belt, undid the button and the zipper on his jeans, and helped him pull them off. He shoved off his boxer briefs too, and his dick sprang free. He felt her grip him in her hand. She cupped his balls in her other hand. Her mouth descended over him, and he threw himself back against the couch.

Her tongue moved around the head. She licked and caressed him, she formed her lips into an "O" and teased him, pulling him in and out of the warmth and wetness. She worked him with her hands and her mouth until he felt himself coming, and then she'd pull back and wait until he begged her through clenched teeth.

"Oh, shit. Fuck. I . . . Jesus. More. Suck me."

"Are you sure?" He opened his eyes enough to see the teasing smile move over her lips. "Maybe we should relax for a few minutes."

She moved her hand slowly up and down his shaft until he thought he was going to burst, and then she'd back off again. She was killing him with pleasure. It wouldn't be a bad way to go. He was putty in her hands, harder than he thought possible, and the slightest touch was going to send him over the edge. Kendall squeezed him once more, her mouth descended toward him, and through the haze of extreme pleasure and desperate need, he didn't care if he woke up the neighbors, let alone his parents.

"Oh, Jesus," he ground out.

Kendall bent over him one more time. Seconds later, he felt like his head was about to separate from his body as his orgasm ripped through him. He let out a long, loud groan and slumped into the couch cushions. He tried to catch his breath. Kendall laid both palms on his thighs as she pulled herself up off the floor.

"Are you okay?" she teased.

"I'm great." He grabbed her around the waist to pull her into the couch cushions with him. "How are you doin'?"

She laughed softly. "I'm terrific."

The sweet afterglow of orgasm didn't last. He heard movement on the floor above them. Seconds later, there were footsteps on the staircase, and they both heard his dad's booming voice.

"I'm sure there's still cake, baby. We'll get some and take it back to bed with us."

"You know I love a midnight snack."

His mother sounded like a giggly teenager. His parents had chosen one hell of a time to get out of bed. There wasn't a lot going on between his ears or above his waist as a result of the past fifteen minutes or so, but he managed to realize they were about to be discovered. Luckily, his couch faced away from the kitchen. If they were quiet, lay flat, and held still, they might escape discovery.

"Lay down," he told her, and moved in next to her. He wrapped his arms around her. It didn't matter if he was a grown man: He really didn't care to be caught in the act by his parents. He told himself to breathe.

"They won't see us. Hold still," he whispered.

"I think they heard us. It's bad enough," she whispered back.

He heard scurrying footsteps in the kitchen and his dad's bigger, heavier ones.

"I could have sworn I heard voices down here," his mom said. "Maybe we should take a look around."

Drew heard the refrigerator door open and shut, the cabinet where he kept the plates opening and shutting, and the sound of the silverware drawer opening and shutting. "Bonnie McCoy, you get your cute little fanny back here and quit snooping around. Drew is fast asleep in his room. Nothing is wrong. Let's go back upstairs."

His parents' voices receded as they climbed the stairs. He could hear the click of the bedroom door shutting all the way downstairs. He took his first deep breath in five minutes. He stroked Kendall's face and kissed her on the forehead.

"Portland's starting to sound better and better," he muttered.

AFTER GRABBING THE clothes strewn around Drew's family room and hurriedly dressing themselves, they decided to spend the next few hours attempting to get some sleep in his bed before she had to go to the airport. Kendall grabbed the quilted fabric overnight bag she'd brought out of the entryway of his house, and they hurried upstairs as silently as possible.

Drew's room was huge and thickly carpeted. One wall was dominated by a clerestory window that looked out over his backyard. The king-sized bed he slept in didn't make a dent in the available space. The bed itself had a dark bentwood headboard, no footboard, and was somewhat nondescript. The bedding was simple in design, earth tones, and he had no decorative pillows. The sheets were white. A wooden chest sat at the foot of his bed. He also had a dresser and a flat-screen TV mounted over it on the opposite wall. She smiled at the large glass jug full of change on the floor beside the dresser.

The room included a bathroom, which had the usual high-end finishes—granite countertops, tile flooring, double-glass-walled shower, big whirlpool tub. There was nothing here, though, that expressed Drew's personality or what he cared about besides the stack of books waiting for him in the recessed cubbyhole of his nightstand. She wondered if there were family photos, football mementos, or other items that might show her a little more about who he was somewhere else in the house.

She set her overnight bag down next to the side of his

bed that didn't have the books in the nightstand and said, "May I sleep on this side?"

"You can sleep anywhere you want," he assured her. He'd moved quickly up the stairs, but she noticed he winced a few times as he pulled a pair of shorts and an old T-shirt out of his dresser.

"Are you okay?"

"Just sore from the game. I'll take some ibuprofen or something and be good as new by tomorrow morning." He nodded toward the bathroom. "Would you like to change in there?"

She'd have to do some thinking later about why she felt suddenly shy getting naked in front of him when she'd been spread out all over his couch, let alone just given him a blow job, but that was a puzzle for when she wasn't post-orgasmic and quite so tired.

"That would be great," she said. She grabbed her bag again, headed into the bathroom, and took care of her business. She emerged from the bathroom to find Drew already in bed. He'd turned down the blankets for her.

"Let's leave one of the bathroom lights on in case you wake up, okay?"

"That might be a good idea. Thank you."

They were oddly formal for two people who were so crazed for each other less than half an hour ago they'd torn each other's clothes off and risked getting walked in on by his parents. If Drew hadn't conveniently finished moments before they came downstairs, she would have met them wearing nothing more than toenail polish and a pair of hoop earrings. She slid inside the soft, cool sheets, lay on her side facing him, and hauled in a breath.

"What time is your flight tomorrow again?"

"Ten AM."

"I'll set the alarm on my phone for six AM. Will that work for you? It takes about half an hour to forty-five minutes to get to the airport from here."

"I forgot to call the shuttle—"

"I'll drive you," he said. "My mom and dad are getting picked up in a town car at seven AM."

"Don't you want to spend some more time with them?"

"I'll see them soon." He reached over to kiss her. His mouth was warm and firm on hers, and he didn't linger. "Let's get some sleep."

He clasped her hand in his, rolled onto his back, and was asleep less than five minutes later.

Chapter Thirteen
_____

DREW HAULED HIMSELF out of bed at six AM to get his parents' luggage downstairs and hug and kiss them goodbye. His mom must have been up with the chickens; she was heating up some breakfast sandwiches. The coffee was ready. She was filling two travel mugs when he walked into the kitchen.

"Good morning, honey," she said as she reached up to kiss his cheek. "Did you sleep well?" He saw color rising in her cheeks.

"Sure, Mom. Did you sleep well?"

"Of course I did."

His mom was doing her best to look innocent, but he knew better. She put the lids on the travel mugs, and he reached out to take both of her hands in his. "There's something I need to talk with you about."

"I have to pack up these sandwiches for your dad. You know how hungry he is in the morning—"

"Mom. Mama. Five minutes of your time."

She let out a sigh.

"Come and sit with me at the table," Drew coaxed.

"Don't you want to eat too? I know you want breakfast."

"It can wait." He led her to his kitchen table, pulled out a chair for her, and sat down kitty-corner from her. "Do you feel like you've worked out most of the issues with Dad while you've been here?"

"I don't know how to answer that question—"

"Try."

"Last night was a good start," and she blushed a little more. He pretended like he didn't notice it. "We need to do a lot more talking about what he expects and what I need. We've been married a long time, honey, but we're in a rut. I wish he understood that I'm enjoying my new job and I'd like to keep working, instead of thinking he's competing for my time and attention." She looked down at the table. "I don't want to spend every day for the rest of my life just waiting for him to get home from work."

Drew squeezed his mom's hand. "Do you want me to try talking with him about it?"

"Your dad is pretty old-fashioned. It was one of the reasons why I fell in love with him. I knew he wanted a wife that stayed home. That worked out well when you kids were little and he was building his client list, but the house is empty most of the time now. He wants to be the provider. Just because I make a little money at what I do doesn't mean he's not doing an excellent job." She looked into his eyes. "I want something that's mine."

Drew squeezed her hand again. "Mom, I've been think-ing about what you've told me and what Dad's told me. I understand that you'd like to shake things up and try some-thing new, but I want you to consider something as well."

"What's that? Honey, I have to get that stuff out of the oven—"

He got to his feet, crossed to the oven, grabbed a hot mat, and removed the pan of breakfast sandwiches, set-ting it on another hot mat to cool. He switched off the oven.

"How's that?"

"Thank you," she said. He sat back down at the table.

"I want you to do something for me, Mom. As I told you the other night, I'm willing to pay for a chef a few nights a week, send you some restaurant gift cards or whatever you and Dad might like so you can spend a little time together talking this out. I'm also willing to pay for some sessions with a counselor."

"We don't need *therapy*—"

"Okay, then." He looked into her cornflower-blue eyes. "I want you to tell your boss you can't work on Sun-days. I'd prefer you didn't work on the weekends at all, but that's between you and Dad."

"Everyone works on the weekends there."

"It won't hurt to ask. Mom, when you made the deal with Dad that you wouldn't work, he thinks you changed the rules on him. I think it's great that you have a job that you enjoy, and I will keep telling Dad that he needs to join the twenty-first century." His mom let out a soft laugh. "I know things at home are not the same as they were when we were all little and you had your hands full, but he wants the same girl sitting next to him on the couch while he watches the game."

"I suppose so."

"Of course he does. Someday, my kids will be sitting on that couch with you."

She gave him a somewhat misty smile. "Yes, honey, they will."

He took her hand again. He still remembered holding her hand when he was little and learning to cross the street, ride a bike, or when his parents were chaperones at his senior prom and he asked his mom to dance. Someday, he'd walk her up the aisle to her seat when he married the woman of his dreams.

He hoped that woman was Kendall.

KENDALL HEARD THE front door of Drew's house slam and heavy footsteps on the staircase landing outside of his bedroom. She'd awoken when Drew's dad called out to his wife while he was looking for a clean pair of shorts, and she got into the shower as quickly as she could. If she was going to encounter Drew's parents, she'd prefer to be fully dressed at the time.

Drew opened the bedroom door and hurried across the room, wrapping his arms around her.

"My parents are on their way to the airport. I love them, but it was time for them to go home for a while." She grinned as she rubbed her face into his chest. "Did you get some sleep?"

"I did. Did you?"

"I smelled your perfume all night. I hated wasting a minute with you." They held each other while minutes passed.

"I wish I didn't have to leave."

"I wish you didn't, either." He let out a long breath. "So, we're meeting in Portland next Monday afternoon?"

She had personal days. It wasn't a great thing to take a day off at the height of football season, but she was going to do it if it meant meeting up with Drew and spending some more time with him. "Maybe I should come back here," she said. "You can show me around Seattle."

"It's a date, if we make it out of my house."

She let out a laugh. "That might be a challenge."

AN HOUR LATER, Drew pulled up in the departures lane at Sea-Tac Airport. He maneuvered his Subaru Outback into one of the parking places closest to the curb. The departure lane at Sea-Tac was crowded. Passenger cars and taxis wove in and out of the vehicles slowing and stopping to disgorge those flying to destinations all over the globe on an overcast October Monday morning. The announcement that all parked cars would be impounded and towed droned on the overhead speaker in the background.

There were hundreds of people on the sidewalk feet away from Drew's car, but nobody seemed to notice the tall guy with the long blond ponytail and the curvy dark-haired woman who'd wrapped her arms around his neck.

"I don't want to say goodbye to you," she said. Her voice broke as her vision blurred with hot tears.

"We'll see each other next week," he murmured into her ear. "I promise."

"I'll miss you."

"And I will miss you. So much."

Drew's mouth covered hers. He angled his head to slide his tongue into her mouth, and she tasted the water he'd been drinking a few minutes ago. His kiss was tender and gentle. He didn't need to eat her face off for her to realize how much he wanted her. She fisted one hand into his ponytail. He leaned his forehead against hers to catch his breath. Her heart was pounding, her knees had turned to water, and she didn't want to go.

They heard a knock on the driver's side window and an unfamiliar male voice.

"Is this your car, sir?"

"Excuse me?" Drew said. He hit the button to lower the driver's side window.

"Is this your car?" A cop nodded toward Drew's Subaru. "You have thirty seconds to move it or I'm giving you a ticket."

"How much is the ticket?" Drew asked.

"A hundred and fifty dollars."

"Go ahead. I'll pay it."

Drew's mouth touched Kendall's again. He pulled her closer. She let out a little moan. She couldn't get enough of him, he couldn't get enough of her, and the cop spoke one more time.

"Okay. Here's your ticket. Move your car in the next thirty seconds, or I'll have it towed, Mr. McCoy. And, oh yeah: Go Sharks."

Three hours later, Kendall hurried through San Francisco International Airport to the baggage claim area. She needed a cab to get to the office. She grabbed her phone out of her bag and hit Sydney's number.

"Hi there. How's it going?" she said when Sydney answered.

"Your lunch meeting cancelled, so if you're here by one PM, things are cool. You got another phone call from Sherman Washington's agent."

"That guy's aggressive, isn't he?"

"His client wants to leave the Sharks. Does Drew know anything about him? You might want to ask before you talk with the guy."

"That's a thought. How are you doing? How was your weekend?"

"It was great. I went out, I had fun. I got away from the studying for at least a couple of hours. I loved it." Sydney paused for a moment as Kendall stepped out onto the sidewalk where the cabs were lined up. "There's one more thing. Cell phone pictures of Drew McCoy kissing a dark-haired woman in his car at the Seattle airport have been trending on Twitter for an hour or so now."

"Oh God. Oh, no."

"You're 'unidentified' so far, but the hunt is on to figure out who the woman is."

"That ought to make the afternoon meeting fun and interesting, don't you think?"

Sydney let out a snort.

DREW STROLLED INTO the practice facility after making his way through surprisingly hellacious traffic. He was still on time to get checked out by the trainer and the team doctor, so he hurried to his locker to pull on some warm-ups and a team logo T-shirt. He could lift afterward.

If he didn't know Kendall's schedule was more insane than his (and there would be serious consequences if he blew off today's health check) he would have followed her onto the plane this morning. He'd be fine lounging in her backyard with a book until she came home from the office. He wanted to spend more time with her. The memory of last night on his couch was enough to make him turn his back and face his locker until his dick settled down a bit. Getting laid was a great thing, but he wanted to spend more time talking about almost anything with her first.

He hung up his street clothes and grabbed some cross trainers out of the drawer beneath the bench. He heard Derrick's voice before he saw him.

"Well, look who's here, Taylor." Derrick let out a belly laugh and sang out, "Drew and Kendall Tracy sittin' in a tree. K-I-S-S-I-N-G." He swiveled his hips and made a thrusting motion to accompany his words, which caused Seth to hoot with laughter. "I told you I'd find out who you were staring at, dawg. No wonder you didn't want to go to Element with us last night. You're all over Twitter now." He waved his smart phone in Drew's direction and nudged Seth with an elbow. "Does Coach know you're sleeping with the enemy?"

Drew's stomach dropped out. He knew there was a pretty damn good chance that somebody else was going to put two and two together when he'd kissed Kendall in the drop-off area at a busy international airport, but he was hoping against hope the people at the airport this morning were too fixated on getting where they needed to go to care. He couldn't regret kissing her, but he regretted the fact she was probably going to pay for it with her colleagues. His teammates would give him shit until someone else started dating someone even higher profile. Luckily, this happened on the regular.

"You're kidding me. Kendall of the Miners? The MINERS? You couldn't find yourself a nice Sharks fan to spend some time with, McCoy?" Seth plunked himself down in the locker next to Drew's. "How long has this been going on?"

Zach Anderson strode into the area. "What the fuck are you talking about?"

"Our boy Drew was in a lip lock this morning at Sea-Tac with the lovely Kendall, interim GM of the Miners."

Zach rolled his eyes a little. "That's all you've got, Collins? From the way you were carrying on, I thought he did the horizontal mambo with your ex."

"Don't mention her," Derrick warned. "Just stop now."

"Too soon?" Zach shot back. Drew had to laugh, and Zach gave him a hard stare. "Oh, laugh it up, buddy, but your ass is in a sling. Is this true?"

"No comment," Drew said.

Derrick tapped the screen on his phone a couple of times. "Such a lovely picture, and so classy. Wait until your mama sees your hand on her breast in front of God and everybody."

"You think you have problems now?" Seth said to Drew. "Forget about the coaching staff. Wait until the fans find out. All those women who've tried to pick you up . . ."

This was greeted with uproarious laughter and more shit from his teammates, who were drifting in to start their day.

"Works for me," Clay, the rookie, shouted from across the room. "I'll take his leftovers. I'm not proud."

"Some woman told me McCoy turned her down because he's 'sensitive.'"

"It's too bad he couldn't find someone who isn't with a piece of shit team . . ."

"You'd want her too," Terrell, the safety, chimed in. "Who gives a fuck who she works for?"

One of the assistant coaches waded into the scrum. "Go see the trainers. McCoy, you come with me."

Chapter Fourteen

THE SHARKS' DEFENSIVE coordinator, LeRoy Bradley, pulled Drew into a corridor outside of the team's locker room. Drew had always had a good rapport with the guy. He was conscientious, thorough, prepared the defense each week for what they might face from their opponents, and didn't get involved in the squabbles that happened between highly competitive teammates. Right now, LeRoy folded his arms and narrowed his eyes.

"Is it true that you are seeing Kendall Tracy of the Miners?"

Drew wasn't going to bother asking him where he got his information. "Yes."

"How long has this relationship been going on?"

"A couple of weeks."

LeRoy shook his head. "Will you be asking for a trade to San Francisco?"

"No. I'm not interested in playing for the Miners."

"Have you been discussing team business with her?"

"Hell, no."

He'd given Kendall advice. He hadn't divulged team strategy or anything else the coaching staff would consider confidential.

"McCoy, I'm not joking. If we find out she's seen your playbook or you've been discussing our game planning with her, you're not going to like the consequences."

"With all due respect, LeRoy, do you discuss that stuff with your wife?"

"She hates it."

"I have other things to talk about with Kendall besides football, too."

Drew knew he was going to get grilled, but that fact didn't make his current situation any more enjoyable.

"It's hard to believe you couldn't find another woman to date in the Puget Sound area. You also have to wonder what she's thinking too. Wait until their front office finds out."

Drew's stomach churned. He knew there would be consequences for Kendall when and if their budding relationship came to light. These guys considered it a betrayal, but her team would consider it an act of treason.

LeRoy nodded down the corridor. "Coach wants to see you. You're going to be asked the same questions. There's also a good chance you might get benched on Sunday."

Drew expected as much, but he'd make his arguments to the head coach instead of discussing it in an open area where any of his teammates could overhear the conversation. He followed the DC to the head coach's office. He stepped inside to see most of the coaching staff and a few of the front office boys.

"McCoy," Coach Stewart said. "Have a seat."

SYDNEY STROLLED INTO Kendall's office as Kendall was attempting to enter data on a spreadsheet and eat half a turkey sandwich at the same time.

"Your secret is out," she said. She sat down in one of the chairs in front of Kendall's desk.

"What's happening?"

"They're meeting to discuss how they're going to handle it."

Kendall's heart skipped a beat and she felt the cold fist of dread forming in her stomach, but remaining calm and taking some deep breaths was the best thing she could do for herself right now. She'd had plenty of time to think on the flight back to San Francisco and while she'd been working at her desk most of the afternoon.

Her private life was her own. She and Drew were consenting adults. It was really nobody else's business who she was romantically involved with.

"It might be nice if I were included in that meeting," she said.

She took another big bite of her sandwich. No matter how hard she tried, she couldn't make anything this good at home. Maybe the guys at the deli would share their secrets with her. Concentrating on the sandwich was a hell of a lot more fun than dwelling on what was about to happen to her at the hands of the Miners' owner and her co-workers.

"Maybe you should attend the meeting anyway," Sydney said. "They're in the main conference room." She grabbed Kendall's iPad and handed it to her. "The rest of your sandwich will be here when you get back."

"Would you like to attend as well?" Kendall knew she'd need a witness to what was said.

"I'm right behind you," Sydney said. She wrapped up Kendall's sandwich to stow it in the mini-fridge in one corner of the office, grabbed her own tablet, and followed Kendall down the hall.

Kendall grabbed her suit jacket, pulled it on, and strode down the hallway to the conference room. She pushed the door open hard enough for the doorknob to bounce off of the wall behind it. The seven men surrounding the table fell silent as she walked into the room.

"Thanks for inviting me to the meeting, guys. What are we discussing?" She put her iPad down on the table in front of the only empty chair, pulled it out, and sat down. They'd called out the big guns for this meeting; both the team's owner and the CEO of the Miners, George Simmons, were there.

George glared at her. "We understand you're involved in a romantic relationship with Drew McCoy of the Sharks. You've put us in a very unpleasant position as a result, Ms. Tracy."

She lifted an eyebrow. "You've been calling me Kendall since I was sixteen years old, George."

"Part of the expectations for your job, interim or not, is to sign McCoy on the offseason. It'll be difficult to obtain his services when we're getting sued for sexual harassment." George steepled his fingers. "How did you think this was going to end?"

"I don't understand what you're talking about."

"You can't work for the team and sleep with a player from another team," the Miners' owner said.

"My personal life really isn't anyone in this room's business," Kendall said.

Jerry Berggren, an older, overweight man with a permanently red face, pointed at her and shouted, "It is when you're fucking around with the biggest free agent acquisition this year."

"That's enough, Jerry," George said to him. "You need to apologize. That was inappropriate."

"I'm not apologizing to her," Jerry snapped.

"Your comments violated labor laws," the team's lawyer said, and he put his face in his hands. "I suggest you all calm down a little. Kendall's right. Her private life is none of your business."

Kendall heard the door behind her open: Sydney walked in. She couldn't miss Jerry's comments; Kendall was pretty sure people in the next county could have heard him clearly. Kendall saw Sydney sit down in a spare chair in the corner of the conference room.

"She had one job: Sign McCoy. She's already failed at it. The franchise is more important than her inability to find a date," Jerry said.

"Maybe we'll get him for less money because of the side benefits," Leonard, the acting director of football operations, snarled.

"Enough," the team's attorney snapped. "You're all over the line."

Five other men started talking at once about how Kendall wasn't the best choice for the job, how she would make them the laughing stock of the league when this got out, how she (and every other woman) could never be trusted in any pro football franchise leadership because they couldn't keep their personal lives out of the office. Kendall saw Sydney's mouth drop open out of the corner of her eye. She was holding her iPad at an angle too. In other words, she was recording what was being said.

If they all thought Kendall was going to burst into tears and slink out of the conference room, they had another thing coming.

The typically shy and introverted Bruce, the Miners' team attorney, was on his feet by now. "Quiet!" he roared.

"We could fire you," George Simmons told him.

"Go ahead. You'll be served with a suit as quickly as I can file it," Bruce said. He shook his head and picked up his things off of the table in front of him. "The fact you're now being recorded means Ms. Tracy has an open and shut case for a hostile work environment and several other violations of federal employment law. I—"

The director of scouting pointed at Sydney. "Shut it off! Shut it off, goddammit! You don't have the right to record me or anyone else here!"

Sydney smiled at him. "No," she said.

"We'll fire *you*."

"Go ahead," Sydney said. She sat up in her chair. "I'm sure the HR department will be really interested in your comments to Ms. Tracy and to me over the past ten minutes or so."

"It sucks, doesn't it?" Bruce said to the six men who were now either gaping at Sydney or whose mouths were opening and shutting like goldfish. "You might want to start with a sincere and abject apology for your comments."

Kendall glanced over at Sydney. She wanted to walk out right now, pack up her desk and leave, but Sydney wouldn't have a job if she did. Kendall had enough in savings to be okay while she looked for something else. If she got really stuck, her parents would help too. When the word hit the street that the woman who'd done such a great job over the past four years managing San Francisco's salary cap was available, she wouldn't be out of work for long.

She wasn't going to let any man talk to her the way her colleagues had today. She also wasn't going to sit quietly while they mistreated Sydney, either.

"We need to talk," Kendall mouthed at her.

Sydney gave Kendall a quick nod. The attorney was heading toward the conference room door.

"Where the hell do you think you're going?" George barked at him.

"I quit," he said. "Good luck finding other representation." He pulled the conference room door open and slammed it behind him. Silence descended over the room.

DREW'S MEETING WAS quick and to the point. Coach Stewart asked him the same questions the defensive coordinator asked him. Drew's answers seemed to satisfy him, but the coach leaned over his desk to fix Drew with a long stare.

"McCoy, I don't get to pass judgment on your love life because everyone involved is a consenting adult, but I am telling you right now I am not happy about this. I know you've said you're not discussing team business with Ms. Tracy, but things have a way of slipping out when we don't expect it." He let out a long breath. "I'm not going to bench you for Sunday, but you won't be seeing a lot of playing time. You also need to decide if this relationship is important enough to jeopardize your career over."

"I don't see why that would be an issue." He knew it would be an issue, but backing down wasn't an option.

"The Miners are our biggest rivals in the league. There was nobody else for you to get involved with?"

"Coach, we met. There was interest. We are pursuing it. End of story."

The coach shook his head. "We can talk more at another time. Thanks for stopping by."

It really wasn't Drew's choice to "stop by," but he got up and stuck his hand out to shake the coach's hand.

"Thanks, Coach."

Fifteen minutes later, Drew had got the thumbs up from the trainers as far as his condition after last Sunday's game when the cell in his pocket rang. He grabbed it out to take a look on his way back to the team gym. He recognized the number of one of the local sports talk stations. He hit the "talk" button with one finger.

"McCoy," he said.

"Hey, Drew, it's Mike from The Score." He'd talked to the guy multiple times in the past, so it wasn't a surprise he'd call. "Have you got a few minutes for us this afternoon?"

"I'm on my way in to do some lifting right now."

"We're trying to clear up a nasty rumor over here. We heard you're dating the Miners' acting GM. True or not?"

"No comment."

"Our phone lines are on fire right now. Why don't you give us ten minutes or so at three o'clock to clear things up and set some people straight?"

"Mike, I enjoy chatting with you guys, but my private life is kind of off-limits right now."

"You have to know Sharks fans are going nuts. They think you're angling for a trade or something."

"No. I have no interest in playing for the Miners, now or in the future."

"Well, then, what the hell are you doing, guy? It's like the Montagues and the Capulets with shoulder pads. The Sharks hate the Miners, and the Miners return the favor."

"I get what you're doing here, Mike, but I don't think giving an interview today would be a great idea."

"Will you call me back when you change your mind?"

"Yeah." Drew pulled in a long breath. "I'll do that."

Drew wasn't as reclusive about his personal life as some of his teammates were, but he'd rather talk about football than who he was dating. He wasn't so sure Kendall wanted to discuss their relationship with any member of the media, either. He wished one more time he'd chosen somewhere a bit more private to kiss her goodbye this morning.

His phone chirped with an incoming text.

All Hell's breaking loose here. I miss you.

To say that the next few days were a challenge for both Kendall and Drew would be an understatement. Kendall and Sydney spent the rest of the afternoon talking with the team's attorney, who had just quit. They were in Kendall's office with the door shut planning what to do next. Kendall didn't want to run away with her tail between her legs, but finding out once and for all what the guys she worked with really thought of her made her wonder if she'd be a lot better off somewhere else.

She'd planned to stay with the Miners as long as possible. She enjoyed her former job. She'd never wanted the GM job in the first place. She was more than happy to let one or more of the assholes at the conference table today take the job, if they wanted it so badly. She'd decided in the past couple of hours that she deserved better than to work with a bunch of guys that feared and mistrusted women, but she'd like to have something else lined up before she made her move.

"Would you like me to help find you another job?" Kendall said to Sydney. "There are several people I know that would hire you in a heartbeat. I'm not leaving until I know you're going to be okay."

"You have to leave," Sydney argued. "You can't stay here

and put up with that crap daily. Plus, I have documenta-tion." She held up her iPad. "Let them offer you an obscene amount of money first, a formal apology, or both."

"They're not going to offer me a thing. They believe they can gut it out and force me to quit first."

Sydney was already shaking her head. Kendall's desk phone rang and she picked it up.

"Kendall Tracy."

"Hi Kendall, this is Miles from HR. I'm wondering if I could have a few minutes of your time this afternoon."

"I'd prefer to meet with you tomorrow—"

"The team attorney just walked in here and quit. So did his administrative assistant. I'd like to talk with you about what happened in the meeting today."

Sydney waved a little to catch Kendall's eye and said, "We'll take the meeting. Be here in ten minutes, please."

"Great," he said. "I'll see you then."

Kendall hung up her phone. "What was that?" she said to Sydney.

Sydney held up her tablet. "You don't have to say a thing, Kendall."

"We can't use that. We didn't ask permission before recording it."

"Let them worry about that," Sydney said. "The guys in that meeting earlier should be on their knees praying I haven't called every sports media outlet on the planet by now."

Kendall's phone chirped with an incoming text.

Is there anything I can do to help?

A FEW DAYS later, Drew ran out onto the field in Dallas in front of a sold-out, cheering crowd. He was thankful for the distraction of a game. What he hoped would be a one-day non-story had ballooned into wall-to-wall discussions on Seattle talk radio and what appeared to be the destruction of Kendall's future with the Miners.

When he offered to fly to San Francisco on Tuesday, she said, "You have a game. I'll be fine. We'll see each other Sunday night. I'll be at your house as soon as I get back from Green Bay and get a flight out of SFO." He heard the strain in her voice and kicked himself again for a stupid mistake. "As of this morning, I have three offers from other teams on the table."

"Is that good or bad?"

"You tell me," she said, and for the first time in days, he heard a smile in her voice. "Oakland, Arizona, or Miami. I'm sort of partial to Oakland right now, because the Miners' owner just about stroked out when they called him to ask for permission to contact me."

"He's not happy with that idea?"

"Nope." She pulled in a long breath. "How are you doing?"

"Things are fine. I miss you."

"I miss you too. Will you introduce me to Nolan?"

"Absolutely."

There was so much to say and never enough time to say it in. She'd be at his house on Sunday night, and they could spend most of Monday holding each other and talking. He was looking forward to it.

After giving him a lot of shit about his and Kendall's romance, his teammates (to his surprise) closed ranks around him.

"I'll give her a chance because of you, dawg," Derrick told him. "If she says one word about how the Miners are a better team, though, it's on."

"I heard on the news she's getting a lot of shit from their organization. She deserves better," Seth chimed in.

"You guys are getting soft," Zach joked, but slapped Drew on the back. "We'll get through this."

They would. His teammates lined up on the field for the kickoff. Drew was listed as a starter, but fully expected his backup to take his place when the defense took the field. To his surprise, Coach Stewart turned to him, pointed at the field, and said, "Get your ass out there."

He ran out to join the huddle before Coach changed his mind.

The first few plays went perfectly. He missed batting down the Dallas QB's pass on the first play, but he helped the defensive line drop Dallas's QB for a loss twice. The Sharks fans in the crowd went crazy. He waved to acknowledge the cheering. The defense huddled up to talk about how they wanted to stop the Dallas offense on third and fifteen, and Derrick gave Drew a nod.

"Here's your big chance, guy. Sack his ass," Derrick said. "I can't wait to watch him cry like a little girl." He pantomimed rubbing his eyes with two grimy fists. "Waaa, waaaa."

"What about *you*? They want to see that sexy sack dance on national TV," Drew responded.

"I've got the play. Shut it so I can tell you shitheads what we're doing," Seth said. The middle linebacker was considered the quarterback of the defense. His helmet had a two-way speaker in it so he could talk with the coaching staff while the team was on the field.

"Oooh. It gets me really hot when you take charge," Clay, the rookie, said to Seth. The other nine guys started laughing.

"The DL coach says he's had enough of your BS, guys. Here's what we're doing." Seth gave the play, told them how to line up, and the defensive line jogged back to get in their stance. The linebackers shifted as they watched the QB's eyes. The guy had signed a hundred million dollar contract extension on the offseason, but he was still too dumb to stop signaling who he was about to pass to with his eyes every time he lined up behind center.

The ball was snapped from center, and Drew ran through a gigantic hole the defensive line made for him and reached out to grab the QB's jersey to pull him down onto the turf. Something went wrong between "You're mine, dumbass" and the sack dance he'd been planning on.

Drew's world crumpled in less than five seconds. His cleats stuck in the turf, his arm wrenched at an unnatural angle as he tried to yank another man off of his feet, and the ripping, popping sound he heard from his shoulder was so loud that he wondered (before he fell onto the turf, overwhelmed with pain) if the fans heard it in the stands.

Bodies crashed into each other all around him. One of Dallas's linemen barely missed stepping onto his leg, and

Drew curled into a protective ball. He could see his teammates frantically gesturing to the Sharks sidelines for the team doctor and the trainers as the play ended. Derrick dropped to his knees, unbuckled Drew's chin strap, and eased his helmet off his head.

"Take it easy, McCoy. We're here." Derrick shielded Drew with his body. "We got you. Breathe, buddy."

Seth helped him ease Drew onto his back. "You're going to be okay," he said. "Terrell got his ass for ya, guy."

A couple of seconds later, they heard Terrell shouting at the Dallas QB, "There's more where that came from, candy ass."

"That's my boy," Derrick said approvingly.

"Damn right," Seth said. "C'mon, buddy. Breathe."

Drew was in so much pain it was hard to get a breath. He grabbed his now-limp arm with his other hand as the doctor and the trainers dropped to their knees around him.

"Breathe, Drew," the doc said. He was already gesturing for the paramedics and their rolling gurney. Drew managed to pull some air into his lungs. He could see his teammates gathered around. Some had taken a knee. Others appeared to be praying. He'd done that maneuver a thousand times during games before. He wondered how it went so wrong today. Coach Stewart's face swam into his vision.

"McCoy, I'll meet you at the hospital. I'm not going back to Seattle without you," he said. He squeezed Drew's gloved hand as the paramedics transferred him to the gurney, strapped him in, and pulled up the wheels. "You're going to be fine," he said.

"Thanks, Coach."

Through the haze of hellish pain, Drew knew the coach was lying through his teeth, but he wasn't going to argue about it right now. He had no control over his arm. It wasn't a dislocation or a sprain. He made the extra effort to flash a "thumbs up," and he heard applause from the stands as he was taken off the field and loaded into an ambulance. The paramedics looped a cannula beneath his nose for oxygen, made sure the gurney was secured, and the ambulance screamed through the streets of Dallas on the way to the hospital.

"Do any of you guys have a cell?" Drew asked.

"I do," one of the paramedics said. "What's up?"

"Will you call my parents?" He gave the number. The guy dialed and held the phone up to Drew's ear.

His mom answered on the second ring. "Mom, I'll call you as soon as I know something," he said.

He could hear the tears in her voice. "I'll get there as soon as I can, honey."

"Don't." Shit, he hurt, but he had to get this out. "I want to see you, but come to Seattle instead. I'll pay for the ticket."

"We love you."

"Love you too."

A FEW HOURS later, Drew's worst fears were confirmed via MRI: He had a torn labrum and a partial rotator cuff tear too. "Your shoulder's a mess, buddy," the team doctor told him. "You'll be having surgery in Seattle as soon as we can get you back home."

Drew was pretty doped up on big-time painkillers, but he knew what the doctor's words meant: He was done for the season. Even worse, his pro football career might be over.

Chapter Fifteen

WHILE DREW WAS doing battle on the turf in Dallas, Kendall staked out a place on the Miners sidelines at Lambeau Field and patted her coat pocket to make sure she still had her phone. Green Bay was known for cold. Today was no exception. It was mid-October, snow flurries were predicted, and she was already freezing her ass off.

She didn't want to be here today, but she was still employed by the Miners. She was somewhat amused by the questions she'd received in team press conferences this week about the fact the team had stepped up their search for a GM candidate. Considering the fact she'd told them to do so, it wasn't news to her. There were also leaks from within the Miners organization. The censored version of her colleagues' remarks to her during their discussion brought an on-site surprise visit from the league commissioner two days ago. If things were bad before, they'd officially hit rock bottom after a few of her colleagues were told the league was opening an official investigation. There would be hell to pay.

After working hard for the past sixteen years to attain a front office position she enjoyed, she wasn't sure she wanted to stay with the Miners in any capacity. She knew that other teams around the league had been dragged into the twenty-first century by the fact women now made up forty-eight percent of the league's fan base, but the Miners' front office was resisting this fact with every weapon at their disposal. She hadn't seen anything like this until she was welcomed into the front office group. A woman in their ranks was obviously more threatening than she had ever imagined. She expected opposition to being the first female executive on their org chart, but she didn't have to take blatant disrespect and disregard for federal employment laws.

Kendall had made the trip on her own this weekend. Sydney was back in the San Francisco area getting ready for her finals. Drew wasn't available by phone right now. She could call one of her girlfriends and whine about her situation, but her friends had their own problems. Hers seemed small in comparison to dealing with husbands, young children, and making ends meet when there was more month than money.

She tugged the hood on her Miners-logo fleece jacket up once more and stamped her feet a few times, hoping the blood moving would bring a little warmth. She felt her phone vibrating but didn't pull it out of her pocket.

Seconds later, she felt it vibrating again. She pulled it out and stared at the text on the screen.

DREW IS INJURED. HE'S ON HIS WAY TO THE HOSPITAL IN DALLAS. CALL ME. SYDNEY

Kendall's stomach dropped, and she felt a surge of adrenaline seconds afterward. She turned and ran into the tunnel the Miners emerged from. Hopefully she'd have some cell bars and even a bit of privacy in here. She held her phone up, twirled around a few times, and realized it was fruitless. No bars. She'd have to get outside again to find cell coverage, and the only way she'd get any solitude for a conversation was to walk out of the stadium and stand on the sidewalk. She was wearing an all-access badge, but stadium security would be less than interested in re-admitting anyone who left the stadium and tried to come back in.

Drew was hurt. The fact he was on his way to the hospital was even worse. If it was something minor, the team would use the on-site X-ray machine in Dallas and patch him up when he got back to Seattle. She darted through the tunnel on her way to the elevators. She needed a place to make a phone call. The fans were in their seats. The media was in the press box. The elevators were deserted as a result.

The media was in the press box. She hit the button for that floor and prayed. If anyone in this stadium had cell and Internet access, it was them. They also had information from every game being played in the league. The el-

evator stopped minutes later, and she got out. She spied
Paul Smith leaning against the wall outside of the press
box door, using his smart phone. Paul had been reporting
on pro football for twenty years now. Besides being excellent at his job, he'd always been friendly and cooperative
when he'd chatted with her for a column or an exclusive
on the Miners. She hurried over to him.

"Paul, do you have a minute?"

He grinned at her. "Sure, Kendall. What's up?"

"Do you have any more information about Drew Mc-
Coy's injury in Dallas today?"

He glanced at his smart phone again and shook his
head. "The preliminary stuff I'm seeing on Twitter right
now from the game states the team is afraid it's a labrum
tear with rotator cuff involvement. They'll know more
after he's at the hospital."

"My assistant texted me." She held up her phone. He
gave her a nod.

"I'm guessing Drew's not answering his phone
right now."

She let out a breath. "Nope."

Paul reached out to pat her upper arm. "You realize
you just told me the rumors of personal involvement between you and McCoy are true."

She swallowed hard and gave him a nod. "I'm guessing it's too late to say this isn't on the record." She clasped
her arms behind her. "Is it too late to make a deal?"

"What did you have in mind?"

"Off the record source information instead?" she said.
Every sportswriter covering professional football was

dying for a credible source that would discuss this past week's fireworks in the Miners' front office. The Miners' owner had threatened the job of anyone found to have divulged information. Sometimes it was good to have nothing to lose.

"You're on," he said. She reached out to shake his hand. "Let's see what else we can find out about McCoy until someone at the hospital answers their damn phone, shall we?"

Kendall called Sydney back. "I'm getting some more info. Thank you for the text."

"You're welcome," Sydney said. "Do you need me to get you a plane ticket?"

"They'll bring him back to Seattle as soon as they can get him released. Maybe I should go there instead." Imagining how much pain Drew had to be in made her want to cry. Even worse, if the reports Paul was getting were accurate, Drew's pro football career might be over.

She needed to get to him. First, though, she needed to handle a few things with the Miners.

DREW FLEW BACK to Seattle the next day with Coach Stewart in the Sharks' owner's private jet. He was still under the influence of hospital-grade pharmaceuticals, but he'd seen the X-rays and the results of the MRI he'd had late last night. It didn't look good for his shoulder or for his future career.

The coach spent most of the plane ride watching game film. Head coaches were expected to keep a distance of sorts from their players so they could dispassionately deliver bad news. Coach Stewart must have been of the opinion that management style was stupid.

"We'll be home in a few hours, McCoy." He glanced over at Drew. "Are you hungry? Thirsty? Need more pain meds?"

Drew managed to crack a smile. "I'm good. Maybe I should try to take a nap or something."

"That's always a great idea. Plus, you'll want to be rested for your welcoming committee," the coach joked. The "welcoming committee" would consist of whoever was taking him for yet another MRI and more testing.

Drew's phone was in the garment bag that had been stowed in the luggage hold by a Sharks employee. He'd talked with his mom a little last night from the hospital. Her employers were nice enough to give her a couple of weeks off so she could take care of him post-surgery. She'd be at his house when he got home later, but he hadn't been able to text Kendall yet. He wasn't allowed the use of his cell phone in the hospital room. He knew she had her own problems, but he needed her. She probably couldn't leave work for a day right now. He got that she loved her job. He loved his job too. If he really wanted to make a relationship endure between them, though, they would have to discuss how to handle each other's schedules.

This type of emergency would probably never happen again, but it might be nice to have a plan when she was seven hundred air miles away from Seattle and he couldn't get himself on a plane without significant assistance. Injuries weren't unheard-of in his job. As a matter of fact, the injury rate in the NFL was one hundred percent.

It wasn't *if* he got hurt, it was *when* he got hurt, and how badly. Teams invested huge sums of money in the best medical care and conditioning staff they could obtain. The league's go-to surgeon was located in Georgia and insisted patients fly to him if a procedure was needed. Drew wanted the best surgeon he could possibly get, but he also didn't want to spend the next four to six months rehabilitating in Georgia.

"I'm guessing I have another doctor's appointment when we get home," Drew said to Coach Stewart.

"That would be a yes. Dr. Ellis will do the procedure," Coach Stewart said. "His office is on Capitol Hill, and you can rehab with us. We talked with him earlier. He'd like to perform the surgery on Wednesday morning. He's operated on several of your teammates with a lot of success, as well as guys from the baseball team and the soccer team. Would you like to talk with him beforehand?"

"Yeah, I would."

Drew shifted uncomfortably in the airplane seat. He knew he'd had enough medication to knock a bear on his ass, but he felt a sharp twinge of pain whenever he moved the right side of his body. He shouldn't bitch. If he was in a traditional airline seat, they would have had to sedate him to get him home. He was looking forward to seeing his mom, but he really wanted Kendall right now.

He knew he wouldn't be dazzling company. Holding her hand might be nice. He'd appreciate her simply being in the same room with him.

Four hours later, he stepped gingerly off of a small staircase and was strapped into a black Suburban with tinted windows.

"Hey, Drew. Heard you're a little under the weather," the guy behind the wheel said. Drew recognized him as part of the Sharks' security detail. "I'm Chuck. I'll be taking you to the surgeon's office."

"Thanks. I feel like shit."

One of the Sharks' training staff got into the front passenger seat.

"Good to see you, McCoy."

Drew gave him a nod and flinched. He couldn't move at all without pain. His shoulder was in a sling, but it wasn't helping.

The coach tapped on Drew's window. "We'll talk with the surgeon as soon as he's done chatting with you. Take it easy." He gave Drew a fist bump on the hand that still worked and got into another black Suburban.

The visit with the surgeon was relatively quick. Drew liked to think he would have been able to ask a few more substantive questions if he was a little more with-it, but he took a look at the testimonials from other pro athletes the doc had operated on previously and gave the go-ahead for the surgery. He got a sheaf of paperwork in return, which needed to be filled out and returned prior to showing up at the hospital at six AM on Wednesday morning.

Chuck, the security guy, was nice enough to retrieve Drew's smart phone out of the garment bag he'd loaded into the back of the vehicle at the airport. He handed it to

Drew for the ride home. Drew scrolled down the contacts with one hand until he found Kendall's number, clicked on it and the speaker function, and listened to it ring.

"Kendall Tracy," she said.

"It's me," he said.

"Where are you?"

"I'm on the way home. I'm having surgery on Wednesday morning." He pulled in a breath. "What's new with you?"

"Things aren't good, but I am more worried about you."

"I'll be fine," he said, and he heard her let out a long breath. The guys in the front seat were pretending like they were ignoring his phone conversation, which was nice of them.

"I have some meetings today and tomorrow. I will be there by the time you are out of surgery on Wednesday morning. Did your mom come back to Seattle?"

"Yes. She's probably baking a cake as we speak."

"Drew, I'm so sorry. I should have been there with you—"

"You couldn't have been on the field," he tried to joke. "You needed a pass for that."

"I could have sat with you in the hospital, or gotten you something to eat, or fixed the pillows." To his shock, he heard tears in her voice. "Anything."

He clicked the speaker function off and brought the phone up to his ear. "I'll still be here on Wednesday. Maybe you'll be there when I wake up from the surgery."

"I could hold your h-hand."

"I'd like that." He flinched again as Chuck drove over

a speed bump which caused a fresh spear of pain through his shoulder. "So it's a date?"

"It's a date."

KENDALL HAD SPENT the past several days attempting to concentrate on the work that had to be done instead of dwelling on the comments made to her during the disastrous meeting she'd crashed. She'd also succeeded in finding Sydney an assistant job at Google with one of Kendall's former sorority sisters. Sydney's last day with the Miners would be tomorrow.

Kendall knew she wasn't going to be able to find as capable an assistant at wherever else she ended up, but to keep Sydney here to ride it out with her was wrong.

"Are you sure?" Sydney said for the one hundredth time in the past week. "You're going to be alone here. I don't feel good about your having to deal with those idiots by yourself."

"I can handle it," Kendall said. "I'm leaving at noon to go to Seattle anyway. I'm hoping they'll make an announcement they've hired a new GM by the end of the week. I'll take another job and get out."

"Do you know which job you're going to accept?"

"No, but I wouldn't have to move if I went to work for Oakland. My parents would probably be happiest if I took Arizona's offer. I don't want to live in Miami."

"Did you ask Drew what he thinks?"

"Not yet. I can talk with him tomorrow. I know he doesn't want to leave Seattle, so that might be a problem for me." She propped her elbow on the desk and rested her chin in her hand. "We'll be meeting in the middle a lot."

She was turning her life upside down for a guy she'd met three weeks ago, and they'd been on only a couple of dates so far. If any of her friends were telling her the same story, she'd tell them to slow down and think before acting. She realized that it was a little nuts for her to consider which job offer would work best for her skipping off to Seattle to see Drew as often as possible.

Above all, she wanted to spend more time with him. She knew he was interested, and she was into him too. The sex was great. He made her laugh. She had no idea, however, if they had what it took to build a life around. She'd been burned enough as the result of her experience with a married man. If things got any worse, she'd be doodling "Kendall McCoy" on her Trapper Keeper. It took a lot more to make any relationship work, though, than almost overpowering physical attraction and the fact they both liked to read. They'd be dealing with the day-to-day of real life for two people who worked an hour and a half plane ride away from each other.

The best thing she could do now was finish up the work on her desk and go to Seattle. She could spend time with Drew and maybe get some answers to the questions she had about any future they might have together. She pulled up the salary cap spreadsheet she'd been working on and forced herself to concentrate. The sooner she was finished, the sooner she'd be on her way.

KENDALL SAVED HER work to a thumb drive a few hours later and stuck it in the zippered pocket of her handbag. She knew she'd need the information to answer questions and be up to speed for the Friday morning conference call she'd agreed to as a condition of her staying in Seattle until Saturday morning. She'd meet up with the Miners in Atlanta on Saturday night for Sunday's game.

Sydney walked into her office with reddened eyes and a shredded tissue in one hand.

"Don't cry, or I'll start crying," Kendall said. She reached out to embrace Sydney. "You'll be running your new office in a week or so."

"Thank you for everything," Sydney said in a tear-filled voice.

"No, thank *you*. I hope you know I'm your friend."

"Uh huh," Sydney said. "You're my friend too."

"If you ever need a job, I hope you'll call me first," Kendall said. "I know you'll be here through grad school, but if you want to relocate . . ."

"I think you're going to end up in Seattle after all. The University of Washington has a pretty good grad program," Sydney said. Kendall let out a laugh. "I hope I'll see you again soon."

"I'll call you when I get back from Seattle."

Sydney gave her one last squeeze and grabbed Kendall's coat, the tote bag with her tablet and phone, and her quilted cloth overnight bag off of the coat rack that sat in one corner of Kendall's office. "Ready?"

"Ready," Kendall said. She gave Sydney one last hug. "Thank you."

"Anytime."

Kendall sprinted to the elevator bank. Outside of the Miners' corporate offices, she hailed a cab, flung herself and her belongings in the back seat, and said, "San Francisco International Airport." The city whizzed by, but she hardly noticed. She wanted to get to Drew. She could be fussing over him and holding his hand instead of having another thrilling encounter with airport security.

For the first time in her life, she made it to the airport in plenty of time. While working on her tablet in the airline's MVP club, she felt her phone vibrate. She grabbed it out of her handbag, glancing at the screen. The display showed it was Sydney.

Kendall hit the "talk" button. "You can't possibly miss me already," she teased.

"There's a problem," Sydney said.

"What happened?"

"Rocky Hill got arrested again two hours ago for beating up his girlfriend in the lobby of the Bellagio. He's in jail in Las Vegas. Jerry Berggren should be passing you momentarily in the airport. He's going to bail him out."

"WHAT?" Kendall knew she couldn't scream in a crowded airport, but she really wanted to. "I knew this would happen. I *knew* it. I told those guys we needed to cut him, and they all fought me—"

"There are already media trucks parked around the building and your desk phone is ringing continuously. I don't know how the media knew before we did. Hill called us twenty minutes ago." Kendall pulled the phone away from her ear and noted the "missed call" symbol on her phone's screen. "I keep hearing doors slamming and people yelling in the hallway."

Kendall closed her eyes. She didn't want the Miners to bail the guy out. She was cutting him and she wasn't accepting any arguments about it, either. It couldn't wait until she came back from Seattle. It needed to happen now, and she was going to spend the next day or so being the public face of the organization while she had to stand up in front of a mob of press and admit she didn't have the spine to make her co-workers realize why Rocky Hill might be an All-Pro, but he was a public relations nightmare for any organization stupid enough to sign him. It was going to be a shit storm. She had no other choice than to get her ass back to the office.

DREW WAS PREPPED for surgery by what seemed like an army of nurses and the anesthesiologist. The anesthesiologist administered the first sedative, and the surgeon and nurses gathered around the table in the operating room and laid one hand each on the blanket covering him. They all grinned at him.

"Go Sharks," someone said.

"Yeah," he responded. He was already a little sleepy. That anesthesiologist knew his shit.

"Drew," the surgeon said. "This is going to go perfectly and you're going to have a quick and complete recovery. We'll see you when you wake up."

"Thanks, Doc." He tried to wave at all of them a little, and it was the last thing he remembered before he awoke in a dimly lit recovery room with two nurses peering down at him.

"Drew, it's time for you to wake up," one of them said.

"Nooo," he said, and he tried to shake his head. His throat was raw. It friggin' hurt. "Where's my mom?" he tried to say. He couldn't get anything out but a whisper, and his throat was so dry.

"We'll let your mom come in here as soon as we get your vitals and help you walk a little."

"Walk." Not only no, but hell, no. He was staying in this nice warm bed.

"Yes."

"Where's Kendall?" No sound came out. He needed some fucking water, which didn't seem to be making an appearance anytime soon. "Water."

"We'll let you have some ice chips in a few minutes." He'd almost forgotten how much fun it was to wake up post-op. He'd love to go back to sleep for a few hours, but these two were all over him every time he closed his eyes again.

"Oh, no, Drew. You need to get up and walk a little before we let you have ice chips or something to eat. How do you feel about graham crackers? We've got some apple juice for you too. You can have a snack right after we get you to your room." Maybe he got dropped off at the local preschool or something. Graham crackers and apple juice? He'd prefer beer.

The nurses were helping him to a sitting position. His shoulder was packed and immobile. He couldn't use his right arm at all. He didn't even want to think about how he was going to pee when he went home. It wasn't like he was asking his mom to help him out on that one.

Shit.

If he forced himself to walk a little for them, he could get out of the recovery room and find somewhere with refreshments and ESPN. He hoped these two nurses lifted weights or something; they didn't look strong enough to keep a 250-pound man upright.

"Here we go," the brunette nurse said. She wrapped her arm around his waist, careful to avoid his packed shoulder. Her blonde colleague slid one arm around him as well and steadied his arm by taking his (good) hand. "We'll take it easy today. No wind sprints."

Like that was funny right now.

Half an hour later, the nurses and his surgeon signed off on his returning to a hospital room for the night. They wanted to monitor things with his shoulder. Whatever. He wanted to know where his mom was and where Kendall was, and not necessarily in that order. The nurses wheeled in his bed, set up all the various accoutrements someone who'd been out of surgery for an undisclosed amount of time seemed to need, and tucked a blanket around his legs as they raised the head of his bed to a sitting position.

"Okay, Drew, we promised. Your snack is coming up."

They doled out a couple of graham crackers and a small plastic bottle of apple juice. He glanced out the window. Dusk was falling. In other words, he'd been in the recovery room a hell of a lot longer than he thought, and he was pretty hungry as well.

His mom breezed through the door to his room seconds later, trailed by his dad.

"Honey!" She hurried across the room to kiss his cheek. "How are you feeling? I wanted to sit in the recovery room with you, but they wouldn't let me. I was so worried. The surgery took a lot longer than the doctor told us and we knew nothing until about an hour ago."

"Your shoulder was a challenge, Son," his father said. He reached out to grasp Drew's still-working hand.

"The doctor says he thinks it will heal up, but it might take longer than he anticipated," his mom said. "You might also need an additional surgery later."

His throat still hurt like a mother, but hand gestures weren't working at the moment for the questions he wanted to ask. "Is he going to come and talk to me about this anytime soon?" Drew said.

"Of course, honey. Is that all they gave you to eat? You must be starving." She began rooting through her purse. "I know I have some crackers or something in here . . ."

The brunette nurse chose that moment to walk back into Drew's room.

"He's hungry," his mother told her. "He needs more food."

"Let's see if he keeps what we just gave him down first," the nurse said. "Can I find you another chair or two, Mrs. McCoy?"

"That would be great."

Two sturdy folding chairs materialized minutes later.

The nurse was checking his IV again, taking his pulse, blood pressure, and listening to his heartbeat. She put a small plastic basin next to him in the bed.

"Let's hope we won't need this," she said. In other words, he might puke up his snack.

Drew gave her a nod. "I hope not as well."

"I'll be back in a few minutes," the nurse said, and she hurried out of his room.

"Mom," Drew said. "Is Kendall here? Have you seen her yet?"

His mother reached out for his hand. "She called your phone earlier. There was an emergency at her office, and she missed her flight."

"Did she say what happened?"

"No, she didn't."

"Is she still coming?"

"I don't know."

His heart dropped into his stomach. Why didn't she tell his mom she'd be on a later flight or she'd be calling him later? She'd been so insistent that she would be at the hospital when he woke up. He was going to live, but he'd looked forward to waking up and seeing her.

It was middle school puppy love crush time, but he wanted to hold her hand when he didn't feel well. He'd like to be a tough guy about all this, but right now, he couldn't. He was glad his parents were there, but he wanted Kendall.

He grabbed the remote control velcroed to the railing around his bed. He clicked the TV on, but no picture appeared. "The TV's broken," he said.

"I'll get the nurse," his dad said. He got up from his chair and walked out into the corridor outside of Drew's room.

"She told me she was going to be here," Drew said.

"I'm sure she will be, honey. She had to deal with something."

Drew frowned at the small sign posted next to his bed. He wasn't allowed to use his cell phone in here. There was a landline phone, at least. He picked up the handset and stabbed in Kendall's cell number. His call bounced to the hospital's operator.

"I'm so sorry, but you can't make long distance phone calls from your room, Mr. McCoy," she said.

He wanted to ask how the hell she knew who he was, but that was too much for someone still a bit woozy from the day's adventures.

"I can't use my cell phone in here, and I need to make a call."

"Is there anyone who can step outside the hospital and make that call for you?"

"I'll work on that. Thank you," he said and hung up.

"What's the matter?" his mother asked.

She was currently reading the menu that had just been delivered by another one of the nursing staff. It was nice to know the hospital was going to allow him to eat actual food sometime in the next few hours. He was hungry, he was still tired, he was pain-free, but he knew the latter would change in a big way when the anesthesia wore off. Maybe he should consider getting some sleep until then.

"I tried to call Kendall and they won't let me. I can't use my cell phone in here, either."

"Let me call her," his mother said. She produced Drew's phone out of her purse and stared at the screen. "How do I hit 'redial'?"

Drew managed to unlock the screen and find the correct number for her. She scooted out into the corridor while Drew leaned back against the pillows.

IT WAS SHAPING up to be one of the worst days of Kendall's life, and it wasn't over by a long shot. She was back in the Miners' offices after taking a cab from the airport. She had no other choice but to return, and she was upset and frustrated over this fact. The director of player personnel ignored her phone calls and was in Vegas bailing out Rocky Hill. Her phone was on perma-vibrate in her pants pocket. She didn't even want to look at it right now. Sydney was currently answering her desk phone while she notified the Miners' department heads that she would like to meet with them in half an hour in the conference room.

Kendall was using Sydney's cell phone to reach Rod Carpenter. She was cutting Hill as quickly as she could find him, and she'd announce this fact at the meeting she'd just called.

The Miners' PR group filed into her office and waited for Kendall to end her call. Sydney glanced up, gestured for them to wait while Kendall ended her call, and went back to her phone call. They'd have to duke it out over the two available chairs in front of Kendall's desk.

"I'm very sorry, but Ms. Tracy is not available for comment right now. May I take a message?" Sydney said for the fifteenth time in fifteen minutes. "I'll make sure to pass that on," she said. "She will call you back at her earliest convenience."

The PR department would be scheduling a press conference when she could announce she'd cut Hill, and she'd answer most of the press's questions at that time. She would deal with the director of player personnel later on. She'd been overridden for the final time. She needed to stand up on her hind legs.

She called Rod's phone for the third time in fifteen minutes, and miracle of miracles, he picked up. She hit the speaker function as he spoke and put her finger up to her lips so Rod wouldn't know there were others listening to their phone call.

"Sydney, I don't have time for this right now—"

"That's nice, because this is Kendall. Where are you?" She could hear him gulp at the other end of the phone.

"I just paid the bail and Mr. Hill will be on his way back to San Francisco as soon as I can get him there. This is just a misunderstanding."

Misunderstanding, my ass. She wasn't harboring that guy for one more minute than it took to get rid of him. Either one of them, actually.

"Didn't I tell you I didn't want you bailing him out of jail in the first place, Rod? Why did you think you could defy me?"

"He's an All-Pro. We can't get through the season without him. We're having enough trouble on the offensive line already—"

"How much more trouble are we going to be in when

the security camera recording of the incident is made public? The witnesses are already talking to the media as well. No." She could hear a male voice in the background.

"Hey, Rod, great to see you. Sorry about all the excitement."

"Don't worry, Rock. We'll be on our way in a few minutes. Why don't you have a seat?"

"NO," Kendall said. "Put him on the phone right now."

"Maybe you should cool off for a while before you talk with him," Rod said.

Kendall saw red. Enough was enough, and she'd had enough.

"Let me make it easy for you, Rod. You either put him on the phone right now, or I'll fire *you*. How's that?"

"You can't fire me—"

"Yes, I can, and I will unless Rocky's on the line in five seconds," she said.

Rod's voice was nervous. "Hey, Rock, the boss lady would like to chat with you for a minute. C'mon over here, will ya?"

"I don't have to talk to that bitch. Tell her to talk to my agent."

"No can do, buddy. She insists."

A few seconds later, she heard Rocky Hill's "What the fuck do you want?"

For the first time since she'd walked in the building that morning, she smiled.

"Hi Rocky, it's Kendall Tracy. I'd love to do this in person, but it can't wait. You're cut from the team. We've disabled your playbook tablet already, so there's no need to return it. We'll pack up and mail the items in your locker to the address on file. Sorry it didn't work out."

She heard a few seconds of silence, and then the man who (allegedly) beat up his one-third-his-size girlfriend in the lobby of one of the most famous hotels in the world recovered his voice.

"I'll make you pay for this, bitch." He took a noisy breath. "You'd better watch your back, because I'll be there when you least expect it, and I'll make sure that pretty face isn't quite so pretty anymore. You dig?" His voice was low, chilling, and furious. Kendall heard the other Miners employees in the office gasp.

"Yes, Rocky, I dig. Thanks for the warning." She didn't bother waiting for him to speak. She hung up, glanced around, and said, "Did you all hear that?"

The five PR department employees and Sydney all nodded.

"Great. I hope you'll back me up." She picked up Sydney's phone again, dialed 911, and asked to speak to the Las Vegas Police Department.

AN HOUR LATER, Rocky Hill was in custody again for threatening Kendall. Rod was on his way back to San Francisco. He'd be fired as soon as he returned to the office and Kendall could get the company property in his possession back. Kendall walked into a crowded conference room and stood behind the chair at the head of the table.

"I'd like to thank Sydney and the PR group for their assistance with what's going to happen this afternoon and tomorrow morning." She glanced around at the thirty people. "I have scheduled a press conference for later today. We'd like to get out in front of the information as much as we can, and I'd like as many of you as possible to be on hand for this." She saw nods from most of the employees. The front office guys looked on stonily. She knew all hell would break loose when she fired Rod, but it was unavoidable.

She pulled in a long breath. "Rocky Hill allegedly assaulted his girlfriend in the lobby of a hotel in Las Vegas a few hours ago. She is in the hospital. He was arrested. I have cut Rocky Hill from the team." She waited for the gasps (and some applause) to die down. "Due to his threats against my safety, he is back in jail. He is not allowed in the building under any circumstances. The San Francisco Police Department will be coordinating security here and at the stadium until further notice. There will be more information as it is available."

"Our offensive line—" the offensive coordinator sputtered.

"You'll need to find another guard. I will not reconsider." She glanced down at her notes. "The Miners' owner will be in attendance at the press conference today as well, which will be held in the auditorium at five o'clock. We'll make a statement and answer questions." She glanced at the offensive coordinator and the head coach. "If you could possibly work on bringing in some guys for a tryout tomorrow or Friday, I'd appreciate that."

"We have a game on Sunday. In Atlanta."

"I realize that. Let's plug in Rocky's backup and see if there might be someone available on the West Coast, for starters." She glanced around the room again. "Any questions? I'll be in my office if you need to talk with me." She gathered up her notes, her tablet, and a bottle of water and walked out of the conference room.

Her phone rang again seconds later. She glanced at the screen long enough to see it was Drew. *Oh, God.* She had a million things to do, and virtually no time to accomplish them in. Plus, she felt guilty. She should have been there when he woke up from his surgery. He was probably so hurt and angry with her, and she deserved it.

She swallowed hard and clicked "talk" on the screen.

"Drew?"

"Hi Kendall, it's actually Drew's mom, Bonnie. Do you have a moment to talk?"

"Is he okay? How is he?"

Kendall knew she should have asked how Bonnie was and the usual small-talk pleasantries when someone she'd never met called, but Drew's mom on the phone . . . maybe he couldn't speak for himself. Maybe it didn't go well. Her heart moved into her throat. A cold fist clutched her stomach.

"He'll be fine," Bonnie said. "He's asking for you."

She closed her eyes with relief and concentrated on taking a breath so her knees wouldn't buckle.

"I'm so sorry I'm not there yet. Things here are not good, and I have to fix a lot of problems before I can get back on a plane," Kendall said. "I–I'm so sorry." She held in the sigh of frustration and anger. She was trying to concentrate on the eleven-hundred things that needed to happen in the next hour, but right now, she needed a few minutes to compose herself. She wasn't going to get it. She headed toward her office while conversations swirled around her. "Is there any way I could possibly talk with him?"

"He's not allowed to use his cell phone in the room, so I'm outside of the hospital right now. Would you like his room number? There's a phone in there."

"Oh, yes, please."

Kendall skirted her desk, plunked down in the desk chair, and grabbed a pen and the first piece of paper that lay atop her desk: the receipt from today's turkey and pro-volone sandwich. Bonnie gave her Drew's room number and the hospital's main number.

"I hope we'll get to meet you soon," Bonnie said.

"I hope so too, Mrs. McCoy."

"Call me Bonnie," she said. She let out a sigh. "The doctor said Drew might be in rehab for as long as a year."

Hot tears rose in Kendall's eyes. In other words, the injury was a hell of a lot more than just the labrum tear and was most likely the end for Drew's NFL career.

The Miners' PR director breezed through the door of her office and said, "Hey, Kendall, I need to talk with you—oh. I didn't see you're on the phone."

Kendall made the arm motion that meant "I'll be with you in a minute." She heard Bonnie say, "It sounds like you're pretty busy. Maybe we should talk later."

"I will call Drew as soon as possible. I promise I will

be there as soon as I can get out of here and get on a plane," Kendall said. The misery of being somewhere she didn't want to be right now and grief over Drew's situation threatened to engulf her. "Bonnie, again, thanks so much for calling me."

"I'm happy to do it, Kendall. We'll look forward to seeing you soon."

Two hours later, Kendall had spent a few minutes in the ladies' room with a bottle of Visine, a hairbrush, and a lipstick. She was currently standing in front of an auditorium crammed with a couple of hundred media professionals, most of the Miners' front office and coaching staff, and she glanced down at the notes Sydney had put in her hand fifteen minutes before.

She read the same statement she'd made in front of the gathered Miners' staff earlier today and added the information that the Miners had been in touch with Rocky Hill's victim and were assisting her with advocacy and medical care. In other words, the Miners were advised by their brand-new team attorney that they should offer Hill's now ex-girlfriend a settlement and the assistance of an attorney to file a civil suit against Mr. Hill to recoup the costs of her medical care, but Kendall wasn't going to mention that in public.

Kendall saw the file of the security camera footage from the hotel earlier that afternoon. It made her want to vomit, and then she wanted to scream. Even if she'd cut his ass when she originally wanted to, she wasn't sure it would have helped, but now it was all about protecting the franchise from liability.

"The Miners have also made a donation to the National Coalition Against Domestic Violence. Our organization is committed to doing what we can to assist women and children affected by domestic violence in our community."

Those words were so empty. If the league was really committed to ending domestic violence, they'd stop signing guys who had been arrested and charged with a domestic violence related crime as early as college. One thing's for sure: She wouldn't sign a guy like this again. The team had known he had an arrest when they'd made him an offer. He swore he'd never do it again.

Words were cheap.

Kendall glanced out over the assembled crowd. "Are there any questions?"

There were questions, waving hands, and shouting from all over the room.

"Why didn't you cut Hill after his last DV arrest?"

"Did anyone in your organization know he'd been arrested on a DV complaint in college?"

"Did the Miners require Hill to take anger management classes or work with a therapist after his last arrest?"

"As the only female GM in the league, do you consider Hill's alleged behavior a personal failure?"

Kendall gripped the sides of the lectern and took the deepest breath she could with the invisible steel bands tightening around her chest. Damn right it was a "personal failure."

She unstuck her hands long enough to pick up the bottle of water in front of her and take a sip. She knew

Hill's victim had signed paperwork holding the team blameless when she accepted the financial settlement that had been hammered out in less than an hour earlier in the afternoon, but she also knew her next comments were most likely not going to be well-received by anyone with the Miners.

She nodded at the sports reporter from Yahoo that had shouted out the question about her being the only female GM. "I'll answer your question, but I'd like everyone to have a seat first." She waited until the rustling of two hundred-plus people sitting down stopped. The only sound she heard was the clicking of cameras. She took another breath, willed herself to be calm, and looked into the TV cameras.

"Yes. I consider what allegedly happened in Las Vegas this morning between a former Miners player and his girlfriend to be a personal failure. I have already spoken with her and offered my heartfelt apology as well as an apology from the organization. Mr. Hill has been charged with this type of incident before. I urged the team to part ways with him at that time. I was overruled." She forced herself to breathe. "As a team executive and as a woman, I don't want anyone playing for the Miners who believes it's appropriate to—allegedly, of course—hit a woman. When we all continue to ignore these incidents or excuse them because the guy's a 'great player' or 'irreplaceable,' our words about stopping the spread of domestic violence or support for its victims are empty." She shook her head. "This will not happen again on my watch. Maybe other franchises choose to turn a blind eye. I won't."

She glanced around the auditorium. "Next?"

It started slowly. She heard one pair of hands clapping, probably Sydney's. More joined in. She felt a hand on her forearm. The Miners' owner had stepped forward and stuck out his hand to shake hers. More cameras went off. She'd like to believe he supported her comments, but she knew it might be a different story when the cameras were off and they were alone in the team's conference room. She wasn't going to dwell on it now; she needed to answer questions, mop up, and get her ass on a plane.

When the press tired of asking questions about this morning's incident, they turned their attention to the Miners' struggles this season. Why would a team that won it all the year before find themselves at 3–5 mid-season? How did she intend to patch the existing holes on the offensive and defensive lines? Did she believe the team would be able to address some of the more glaring needs on the roster through the draft, or were they planning on spending some money in free agency?

"Will the Miners be going after Drew McCoy of the Sharks on the offseason despite his injury?" a reporter in the back shouted.

"How will McCoy's possible signing with the Miners affect your off-the-field relationship?" another reporter called out seconds later.

"The Miners are interested in Mr. McCoy, but we'll also be taking a look at multiple free agents on the offseason. There are lots of games to be played this season before speculating on whom the team would like to sign for next year."

"What about the fact you're romantically involved with him?" A woman in the front barked out.

"No comment," Kendall said. She heard several more reporters shouting questions about how both teams reacted to their relationship, etcetera. She gave those in the auditorium a nod. "Thanks, everyone. If we have further information, we'll let you know." She walked off of the small stage, pushed through the door leading to the corridor outside of her office, and took a deep breath for the first time in an hour.

"Ms. Tracy," the Miners' owner said from behind her. "I'd like to see you in the conference room, please."

"Of course," she said.

The team's employees were going back to work all around her. She was surprised and gratified to get a few pats on the back, some handshakes, and "Good job, Kendall" from more than one of them. They all had no control over what the media would report on the issues facing the team, but she'd done her best to put a good face on it.

Kendall reached out for the conference room doorknob. The director of player personnel, Rod Carpenter's, hand closed over it first. He glared at her.

"Hello," she said to him.

"Hello to you, Ms. Tracy," he said. "It was nice working with you."

Her hand froze in mid-air. She stared at him. "Excuse me?"

"You're about to be fired." Rod's smile was smug. "I'm sure you'll catch on somewhere else."

She bit back the name she'd like to call him. She heaved a sigh, shoved the door open, and walked through it. The department heads were filing in. The owner gestured for her to sit in the chair at the head of the table. It was a bit of a surprise, but she accepted it. It took a few minutes for everyone to be seated, and the owner got to his feet.

"When I walked into the building today, Kendall, I was considering buying your contract out and urging you to go to another team. The transition has been rough. I know you took this job because we were in a tight spot." He tapped his fingertips on the table in front of him. "It wasn't your first choice, either. I have been impressed, though, at your handling of situations the team has needed to face for a while now. I believe your actions today and your comments during today's press conference defused a pretty explosive situation. That being said, I'd like you to stay on as GM. I'm happy to negotiate a mutually satisfactory salary and benefits package commensurate with your responsibilities, and you can make your own decisions as far as staff and assets."

The room was silent. He stuck out his hand. "Will you accept?"

Chapter Sixteen

KENDALL STARED UP at him in shock. Either he was spooked over having nobody at all to run the team if she took one of the three offers she currently had on the table, or he'd heard from his lawyers, and it wasn't good news. Mr. Curtis had never seemed especially supportive. She knew the other guys she worked with were probably bending his ear to hire one of them.

The other guys at the table were all staring at her too. Most looked disgusted. Sydney grinned at her. "Well, boss?" she said.

"I'm not taking the job unless you're still here," Kendall said to Sydney. The owner's hand was still outstretched to her. "I have conditions," she told him.

Mr. Curtis lowered his hand. "So we'll need to talk a little before you can shake my hand and tell me you'll stay."

"Will I have the ability to make decisions about team and front office personnel without interference?"

"Yes."

"I can hire and fire as I see fit," Kendall said.

"Yes. It's in the job description of a GM to do so."

"Okay, then. Since I still hold the title, I'd like to start now." Kendall grabbed her phone out of her pocket and sent the Miners' network administrator a text:

Please disable Rod Carpenter's Internet access/security passes ASAP. Text me when you're finished.

"I'd like Sydney to stay, and I'm going to make it worth her while to do so."

"I approve," the owner said. The other guys at the table were still silent. One was fiddling with his phone. Kendall would almost bet her house he was currently accepting an offer from another team. "Anything else?"

Her phone chirped with an incoming text from the IT guy:

Done. Anything else?

She texted back:

Not right now. Thank you.

"I'd like to dismiss everyone from this meeting but Rod Carpenter and Mr. Curtis."

"I have things to do," Rod said. "I can't sit here all day,—"

"Sit down, Rod," the owner said.

He dropped back into his chair. The other department heads filed out of the room. The door clicked shut behind them, and there were a few seconds of silence.

Kendall glanced down the table at Rod. "You're fired. Please turn in your tablet, your corporate credit card, and the keys to your company car right now."

"You can't do this. You can't fire me!" By now, he was up out of his chair and pointing at Kendall with a shaking finger. "She can't fire me!" he told the owner. "She doesn't have the authority. Tell her!"

The Miners' owner shook his head. Kendall dialed zero on the conference room phone. "Please send security in here to help Mr. Carpenter clean out his desk and escort him out of the building. I want him off the property as quickly as possible."

He was still ranting. "I've been with this organization for ten years now! I know everything, and I won't hesitate to use that knowledge! You can't fire me!"

Two uniformed San Francisco police officers entered the room, got on either side of him, took his arms, and hauled him out of his chair. They marched him out of the room.

"Forget helping him clean out his desk. We'll do it," Kendall called after them. "Let's get him out of here as quickly as possible."

A few minutes later, Rod was in a cab headed home, and Kendall turned to face Mr. Curtis. "There are a few other things I'd like to talk with you about."

"I thought so," he said. He held out one arm. "Lead the way, Ms. Tracy."

DREW AWOKE IN his dimly lit and quiet hospital room to his mom's hand on his good shoulder.

"Honey, I'm sorry to wake you, but we've got to go back to your house for the night. Your dad's falling asleep. Will you be okay without me for a few hours?"

"I'm fine, Bonnie," his dad insisted.

"You can't sleep in that recliner, and you know it. You'll be in traction by morning."

His dad let out a snort. His mom kissed Drew's forehead.

"Mom, the nurses are here. I'll be fine," he said. "You and Dad need some sleep. Are you sure you're okay to drive home?"

His house was only twenty minutes from the hospital, but it was late. He knew his mom would sit up all night fussing over him, no matter how many times he told her he was fine and she should go to sleep. Plus, the hide-a-bed thing in the corner of his room didn't look comfortable. They needed some rest. He'd be fine overnight.

"Your dad is sleepy. I'll drive. I'll ask the nurse to come in here and check on you," she said. "We'll be back in the morning. I promise." She smoothed the hair off his forehead with a gentle hand. "We love you, honey."

"I love you too. Call me when you get to my house so I know you made it safely, okay? Owen left some stuff in the fridge for you in case you're hungry."

His mom shook her head. "He didn't have to do that. We'll see you tomorrow."

His dad shook his good hand, his mom blew him a kiss, and they left.

An hour or so later, he wasn't sure why the nurses hadn't been in yet to check on him. Maybe his mom bribed them to let him sleep. He hit the button to sit up a bit in his bed. The window showed full-on darkness outside. In other words, he'd been pretty much out since he had the graham crackers and apple juice post-surgery. He was hungry as hell. An experimental nudge of his shoulder made him clench his teeth in pain. The anesthesia had worn off. He needed a bathroom. And food. And some pain medication. He wasn't sure which was more urgent, but he wasn't going to be able to get these items for himself. He located the nurse's call button in the sheets and gave it a gentle press.

Another dark-haired nurse walked into the room thirty seconds later. "I see you've finally decided to join us," she said with a big grin.

"I wondered what my mom said to you."

"She's a very persuasive woman," the nurse said. "Let me guess what you want right now. What's your pain level from one to ten?"

"It's an eight," he said through clenched teeth. "I also need to visit the men's room."

"Well, alrighty then," she said, and he almost laughed out loud at the expression on her face. "Let's see what I can do for you here." She crossed the room almost silently to wash her hands in the attached bathroom. She stepped out into the hall for a moment, engaged in some elaborate pantomime with another nurse, and came back into his room with a syringe of what he was guessing was pain medication. "I'll put this in your IV first, and then we'll get you a portable urinal. Will that work?"

"I guess. Do you all have something I could eat?"

"I'll get to it. Don't worry," she said. "We refrigerated your dinner, so there's always that option." The nurse harpooned the IV line with the needle and slowly depressed the syringe's plunger.

"I'm guessing a Dick's burger is out," Drew joked.

"It's almost one AM, my friend. Dick's has gone home for the night." She finished administering the pain meds and produced a portable urinal. "Will this do, or do you need me to help you to the bathroom?"

"I'll take that," he said. He let out a sigh as the plastic container vanished beneath the sheet and blanket covering him. "May I ask you a somewhat weird question?"

"I'll bet you're going to ask me if it's freaky to touch some guy's junk I'm not sleeping with."

"Well, yeah. Plus, I don't even know your name."

"I'm guessing your normal policy is to know a woman's name before she starts getting grabby with Mr. Happy." She grinned at him. "My name's Cheryl. And to answer your question, it's part of my job. Obviously, I can't say anything about yours to anyone else due to HIPAA laws, but if that wasn't the case, I'd be telling the other nurses that you're well-endowed," she teased.

He had to laugh. "That would help me get a few dates," he said.

"I don't think you have a problem getting dates, Mr.

McCoy," she said. She extracted the plastic receptacle from beneath his sheet and blanket and disposed of it before turning to face him again. "I've heard about you."

"Is that so?"

"Hell, yeah."

Whatever she gave him was starting to work. Maybe he didn't need to eat after all right now. His eyes slid closed, and Cheryl's voice sounded like it was coming from a long distance away. She was taking his blood pressure and his temperature. Again.

"Okay, Drew. You take a little nap, and buzz me when you wake up again. I'll make sure you'll get something to eat."

"Thank you," he tried to say. He wasn't sure if he spoke aloud or not. He floated on an almost pain-free cloud of warmth and comfort.

DREW FELT A soft hand taking his and a whispered, "Baby, I'm here."

"Mmpht," he said. He smelled green apples. He was dreaming about Kendall. If he opened his eyes, she'd be gone, and he'd be alone. In the midst of the fuzz of being half-asleep and the pain medication, he felt someone lie down next to him in the bed. He felt soft hair brush his chin as she laid her head on his good shoulder and breathed in her sweet fragrance. Shit, it felt so real. He didn't want to wake up and discover it wasn't.

"I missed you so much," he said to the woman in his dream.

"I missed you too," she whispered. "Go back to sleep."

He let out a long breath.

KENDALL OPENED HER eyes the next morning to Drew having a murmured conference with a tall, dark-haired nurse. He still clasped Kendall's hand.

"I'd like some breakfast, but first, I think I need to visit the men's room," he said to the nurse.

"You'll need some assistance for that."

"Are you sure?" he said. "Will I be able to take a shower today?"

"I don't think you're going to be able to get those stylish boxer briefs off by yourself right now, Mr. McCoy," she teased.

"Normally I'd think that was a great thing," he muttered. The nurse burst out laughing.

"How about a sponge bath after your trip to the men's room?" she coaxed. "The doc was nice enough to use some waterproof sutures in your shoulder, so we'll try a shower tomorrow morning before you leave."

"My hair—"

"I have some lovely dry shampoo with your name on it." The nurse glanced over at Kendall and grinned. "Good morning. And you are?"

Kendall shoved her hair out of her eyes. "I'm Kendall."

"I'm guessing you two know each other."

"You could say that," Kendall said.

She probably looked like hell. The hospital was probably used to seeing people in less than magazine cover model condition, but she didn't want Drew to scream and run when he glanced over at her.

"We don't usually let visitors bunk with the patients, but I'll overlook it." The nurse stuck out her hand. "I'm Cheryl. I'm about to go off-duty, but I'll be back at eleven tonight. I'll take Drew to the men's room, and the day nurse will be here to help him with the rest of the items on his to-do list."

Kendall shook her hand. "Is there coffee anywhere?"

"There's an espresso cart in the waiting area," Cheryl said.

"God bless you," Kendall said and shoved herself off Drew's bed. "I'll be right back."

She hurried into the bathroom. By the time she emerged, Drew was slowly making his way across the hospital room. His legs weren't the problem. His heavily-bandaged shoulder was affecting his balance. Kendall was fairly sure the pain meds were creating an issue as well. Cheryl, the nurse, was leading him toward the bathroom.

"Take it easy, Drew. We're almost there."

Drew glanced over at Kendall. "Good morning."

"Good morning," she said. "Want me to get you a coffee?"

She saw his lips curve into a smile. "Hell, yeah. Tall latte, please."

Drew was sitting up in the reclining chair when she walked back into his room, and he was eating what looked like breakfast for five. "I'm a little hungry," he explained.

She put his to-go cup on the rolling table in front of him and pulled a folding chair closer to him. "It looks good." She peeled the wrapper off of some kind of protein breakfast bar she had bought from the barista.

"Want some?" he said. He pushed the tray closer to her while he unearthed another fork from under a second plate.

She held out the protein bar. "Want to share?"

"Sure."

Drew smiled at her. He offered to share his food, but he seemed somewhat preoccupied. Maybe he was just in pain and still tired. He seemed happier to see Cheryl than he had been to see her, though, and the first gnawing tendrils of worry started in her gut. She cut the protein bar in half with a plastic knife and handed it to him.

"Isn't blueberry your favorite?"

"Fruit is good," he said. He didn't meet her eyes. He nudged a plateful of scrambled eggs and turkey bacon in her direction. "Have some."

She took a bite of food that tasted like sawdust in her mouth, chewed, swallowed, and said, "What's wrong, Drew?"

"What do you mean?" He took another bite of fresh fruit salad. He still wasn't looking at her.

"We're talking past each other. We're not talking *to* each other." She hauled in a breath. "Are you mad at me?"

He put his utensils down and sat back in the chair. "Why would I be mad at you?"

He looked into her face, but he wasn't smiling. If she had to give his expression a name, it would be "wary." He wasn't committing himself or his feelings to this conversation. He might have been holding her hand when she woke up this morning, but he wasn't extending himself in any way, shape, or form.

She stared at him for a moment. "Maybe you could tell me how you feel instead of answering a question with a question."

He took a sip of coffee and set the to-go cup back down on the table. "Truthfully, I'm hurt."

"I know I wasn't there when you woke up yesterday—"

"No, you weren't. You didn't call. I thought it wasn't important to you."

"Your mom called me yesterday with your phone. Did she tell you I was in the middle of a gigantic firefight?"

"She said you had an emergency you needed to take care of."

Kendall sucked in a breath. "I did. I cut Rocky Hill yesterday after he beat the hell out of his girlfriend in Las Vegas in front of several hundred witnesses. I had to do a press conference, among other things. I also fired one of the front office staff for defying me when I said I didn't want him to bail Hill out of jail. I didn't leave the office until eleven o'clock last night." She pushed the eggs around on her plate. "I was at the airport to fly out yesterday morning, Sydney called me, and I had to turn around and go back. Didn't you see what happened on the news?"

"The TV in here is broken. The hospital said they'd either replace it or fix it today. ESPN wasn't high on my list right then." He folded his arms in front of him, or at least tried to. She stared at him.

"You have to know that I did my best to get here," she said. "The Miners' owner was nice enough to let me use his plane so I could be here late last night, or actually, early this morning. I left as soon as I could and I didn't do this to hurt you." She hauled in a breath. "You are very important to me."

He gave her a nod. They sat in silence for a minute or so. He glanced away from her and swallowed hard.

"Drew, what's the real reason for this?"

"I don't understand what you're talking about."

"I know you're hurt because I wasn't here when you woke up, but there's something more to this."

He folded his lips, gave up attempting to cross his arms, and folded his hands in his lap. "Are you staying with the Miners?"

"I wasn't going to until late yesterday afternoon," she said.

"What happened then?"

"I had a long talk with the owner. He officially offered me the GM job. He is happy with what I am doing with the organization and the team, and he'd like to have things settled in the next several days. His attorneys have notified him to expect an indictment." She swallowed. "I'm not sure if he will give the team ownership outright to his wife before the paperwork arrives or what is going to happen, but the franchise will need to batten down the hatches to survive, so to speak."

"Where does that leave us?"

She looked into his face. "I will have to live in California for the foreseeable future, if that answers your question."

"If we want to stay together, I'll be living alone in Seattle six months a year."

"Drew, we haven't been on a real date yet. Maybe we should try the meeting in the middle thing you talked about last week before we decide it's not going to work," she said.

"I'll be in rehab for at least six months now, most likely a year. In Seattle." He let out a sigh. "I'm not sure this is going to work, Kendall. You'll be working sixty to seventy hours a week for the Miners. Our GM must be part giraffe; I don't think that guy ever sleeps. You'll be so exhausted on the nights we can see each other that dating will be out of the question—"

"I'll make it happen," she said. "I'll do whatever I have to do."

"What if I want to start a marriage and a life in the house I picked out for my future family? What then?"

He realized he was starting to sound like his dad, but he'd made a plan. He wanted to see his smiling wife in a luxurious house, watch his kids playing in the grass in the backyard, and holidays and birthdays and family celebrations there all year long. Was it a crime to wish for such a thing?

"Why does it have to be your house and your city? Is there any room for compromise at all?" She pushed the plate of eggs and turkey bacon away. "I know you lived in California in college. Would Portland be an alternative? I'd have to fly in for weekends, but we could make it work."

"I can't get on a plane six months a year to go to practice."

The argument could go around and around and never get anywhere. He wouldn't budge. Right now, she couldn't. She'd given Mr. Curtis her word last night that she would stay with the Miners until his legal problems were over at the least. The coaching staff and players needed to know that their world wasn't changing all that much.

She glanced up from staring down at the rolling table to see him flinch in pain.

"Do you need some painkillers?" she asked.

"I don't know when the last dose was. Maybe I should call the nurse."

He started to get up from the chair, and she said, "Let me do it."

DREW OPENED HIS eyes from another pharmaceutically-induced haze to see Kendall asleep in the reclining chair next to his bed. The TV in his room had been replaced while he was out too. Whoever installed it left it on ESPN. The volume was muted and the closed captioning was enabled. He noticed there was a special report coming up about the Miners' current situation, so he hit the button on his bed to sit up a bit and turned the volume low enough that he could hear it, but not so loud it would wake up the (obviously) exhausted Kendall.

The sportscasters started out by showing a clip of the security camera footage from the hotel where Rocky Hill used his girlfriend's face as a punching bag. Even in black and white, the pictures were chilling. The next clip was Kendall answering a question from a reporter asking her if she was ashamed the incident happened while she was acting GM of the Miners.

Kendall looked stricken by his question. She took a sip of water while she gathered her thoughts. When she spoke, her voice was strong and she looked directly into the camera. He was stunned by her admission that yes, she was ashamed. He listened to the rest of her comments with his mouth hanging open. He resisted the impulse to applaud. No wonder the owner of the Miners moved toward her at the podium to shake her hand. She'd defused a disastrous PR situation with honesty and a commitment to the future. She handled a room full of media who wielded questions like pointy sticks and didn't back down to them.

The strong, decisive leader on his television set, the woman who said she wouldn't let anything like it happen again on her watch, stirred a little in her sleep. The sports anchors were now opining on what this all meant for the Miners. He didn't care what they had to say about the whole thing, so he hit the "mute" button again.

He was so proud of her. Even more, it was evident to him that Kendall would dedicate herself to home, family, and her career. Watching her lead a franchise in trouble made him understand she was born for the job, even if she wasn't sure she wanted it. She'd have a husband and a family, but she wouldn't be happy if the only things she had to worry about were what she'd serve for dinner, or getting the kids to their soccer practice beforehand. He knew she would love her family and do her best, but she would also have a career that absorbed and challenged her, whether it was with the Miners or another pro football franchise.

His dad was currently having heartburn over his mom's serving him pasta sauce out of a jar because she was enjoying the opportunity to have a job. His mom wanted a challenge too, and she went out and got it. It wasn't about Kendall's serving him takeout for meals or forgetting to wash his shorts. How was he going to deal with the fact she lived in another state and could not move, let alone the knowledge that she had a lot bigger things on her plate than whether or not things in their house were running smoothly?

If he wanted Kendall, his definition of the perfect family needed to change. They would be handling the details of any future home together. They might have those holidays and birthdays and friends over to visit, but it might not be in a suburb twenty miles east of Seattle. Whether he realized it or not, Drew's dad had taught him a very valuable lesson. Home wasn't a place in which one person worked to meet the needs of her entire family. It was a place in which everyone worked together to take care of each other.

He glanced up to see his mom and dad in the corridor outside the room.

"Shhh," he said, putting one finger over his lips.

"This must be Kendall," his mom whispered.

His dad gave Drew a nod. "Let me go find out if I can get another chair or two," he muttered.

Kendall stirred again and opened her eyes. "Oh. I must have fallen asleep," she said. "I'm so sorry." She smothered a yawn, stretched a bit, and got to her feet. She extended her hand to Drew's mom. "You must be Mrs. McCoy. I'm Kendall."

Drew's mom hurried around his bed and threw her arms around Kendall.

"It's so nice to meet you. You are as lovely as Drew told me."

"He's been bragging about you also. It's wonderful to meet you."

"Call me Bonnie," his mom said, gesturing for Kendall to take the chair. "My husband went to get a couple more chairs so we could sit here and have a good visit."

Bonnie kissed her son on the forehead and said, "Is there anything we can get for you, honey?"

"A new shoulder would be nice."

"I'll do my best," Bonnie told him. "How about some brunch in the meantime? I'll ask the nurse if you can have something to eat. I'll be right back."

DREW PATTED THE bed next to him when his parents wandered out of the room. Kendall perched on it.

"Maybe we could continue our conversation later on."

"I'd like that."

She was thinking the chances of that happening were small to none. Drew's parents would most likely stay until visiting hours were over, and part of the deal she'd struck with her boss was the fact she'd be back in San Francisco by tomorrow morning. The Miners had a bye next week, so she could come back on Friday afternoon and stay until Monday morning.

She wasn't sure how she and Drew could realistically make things work. She couldn't telecommute. She had to be in the Miners' offices at least five days a week to do her job, and most of those workdays stretched into the evening hours. Any relationship they managed to carve out would wither and die due to absence and inattention.

He was also facing the biggest challenge of his professional life. Would he be able to come back from such a catastrophic injury, or would he be forced into retirement? If he had to retire, he might want to move where she was, but she couldn't count on that. He'd be facing the biggest fear of all NFL players forced into premature retirement: Who would he be after a life spent being Drew McCoy, football star? He'd have to start over. Even more, he'd have to redefine himself, and many former players struggled with that challenge.

Drew didn't seem interested in coaching. He'd lose his mind being stuck in a broadcasting booth each Sunday for six months a year. He probably thought he had several years to decide what he wanted to do after football. Those years had evaporated on Dallas's turf last Sunday morning.

He might resent her because she still earned a living from football, and he did not.

Chapter Seventeen

LATER THAT DAY, Kendall pulled the blankets up Drew's chest as she watched his eyelids flutter shut. The nurses had re-packed and changed his dressing about half an hour ago. They'd pumped him full of painkillers before they did it, but the pain etched on his face told her whatever shot they gave him wasn't quite enough. He was exhausted. His parents had left a few minutes ago.

She wished she could stay.

"They're letting me take a shower tomorrow, baby," he whispered. "Can't wait."

She had to smile. "Alone?"

"I'll have a couple of assistants. Maybe you'd like to help too."

"Sounds steamy," she said. "Are you sure you're ready for all that action?"

"Bring it on," he said.

She leaned over the bed and touched her mouth to his

as she stroked his hair. His mom had brushed the tangles out of it earlier and put it back into a ponytail, but it was already rumpled.

"I heard you're getting out of here tomorrow."

"That's what the doctor said."

He was half-asleep. She had to leave. There was so much to say and he wasn't awake to talk about any of it. She'd spent the entire afternoon talking and laughing with him and his parents instead.

Neil and Bonnie McCoy were terrific people. She really liked them. She knew her parents would love Drew. He would joke with her dad and flirt with her mom, and there wouldn't be in-law problems or unpleasantness. The longer she stayed, the more she ignored the truth.

It wasn't going to work between them. Neither of them was willing to give an inch on the compromises needed to make any relationship thrive. She could give up the things she wanted to be with him, but she knew she'd resent those sacrifices. She'd be giving up her own goals and aspirations, and that scared her more than a lifetime of being alone.

He could retire or get himself traded to a team in California, and he'd still be wondering if he'd done the right thing. Bitterness would build.

She knew she was falling in love with him. She knew she might spend the rest of her life kicking herself, but maybe it was best to cut it off before things were even worse—the exchange of "I love you's," the lonely nights spent Skyping or texting when you'd give almost anything to lie next to your loved one and tell him about your day.

She reached over to kiss him one more time. He was almost asleep. Hopefully, he wouldn't figure out she was gone until morning.

"Good night, baby," she whispered. "I'll be back soon. Sleep well."

He let out a murmur of protest, but he was so drugged up he couldn't force himself awake. She watched him relax into a deep sleep. She stroked the roughness of his cheek and kissed the middle of his forehead. She turned to pick up the backpack and handbag she'd brought with her from San Francisco.

She hurried out of his room, took the elevator to the first floor, and pulled her cell phone out of her handbag to let Mr. Curtis's pilot know she was on her way to Boeing Field.

DREW'S BEDSIDE PHONE rang the next morning. He reflexively reached out to grab it and let out a "son of a *bitch*" as he realized that probably wasn't the best career move. He should have put the fucking thing on the table next to his left hand. In those split seconds, he also realized that Kendall wasn't in the room. Her stuff was gone.

Shit.

He knocked the receiver off of the cradle, said, "Just a minute," and finally managed to grab it with his good hand.

"Hello?"

"It's Kendall," she said. "Good morning."

"Where are you? I thought you were going to be here this morning—"

She let out a sigh. "I thought I was too. I'm so sorry."

"When did you decide you were leaving?"

"I had meetings today."

"Wouldn't it have been a good thing to tell me about yesterday?"

He could hear the strain in her voice, but he was hurt and angry. Pissed enough to finally say something about it, as a matter of fact.

"Drew, I'm so sorry—"

"That's what you claim, but I'm not sure you really mean it. I need you right now."

He heard her gasp, and he heard voices in the background.

"Kendall, we're ready to get started," a male voice said.

"I have to go," she said.

He'd make it easy on her. He knew it was childish and he should cut her a little slack for being in an impossible situation, but right now, he didn't want to. He hung up on her.

AFTER A SHOWER that had nothing in common with the "naughty nurses" porn he'd seen at other guys' bachelor parties, Drew's incision was inspected, re-bandaged and wrapped again for the trip home. He was helped into cross trainers, Sharks warm-ups, and a very loose button-down shirt. His mom draped a fleece jacket over his currently useless shoulder and his entourage (nurses, parents, and Sharks security) made their way to the SUV that would be taking him home.

"I thought we'd see Kendall this morning," his mom said as he was wheeled down the hospital corridor.

"She had to go back to San Francisco," he said.

"Maybe you could talk with her later, or she can fly back for the weekend." His mom sounded so hopeful. He knew he was about to break her heart.

Drew had dated a lot of women over the years. His parents had been friendly toward them. His mom even hinted around about a couple of them. In other words, she would have been happy to have a daughter-in-law. Kendall had evidently joined that shortlist. His mom knew what his schedule was like during football season. She didn't understand Kendall wasn't going to be able to get out of going to the Miners' game on Sunday in Atlanta unless she was bleeding from every pore, and even then it was not a certainty.

"Mom, I think we broke up this morning," he said.

His normally calm, quiet, sweet mom grabbed the arm of the wheelchair he was currently riding in and shrieked, "WHAT?"

The small group of people surrounding Drew came to a screeching halt. His dad reached out to slide his arm around his mom's shoulders.

"Bonnie, we can talk about it later."

Drew reached over to take his mom's hand in his good one. "Mom. It'll be okay." His mom pulled away from him.

"*You broke up with her*? That poor girl got on a plane

to spend twenty-four hours with you. Why would you do such a thing? I really like her. Are you nuts?"

"Why would you think I broke up with her? Maybe she dumped me," he said.

"I saw the way she looked at you yesterday. She's in love with you, or my name isn't Bonnie McCoy. I'm ashamed of you, Andrew David McCoy. *Ashamed*."

His mom dropped his arm and walked away from him. He stared after her in astonishment. Maybe the pain meds were making him hallucinate or something. She wasn't that mad when he dented the fender on his dad's month-old truck as a newly-licensed driver.

If (and when) she found out he hung up on Kendall's attempt to apologize, there would be additional hell to pay: His mom would not tolerate rudeness.

After a pause, Cheryl got his wheelchair going again. "It looks like you're in trouble, Mister. Are you sure you want to go home right now?"

"Yeah, I'm sure. Maybe the neighbor can come over and help me take a shower," Drew joked. "I also have a guest room, Cheryl."

"Mr. Cheryl might have a problem with that."

"Tell him it's a business thing."

"God, you're a flirt," she said. He had to laugh.

He was rolled onto the sidewalk in front of the hospital a few minutes later. A small knot of jersey-clad Sharks fans held up "Get Well Soon" signs for him, and they chanted "Go Sharks! Go Sharks!" There were a few members of the media filming his exit from the hospital. It must have been a slow news day.

He glanced up at Cheryl.

"Will you take me over there?"

"I suppose." She grinned at him.

"Have they been out here all day?"

"They've been out here on and off since you were admitted."

He didn't have a pen, but he was willing to bet someone in the crowd might let him use one. The fans burst into applause when he was wheeled over to them. He tried to stand up, but he felt Cheryl's hand on his good shoulder.

"You can't be out of the wheelchair until you're in a vehicle and off hospital property, Buster."

"Crap," he said good-naturedly. A little boy with no front teeth wearing a reproduction McCoy jersey bounced up to him.

"Will you sign my shirt?"

"Of course I will," he said. "I think I need a pen, though."

Someone from the crowd handed him a Sharpie.

"Thank you so much," he said to the woman with the pen.

He saw color rising in her face, and she gave him a shy smile. In other words, she wanted to talk with him, but she was too shy. He'd make sure she got an autograph. He could sign a few more in the meantime. He'd have to use his non-dominant hand. Hopefully, nobody would mind.

He felt his dad's hand on his good shoulder. "Son, I'm taking your mother back to your house. I think she needs to lie down for a little while."

"Is she okay?"

"She's fine. She's a little overwrought. I think she's tired."

Drew's stomach clenched in concern. He wondered if she was getting sick. He couldn't remember the last time she'd freaked out like she had a few minutes ago. Maybe she was stressed out from taking care of him and the ongoing fights with his dad over her job. He was going to find out what was wrong as soon as he could get out of here.

"Do you need my keys?" Drew said.

"No. We've got the other key. We'll see you at home."

"Thanks, Dad."

Drew went on signing autographs until he'd signed for everyone. He gave the pen back to the woman who'd handed it to him in the first place right after he signed her McCoy jersey. "What's your name?" he asked.

"I'm Abby," she said. She gave him another shy smile. She'd waited until everyone else got their turn to talk with him, she didn't complain, and she wasn't wearing a ring. If Collins or Taylor were here right now, he'd be introducing her and letting them slug it out over who got to take her out for coffee.

"You saved my butt, Abby. Thanks." He extended his hand to shake hers and said, "If you'll call the Sharks headquarters on Monday and leave your contact information with the receptionist, I'll make sure you get some Sharks gear on me."

"I would love that!" Abby said. "Thank you so much."

"Oh, no, thank you."

Cheryl leaned forward and tapped his shoulder.

"Listen, big guy, I need to get you in that car to go home. My boss is going to kill me."

"Got it."

He waved goodbye to the Sharks fans, who cheered as he was helped out of the wheelchair and into the black SUV the team's security guys drove. Chuck threw himself into the driver's seat, pulled on his seatbelt, and they were off.

DREW TALKED CHUCK into obtaining a to-go order from Burgermaster on the way to his house. This might have had something to do with the fact Drew offered to treat Chuck and his colleague.

"I need a Tom & Jerry shake," Drew told Chuck. "The hospital food wasn't terrible, but I could go for a cheeseburger too."

"Gotcha," Chuck said. "Is there any place else we need to stop before we take you to your house?"

"I think I'm okay. Thanks for asking."

He reached into the pocket of his warm-ups and scrolled down his contacts list with one fingertip. Every Shark knew Amy Hamilton Stephens, the owner of Crazy Daisy in Seattle's Capitol Hill neighborhood, specialized in smoothing the feathers of infuriated females among other flower-and-gift-sending emergencies. He hit the number and held the phone up to his ear.

"Crazy Daisy," a cheerful female voice answered.

"Hi. Is this Amy?"

"It sure is. Who's this?"

"It's Drew McCoy, and I think I need your help."

He heard Amy laugh, and she said, "Well, this is a first. I usually hear from your teammates. How are you feeling? Didn't you have surgery the day before yesterday?"

"I did, and that's why I need your help. My mom is a little irritated with me at the moment. I'm wondering what you might recommend. I'd also like to send something to the woman I'm seeing, but I'm not sure what she might like."

"An irritated mom is a new one," Amy said. "This might call for fine jewelry. I know you just got out of the hospital, though, so you might not be in the mood for shopping. My brother-in-law knows his way around a jewelry store. Let me call him and get an opinion or two, and I'll call you back. Is the number on my caller ID your phone?"

"Yes, it is."

"I'll think about what the woman in your life might like as well. Talk to you in a few minutes." She hung up.

"Sorry to eavesdrop, but that little Tiffany's box can get you out of a hell of a lot of trouble once in a while," Chuck said. He pulled into Burgermaster's parking lot and parked in one of the stalls. "Maybe you should call your parents and ask if they'd like you to pick them up some food."

"Good idea," Drew said.

Twenty minutes later, the SUV was on its way to Drew's house again with multiple bags of food and drinks, and Drew's phone rang.

"Hey, McCoy," Brandon McKenna said. He hadn't lived in New Orleans for almost fifteen years now, but he'd never lost the accent. "How are you doin'? My sister Amy called. She says you're in a jam."

"My mom is mad at me. I know it's ridiculous."

"Not at all," Brandon said. "I just happen to be at Tiffany's at Bellevue Square right now. If I remember correctly, you live in Clyde Hill, don't you?" The last year Brandon had played for the Sharks, Drew hosted the prefunction for the defensive players' holiday dinner at his house. He was fairly sure his neighbors still remembered it too.

"Yeah. Just off the main drag," Drew said.

"Got it." Brandon let out a breath. "The last time my mama was irritated with me, I bought her a charm bracelet with "Mom" engraved on it. She cried and everything, man. How about I pick up one of those for you?"

"I think I have some cash." Drew was already grabbing for his wallet to see how much cash he had. "How much will I owe you?"

"A couple hundred dollars and I'll drop it by your house on the way home."

"Deal. I'll buy you a beer for your trouble."

He heard Brandon's booming laugh. "I'll take you up on that beer. How about an interview for Sunday's show too?"

After Brandon McKenna retired from the league, he took over Matt Stephens' (also retired from the Sharks) seat on the Sunday morning pre-game show. Brandon was well-liked by viewers and his colleagues. He had no problem getting interviews with players, either: After all, he remembered what it was like to answer the same questions over and over. He didn't ask the obvious, and his efforts were rewarded by the stature of players that would sit down with him and nobody else.

"As long as I don't have to fly anywhere, you've got yourself an interview," Drew said.

"We can do this at your house or at a studio in Seattle, whichever you prefer. Let's discuss it when I get there. I should see you in the next half an hour or so."

"Thanks, Brandon."

"You'd do the same for me, man."

"You're right. I would."

Chuck was pulling several bags of food and drinks from Burgermaster out of the SUV. Drew picked up the duffel bag he'd shoved clean underwear and socks into. There were also some written instructions on what to do with his shoulder, a couple of prescriptions, and a referral to a rehab doc. He knew the Sharks training staff would handle his ongoing care, but it was always good to have a variety of options.

He had hoped he'd make the trip up the stairs to his front door with Kendall. He'd wanted to spend the evening with her, despite the fact all he could do right now was talk. He missed her already. Hanging up on her was a dick move too.

No wonder the women in his life were disgusted with him right now. He felt like shit, but that was no excuse. His mom (and dad) dropped everything to come out and take care of him. The woman he cared for had also gone out of her way to spend even a few hours with him.

He needed to make amends. He'd better start now.

DREW AND CHUCK spread the burger feast over his dining room table. Drew's dad's face lit up as he grabbed a juicy cheeseburger and a chocolate shake out of one of the bags.

"Don't tell your mother," Neil said. "She's restricting my red meat intake."

"I'm already in trouble with Mom." Drew dropped into a chair. "Where is she, anyway?"

"She's taking a nap. We came back here last night and she still couldn't sleep for worrying about you." His dad sat down at the table. "She'll be in a better mood when she wakes up."

"She hasn't acted like that since I was in high school and I missed curfew by an hour." And he never did it again after listening to how scared his mom was he'd been in an accident or something. Maybe he was a mama's boy, but he still called her first thing after the Sharks' plane landed when they traveled to an away game. He loved his dad and he knew his dad loved him, but he knew his mom worried about her kids and grandkids.

"I'll be taking a little nap myself after I finish this, Son."

His dad reached out for a container of excellent fries and one of the small cups of ketchup they'd gotten with the order. Chuck and his colleague were devouring their food. Drew reached into the bag for a couple of cheeseburgers and grabbed his Tom & Jerry shake. He lifted it up to toast.

"Here's to a speedy and complete recovery," Drew's dad said.

"Cheers," the three other men said. The only noise in Drew's dining room for the next fifteen minutes or so was crinkling paper and foil food wrappers and an occasional "Mmm."

Drew's front doorbell rang. "I'll get it," he said and shoved himself to his feet. Damn shoulder.

Brandon McKenna stood on the porch with two small Tiffany's carrier bags. Drew had talked with him several times before, but he knew his dad would love meeting him.

"C'mon in," Drew said. "How about a beer? We've also got cheeseburgers and shakes, if you're hungry."

"My wife would appreciate it if I didn't eat this close to dinner, but I will take a beer," Brandon said. He reached out to shake Neil McCoy's hand. "I'm Brandon," he said. "Good to see you both too," he said to Chuck.

Drew managed to get a beer and the bottle opener one-handed and delivered both to Brandon, who handed him one of the carrier bags in return.

"Your mama should love this. My mama hasn't taken hers off since I gave it to her."

"What's in the other bag, guy?" Drew dug the cash out of his wallet and handed it to Brandon.

"I got my wife a high-heeled shoe charm for her bracelet."

"That's nice," Chuck said.

"What'd you do?" Neil said, and the men sitting at Drew's table burst into laughter.

"Well, it's actually what I *didn't* do." Brandon passed one hand over his face. "I told my bride that I would handle things with our twin sons yesterday so she could go to some shoe sale at Nordstrom with her mama and her sister—"

"That was your first mistake," Chuck joked. Brandon grinned at him.

"I was having lunch with a couple of my colleagues, and time got away from me. When I arrived at home, her mama and sister couldn't break away, and my wife very sweetly told me she wasn't happy about my behavior." Brandon shook his head. "She doesn't like missing a good shoe sale. Plus, our boys are mobile now. A visit to the ladies' shoe department wouldn't have ended well." He glanced around the table. "They take after their daddy."

"Has she forgiven you yet?"

"Let's put it this way: I apologized. She puts up with a lot from the three men in her life. She accepted my apology, but wait until she finds out what else I've got up my sleeve."

"What might that be?" Drew asked.

"The shoe people are visiting our house tomorrow night. I'm taking the twins out for ice cream with their grandpas while my wife, her sister, and our mamas sip champagne, eat appetizers, and buy some shoes."

"That's going to get expensive," Drew said.

"She's worth it. I can't wait to see the look on her face." The other guys at the table teased Brandon a little, but he grinned at them. "My mama didn't raise any stupid children. With that, I'd better be on my way home. Thanks for the beer, Drew, and we'll be here at nine tomorrow for the interview, if that will work."

"Sure," Drew said. He gestured toward his shoulder. "I'll try to find something to wear."

"The production assistants will take care of that. Don't worry about it."

Brandon got to his feet, shook hands with everyone, and hurried out to his car.

Drew walked back into the dining room, picked up the Tiffany's bag, and said, "I'll be back in a few minutes."

"I'll put a shake in the freezer for your mom, Son."

"Thanks, Dad."

Drew trudged up two flights of stairs that he would have run up last week. He needed a little time to think. Maybe he needed to solicit advice from McKenna: The guy was obviously crazy in love with his wife, and he knew they had had to make some pretty big adjustments so his opera diva wife could keep working after their sons were born. If he wanted to get anywhere with Kendall (after he apologized profusely for hanging up on her) he'd better be willing to make some compromises himself.

He tapped on the guest room door next to his bedroom. "Mom? Are you awake?"

"Come on in, honey," she said.

He shoved the door open with his shoulder while hiding the little carrier bag behind his back. "Are you okay? You were pretty upset earlier. I'm sorry for what I did."

He saw his mom's smile in the soft light of the lamp on the bedside table. "Don't worry about it. I haven't been sleeping well since we got here, and I . . ." She shook her head and flinched a little at the movement. "I have a headache."

"Do you need some aspirin or something?" He leaned down to stash the bag next to the nightstand while she wasn't looking.

"That might help."

"I'll get it," he said. He walked into the attached bedroom, filled a drinking glass with water, and grabbed the ibuprofen bottle out of the medicine cabinet. He could still carry stuff in his right hand as long as he didn't try to lift his arm or anything, which hurt like a mofo. He needed some more medicine himself, but he could do this for his mom first.

He sat down on the side of the bed where she lay, put the drinking glass down on the nightstand, and said, "Do you need me to help you sit up a little?"

"I'm okay," she said. He thought she looked pale and worn out, but he wasn't going to tell her that. She pulled herself into a sitting position. He gave her a dose of the ibuprofen and the water glass.

"Do you need me to shut off the light for you?" he said.

"No. I'll be much better in a few minutes." She slid back into the pillows and gazed up at him. "How are you feeling?"

"My shoulder hurts. I'll go back downstairs and get the prescriptions I brought home." She started to sit up and he said, "No, Mom, I can handle it. You rest. Do you need me to get that blanket over there for you?" He nodded at the folded throw that usually hung over the back of an overstuffed chair in the corner of the room.

"I'd like that, honey."

He could get the blanket just fine and bring it back to her, but spreading it over her was a different story with one usable hand.

"This is harder than I thought," he said after struggling with it for a minute or so.

"I'll take care of it," she said. She managed to toss the blanket over her legs and said, "Why don't you relax here with me for a few minutes?"

"Sure, Mom." Maybe he'd retreat to the big chair in the corner. He was surprisingly tired after doing nothing more strenuous than riding around in a car and eating a cheeseburger. Maybe he could get a cat nap while his mom rested.

His cell phone rang.

He reached in, pulled it out, and noted it was the Sharks' headquarters. He clicked on "talk." He hit "speaker" so his mom could hear.

"Hey, Drew, how are you feeling?" Coach Stewart said. "I'm here with the coaches and the conditioning staff. We're wondering how the trip home went."

"Thanks for calling. It's nice to hear from you guys. As far as the trip home, everything's fine and I'll be taking some painkillers in a little while."

He heard some male chuckling in the background and the coach said, "They'll actually help you heal faster. We understand the home health care nurse will be at your house tomorrow to help you with whatever you need."

"That's great."

"You're probably wondering why else we're calling," the coach said. "Drew, we have every hope you're going to recover from this and come back even stronger and ready to play by next season, but we're putting you on IR today. I didn't want you to hear it from anyone else but me." He saw his mom put a hand over her mouth. Tears rose in her eyes. He had to look away; if he saw his mom's tears, he couldn't get through this. "The guys miss you already and are looking forward to your being here to rehab and run as soon as possible."

He heard one of the trainers in the background. "The minute we get a sign-off from your doctor, we'll be in the training room with you. We're going to work you hard, but you'll be ready. We promise."

Drew swallowed past the gigantic lump in his throat. "Uh, yeah. I'm looking forward to it."

"If you have questions or you need anything, please call us. We'll be checking in on you, also. We'll get through this together," the coach said.

Drew knew he was still speaking. He made what must have sounded like the correct comments about motivation and not letting this thing beat him. A few minutes later, they hung up and he sat numbly, phone still clutched in his hand.

His mom sat up and gingerly wrapped her arms around him. He felt her tears falling on his good shoulder as he slipped one arm around her. His phone fell into the bedclothes.

KENDALL FELT THE cold fist of dread in her stomach as she walked into the Miners' offices. She wasn't quite sure what to expect. Today would be (hopefully) mostly mopping up from the day before yesterday's press conference. She also would be expected to observe the workouts of the three players brought in by the new director of football personnel. She'd expected all hell to break loose when she fired Ron, but so far, her e-mail and voicemail had been remarkably quiet.

It was early. There were plenty of chances for things to go to hell in a hand basket.

When she wasn't dwelling on the thousand and one things that needed to get done today, she was still thinking about Drew. It was all she could do to not curl up in the airline seat like a wounded animal and cry. She was asleep last night when her head hit the pillow, and this morning, she had to face the facts: If she was in his shoes, she'd be pissed. She'd more or less shown him that a job was more important to her than anyone or anything else in her life, and if she really cared about him, she would act like it.

He shouldn't have hung up the phone on her, but she got why he did it. She owed him an apology, but he owed her one too.

She'd wanted to get an early start this morning. Her heels clicked on the hardwood floor of the corridor outside of her office. It was seven AM, and her office door was ajar. The light was on\. Who the hell would be in her office at seven? Sydney wasn't usually in until after ten AM each morning due to her class schedule.

Maybe she should back away from her office and call for help. The Miners' private security force was in the office twenty-four hours a day now. Whoever was in her office had the electronic card that got them past the locks and a photo ID badge.

Maybe it was the cleaning crew. Maybe it was someone who'd been in there last evening. Maybe it was one of the security guys. She crept over to the partially open door and peeked through it.

Sydney sat at her desk, tapping away at her laptop.

Kendall shoved her office door open. "What are you doing here? You're supposed to be at school, you goofball!"

Sydney grinned at her. She picked up a tall iced latte and shook the cup a little. "Got you some coffee, boss. And a pastry."

Kendall dropped into one of the chairs in front of her desk and took the proffered Starbucks bag from Sydney. "Are you sure?" Sydney's workload was going to double, and Kendall didn't want her to drop out of school from sheer frustration. "Maybe I should get you an assistant of your own."

"I can handle it," Sydney said. "It's just like eating an elephant."

"One bite at a time," Kendall said. She raised her iced latte cup in a silent toast.

"Oh, *hell*, yeah. Let's get some shit done."

DREW WOKE UP after a restless night and swung his feet over the side of the bed. Seconds later, the phone his mom must have brought in and put on his nightstand rang.

His agent, Lance, sounded too damn cheerful for six AM Seattle time.

"How are you doing today?"

"Everything hurts. You do know it's six o'clock here, right?"

"Sorry, guy. I wanted to let you know that the Sharks' putting you on IR has hit the media, and the team is paying out the guaranteed portion of your contract."

"Okay. Coach called me yesterday."

"Why didn't you let me know?"

"I was a little busy. Hey, Lance, now that I have you on the phone, I have a question or two."

"What's up?" Lance said.

"One: I know I have to show up for the home games for the rest of the season. Am I required to go to away games?"

"No. You're expected to rehab."

"Does it matter *where* I rehab?"

"I'm guessing the Sharks might like it if you stayed in the Seattle area—"

"I'd like to see if I can work with a rehab center in California. I'll fly in for the games."

"Rehab in another team's facility? Please don't tell me you're considering doing this at the Miners."

"No, but there's at least two other teams in the area. What are your thoughts?"

"I'm guessing this means that you're interested in spending time with Kendall Tracy."

Drew pulled in a breath. "She can't move. It'll give us a chance to decide if it's worth working out the logistics to continue. I also need to face facts. I may not play again."

He was proud of himself: At least he could get the words out without bawling like a baby. He didn't know who he was without football, and it might be a while before he discovered what he'd like to do. Fortunately, between his contracts and endorsements, he'd saved enough to take his time and figure out what the future might hold for him professionally.

"Come on, McCoy. You're going to play again. Do you want me to approach the Sharks with your rehab plans?"

"I can do it. I'll bring you in if I need backup."

"Okay, then. Is there anything else I can do right now?"

"Nope," Drew said. "Thanks for listening." After a few more pleasantries, his agent hung up.

Drew had tossed and turned most of the night last night, thinking and weighing his options. Even the pain pills didn't knock him out. The best plan of attack was to rehab and train like he was intent on going back to the Sharks, while preparing for the fact he may not. He knew he wanted Kendall to be included in every plan he made. He'd crawl on hands and knees to California with a duffle bag of clothing between his teeth if she wanted him to, but he hoped some sincere groveling might work as well.

Three o'clock in the morning was a great time to think in an almost-silent house and straighten out his priorities. While his parents slept on in the room next door, he calculated and thought. He knew the only way he might get at least one of the things he wanted—creating a happy family—was accepting the fact that family might be living an hour outside of San Francisco, instead of in a 5800-square foot house on Seattle's Eastside. He'd bought a family house, but it was never going to be a home as long as Kendall didn't live here with him.

He remembered the night his teammate Zach bought the engagement ring for his now-wife, Cameron. He remembered Zach's trembling hands as he pulled the box out of his shorts pocket and showed a roomful of his teammates a gigantic ring, and the joy in his face as he told them he was in love. He reflected on the fact he'd watched their romance bloom from one dorm room over during training camp.

His and Kendall's love story wasn't going to happen under the noses of eighty guys. It would be just the two of them, and he would woo her until she fell in love with him. He'd known her a month, and he couldn't imagine his life without her already. If that was love, he'd take it, and he'd water it, feed it, and let it grow like the flowers in her backyard garden.

He grabbed his phone and tapped out a text to Kendall with one finger.

I am so sorry I hung up on you. Will you forgive me? I miss you.

He could take a nap later. He stood up from the bed, pulled a suitcase out of his closet, and started packing.

HE HEARD FOOTSTEPS from the room next door, his dad's voice as he talked with his wife, and Drew's mom tapped at his door as she poked her head in.

"Honey, are you awake already?"

"Yeah, Mom. How are you this morning?"

She looked at the mostly-packed suitcase on his bed and the scrawled page of notes he'd made with his non-dominant hand during the night last night. She raised an eyebrow.

"Maybe you should lie down for a while. You need some rest," she said. "What's going on here?"

"Is Dad in the shower?"

"No. He's downstairs making coffee."

Drew patted the bed. "Mom, sit down. I'll be right back."

He walked into the guest room, grabbed the little Tiffany's bag from its hiding place, and came back to his room. His mom stared at the bag.

"I have some stuff to tell you, but first, this is for you. Thank you for always being there for me, Mom. I really appreciate it, and I wanted you to have this."

His mom's eyes were huge. "Is this from Tiffany's?"

"Yes, Mom. Open it," he prompted.

"Are you sure?"

"Yes. I'm sure." He nudged her with his good shoulder. "Open it."

His mom bit her lower lip as she reached into the bag and extracted a palm-sized robin's-egg-blue box tied with a double-faced white satin ribbon. "It's so pretty I don't want to take the ribbon off," she said.

"You won't see what's inside until you do," Drew teased.

She admired it for a few minutes and finally pulled the

end of the ribbon, which slipped off of the box easily. She took off the lid and let out a gasp.

A sterling silver charm bracelet was nestled inside, featuring a heart-shaped charm that read "Mom" in flowing script. The only other charm on the bracelet was a small, intricately detailed football.

He owed McKenna some more money, but he could take care of that later. He watched his mom take the bracelet out of the box and hold it in her palm. "Oh, honey. It's beautiful," she said.

"They have a lot of charms, Mom. Maybe we kids should get you one for every special occasion."

"You don't have to do that," his mom protested, but her eyes sparkled. She might need two or three bracelets by the time he and his siblings were through. She unclasped the bracelet and held it out to him. "Help me put it on?" she asked.

It took a few minutes and some maneuvering, but he managed to clasp it around her wrist. She kissed his cheek.

"Thanks, honey. I love it."

"If you want gold, we can take it back—"

"No. I love this." She let out a happy sigh.

"I also wanted to apologize for upsetting you yesterday."

"You didn't upset me. I wasn't feeling well and I–I freaked out, as you kids would say." She fingered the little football charm as she spoke. "I know your love life is your own business. You're a grown man and you should make your own decisions. We really like Kendall, though. Is there any way to patch it up?"

"I'm working on it," he said. "You and Dad have made me think over the last couple of weeks."

"We've been fighting like kids. Really? I'm a little worried about that."

"Mom, it's not what you think. I've been thinking about the fact I always thought I wanted a wife that stayed home too, and it was pretty unfair of me to expect her to fulfill all my needs and wants, and none of her own."

His mom took his hand in her smaller, work-roughened one. "I thought you sided with your dad."

"There's not a side. We're a family. Why should you sit home all day if you find something else that makes you happy, Mom?" He let out a sigh. "I'm glad you're enjoying your job. I'm proud of you. You wanted something more, and you went out and got it." His mom patted his hand. "I hope they'll still let you come back after you had to come out here to hang out with me for a little while."

"The HR person told me there's a federal law that protects a leave of absence taken to care for a member of my family." She twirled the bracelet around with her other hand. "I might have to do some retraining or something when I go back, but I want to go back. It doesn't mean I don't love your dad. I need something for myself. You understand, don't you?"

"Yeah, Mom. I do." His shoulder was twinging. He should get his ass back to bed for a while, but he wanted to make sure he got the next part out. "You might be going back sooner than you think. I'm going to ask the Sharks if I can rehab in California."

"Honey, you just had surgery two days ago—"

"I'll make sure the doctor signs off on it before I get on a plane. I need to find a rehab facility that I can find a place to stay close by. I'll do those things, and then I'm going to go find out what happens when I can spend a little more time with Kendall. If she won't let me in the front door of her house, I plan on groveling."

He heard the "chirp" of an incoming text.

I miss you, too.

Chapter Eighteen

DREW SPENT THE next several days learning to do the smallest things for himself, such as dressing, using the men's room (thankfully, he figured that one out rather quickly), and eating anything that required the use of a fork and a knife. Showering was still a challenge. Someone else needed to secure his hair in the low ponytail he typically wore it in each morning. He couldn't drive. He got picked up in the morning for conditioning and physical therapy, and he was still on painkillers for the aftereffects of a few hours of adventures with the Sharks' training staff.

Luckily, nobody seemed to care that his wardrobe consisted of anything clean he could pull on at the moment, otherwise known as warm-ups and oversized T-shirts. He'd repacked his suitcase for this reality. After a week of dealing with the aftereffects of shoulder surgery, though, he could see the light at the end of the tunnel. It was dim, but it was there. He was going to spend months rehabbing his shoulder, but he would recover.

Drew walked out of his house, locked the door, and stood looking at it for a minute or two. Chuck was behind the wheel of the SUV idling in his driveway. It wasn't nice to make Chuck wait, but it was a ritual of sorts: He'd shut the door on the life he thought he would have. It was time to see what else might be in store.

Two hours later, Drew strolled into the Sharks' head trainer's office after his latest workout.

"Hey, Stan. Do you have a minute?" he said.

Stan had been with the team for fifteen years. He was known around the league for the excellence of his training and conditioning programs. The Sharks had benefited from his expertise. It would be smarter for his career to stay in Seattle for the next several months, but Kendall wasn't in Seattle.

"Sure, Drew." Stan nodded toward the chair beside his desk. "Have a seat. What's on your mind?"

"I've talked with my agent and the coaching staff this morning already. I'd like to rehab in California at least four days a week for the next few months, if that will work for you."

"Are you unhappy with what's going on here?"

"No. Not at all." Drew leaned forward a little and braced one arm on the desk. "There's someone special in California—"

"Say no more," Stan said. "Do you need a recommendation or suggestions on who to work with? I know some guys."

"They know you too," Drew assured him. "They would like to be able to coordinate with you and the staff here, if that will work."

"It'll work." Stan stuck out his hand, and Drew shook it. "Someone special, huh? Maybe you could bring her by sometime and introduce me."

"I'd like that. I'll also keep you up to date with the workouts and what's happening."

"You do that," Stan said. He grinned at Drew. "Guys are dropping like flies, aren't they?" Drew knew his comment had nothing to do with injuries, and everything to do with the fact more than a few Seattle Sharks were now sporting a wedding ring. "I'll see you in June for OTAs."

"Yes, you will," Drew said.

DREW HAD ONE more visit before he got on the plane for San Francisco. He hit the walk-up window at Dick's Drive-In, and Chuck helped him get enough food and drinks for one ten-year-old and a gaggle of nurses into the back of the SUV.

"Thanks for all your help, Chuck," Drew said as he eased himself back into the passenger seat.

"It's my pleasure," Chuck said. "Maybe I need to get on the Tuesday afternoon Children's detail too."

"I think the kids would enjoy that." Chuck and his colleague were in the Secret Service before they decided to open their own security firm. Drew was sure Nolan would love asking Chuck questions about his job.

He felt another pang. As his shoulder healed, he could get a cheap flight to Seattle on Tuesdays. There were so many things he'd miss about his adopted hometown, but Nolan (and Dick's Doubles) was the biggest.

After dropping off most of the food, Drew walked into Nolan's room with a couple of bags and a huge grin. "Hey, big guy," he said. "How are you feeling?"

Nolan was sitting up in a chair. There were a few less IVs in his arm. Drew turned to tap the sign as he always did, and he noted the indentations of fists and fingerprints in the drywall from the sheer number of visitors that had already done so.

Nolan reached out eagerly for the bags. "I'm hungry," he said.

"That's good, because I brought you some food." Drew lowered himself into a chair. "Do you need me to set you up?"

"Nope." Nolan reached into the bag, handed Drew a cheeseburger, and grabbed one out for himself. "Want some fries?"

"Sure," Drew said.

He watched Nolan spread the napkin over the rolling table, shake a few fries out from their paper sleeve, and grab out a small container of ketchup from the bag. He uncapped it and put it where Drew could reach it.

The dark circles under Nolan's eyes had faded. He had fresh color in his cheeks. He was energetic. He was also eating. The fries disappeared rapidly. Nolan reached into the bag to grab out another order of them.

"You seem like you're feeling better."

"I am. The doctor said I'm improving and I don't have to have as much medicine."

"That's a good thing."

"Yeah. My mom's really happy." Nolan had smeared ketchup on his cheek. Drew handed him a napkin. "You had surgery on your shoulder."

"I did. It'll get better. It'll just be a while." Drew propped his feet up on the footboard of Nolan's bed. "No big deal."

"Want more fries?" Nolan asked.

"I'm good. You eat 'em, buddy." He wasn't sure how to broach the subject. Maybe the best thing was to just blurt it out. "So, Nolan, I may not see you for a while. I'm going to work with some trainers and a doctor in California." He saw Nolan frown. "Derrick and Seth already said they're coming to visit you like always every Tuesday. Plus, there's a guy named Chuck that works with us that might stop by too. I think you'll like him."

"I'll see you again, right?" He'd wondered if Nolan's dad had abandoned their family or what the story was. Nolan never talked about it. He had to think of a way to reassure Nolan he wasn't falling off the face of the earth.

"You'll see me when I'm better. I promise." Drew let out a breath. "I'll give you my cell number in case you want to talk."

"I can call you?"

"Yeah, you can call me. If I'm busy, I might have to call you back."

Nolan gave him a nod and passed him one of the

chocolate shakes out of the other bag. "We'll see each other soon," he said.

"Yes. And you're going to run out onto the field with me for the first game."

Nolan grinned at him. "That means we'll both have to get better."

"You bet, buddy." Drew took a sip of his shake. "We will."

A FEW HOURS later, the flight Drew was on descended into San Francisco. The weather was perfect. San Francisco Bay reflected the blue skies above. The Golden Gate Bridge glowed a soft orange in the late-afternoon sun. The pilot set the jet down on the runway as if it were made of cotton.

Drew managed to grab his backpack out of the overhead bin and make his way into the airport. He had a driver waiting, who grabbed his suitcase.

"Where to, Mr. McCoy?" the driver asked as they strapped themselves into yet another black SUV.

Drew read Kendall's address off of his contacts list. He had a place a mile or so from her house. Maybe he should call first.

Maybe not.

The ride from the airport offered some time to make some calls, and to think. It was pretty ballsy to show up at her house without letting her know he was coming. He saw a flower stand as they exited off the freeway in Santa Clara.

"Would you please stop for a minute?" he asked the driver. "I'd like to get some flowers."

"Sure," the guy said.

Drew reached into his pocket for a little cash and bought a bouquet of long-stemmed red roses.

"Go big or go home," he muttered to himself.

"Excuse me?" the woman selling the flowers said.

"Oh, nothing. Don't worry about it." He gave her a grin and got back into the SUV.

He wasn't sure if Kendall was home from work yet, but there was only one way to find out. They pulled into the driveway of her house.

"Would you mind waiting a few minutes? I'd like to drop these off," he said to the driver.

"Not at all," the guy said. He shut off the engine and unsnapped his seatbelt.

Drew slid out of the SUV and mounted the few stairs to Kendall's front door. His stomach was in knots. His heart was pounding. He forced himself to breathe. He hoped he'd know what to say.

Who was he kidding? He'd been rehearsing what to say for the past week. He reached out to ring the doorbell. He waited. He rang it again. A minute or so later, he heard light footsteps and a woman's voice.

"Just a minute," Kendall called out.

The front door flew open. She stared up at him. "Drew," she whispered.

He cleared his throat. "I'm new in town. I was wondering if you could show me around or something. I'm planning on being here for a while, and I want to—"

She threw her arms around his neck before he could get the rest out. He wrapped his good arm around her and breathed in the scent of green apples.

"You're staying?" she said.

"For as long as you want me to."

Her fingers were already in his hair. He saw the sheen of tears in her eyes. "How about always?"

"Works for me," he said.

Epilogue

One year later

DREW PULLED INTO a parking space at the Sharks' training facility. He glanced into the rearview mirror. His passenger had no comment about visiting his workplace, at least so far. He got out of the car, opened the door behind the driver's seat, and looped a black leather baby sling over his head. He pulled his ponytail free of the strap, reaching into a car seat to scoop up his infant daughter, Tessa.

Three months after he'd opened the damn thing at Kendall's baby shower, he was a pro at slipping his baby into it and making sure she was comfortably (and safely) situated against his chest. He grabbed something called a "bouncy chair" out of the car as well.

Tessa gave him a gummy smile and cooed a little. His heart melted. He took her tiny hand in his. "Let's go, gorgeous. We'll find Mommy."

Tessa looked pleased and glanced around as he walked through the front doors of the training facility.

He never knew it was possible to love someone else more than his own life, but now he had two of them: Kendall and Tessa. They loved him too. If he started dwelling on it, he'd be a big-ass tearful mess again. Kendall's pregnancy had been a complete surprise to both of them, but he couldn't remember what his life was like before he saw his daughter's face for the first time. She had Kendall's dark hair and his light blue eyes, a button nose, and a dimple in one cheek. He could look at her for hours. Holding Tessa while she slept on his chest was even better.

Drew paused at the reception desk so Molly could say hello to the baby. Joanna, the former receptionist, spent twenty-five years with the Sharks before being tempted away by Zach Anderson's wife, Cameron. Joanna was now Cameron's assistant. Molly had big shoes to fill, but she was already a team favorite. Maybe that had something to do with the huge platter of homemade chocolate chip cookies she brought in every Friday for the guys.

"She looks just like her mama."

"She does," Drew agreed. "I'm a lucky man." He tenderly kissed the top of his daughter's head. "Have you seen Kendall at all?"

"She should be finishing up with her meeting. Let me find out." The receptionist punched a few buttons on her phone and said, "Sydney, are they out? Okay. I'll let Drew know." She clicked off the headpiece and said, "Kendall will meet you in the training room."

"Great. Thank you so much."

His wife had been hired by the new owner of the
Sharks as their director of football operations five minutes after the other league franchise owners approved
him. She'd managed to turn things around in San Francisco, but she wanted a change, and she wanted a lower-
profile job as well. Drew, Kendall, and Tessa were now
living in the big family house in Clyde Hill Drew bought
before he had any idea his wife and daughter were only a
year away.

Drew walked through the lobby, glancing over at the
two Lombardi Trophies on display and a huge trophy
case full of team memorabilia. He'd spent the past year
recovering from a torn shoulder labrum and rotator cuff,
and the resulting surgery to fix it. It was the greatest year
of his life, but in some respects, it was the hardest. He
was a happily married first-time father, but he wasn't
sure what the future held for him professionally. He was
having a physical today. Shortly afterward, there would
be a meeting to discuss whether or not he could play in
the league again.

His teammates had practice. He had physical therapy.
He missed the camaraderie of the locker room, the laughter, and the pranks. The Sharks had gone thirteen and
three, but missed another trip to the championship game
by a last-minute field goal. The Miners went instead. The
only comfort for Sharks fans everywhere was the fact that
Pittsburgh beat the Miners like a rented mule.

As Drew continued rehabbing and running, he had
something else to think of besides getting back on the
field: his wife and his daughter. The silver lining in his

cloud was the three months he'd spent at home with Tessa. He never dreamed he'd actually find fulfillment in things like cooking dinner for his wife for the first time, or being the guy that took Tessa to doctor's appointments and baby gym and play dates with other people's babies. He now knew how to get baby spit-up out of anything, among other useful skills.

He still wasn't sure about the "play date" thing. Three month olds mostly lay on a blanket and smiled at each other, but if his wife, both grandmothers, and the pediatrician assured him it was a good thing, he'd make sure it happened for Tessa.

He elbowed his way into the trainers' room and came to a halt. The room was full of his teammates, the team doctor, and his wife, who advanced on him with arms outstretched. His teammates were applauding. He glanced around at guys who had no problem trying to remove some other guy's lungs on a football field beaming at his little girl.

"Our little angel," Derrick said.

"Let me hold her," Zach called out.

"We got her a present," one of the guys from the Sharks' secondary said. They held up a tiny pink bedazzled T-shirt with the Sharks' logo, pink fleece warm-up pants, and some baby-sized tricked-out football shoes. "We also got her an early admission letter to USC."

"You do realize I graduated from UCLA," Drew said.

"Is that so? *USC?* The University of Washington might have something to say about that," one of the rookies called out. This started a loud discussion among Drew's teammates as to where Drew and Kendall's daughter would matriculate.

Tessa wasn't ready to commit. She let out a big yawn and squeezed her daddy's thumb.

"This is going to go fine," Kendall said. "We'll be waiting for you when it's over." She reached into the baby sling for Tessa. "I'll take that," she said as she pulled the sling over his head. She kissed him and whispered, "I love you."

"I love you more."

Drew walked out of the room to more clapping and Kendall's voice: "I was hoping she'd want to go to Stanford for undergrad like I did."

Drew could hear the laughing and trash-talking all the way down the hall.

The team doctor was thorough. Drew was poked and prodded and had an MRI. When it was all over, he was asked to wait in the doctor's office. Kendall was already there with the baby.

"How'd it go, champ?" she said.

"I had a blood draw. I wasn't offered a cookie," he said.

She let out a laugh. "I'll bet we could find one on the way home."

"I'll bet we can too." He reached out for his daughter. Kendall handed her over. "How's my daddy's girl?" he cooed to Tessa as he settled her in the crook of his arm.

Kendall moved her chair closer to his. He slung his other arm around the back. A year ago, a family wasn't in his frame of reference, and now he had one. He pulled his wife a bit closer.

A minute or so later, the team doctor walked in and sat down in his chair behind the desk.

"Well, Drew, would you like the good news or the bad news?"

Kendall reached out for his hand. Tessa had already fallen asleep on her daddy's chest.

Drew took a deep breath and braced himself. He hoped the news was good, but he wasn't sure. Mostly, he knew Kendall would face whatever it was with him.

"I'll take the bad news, Doc."

The doctor tossed his file and the CD of information from Drew's MRI on the desk. "Your days as a house husband are numbered, Drew." He grinned at Drew, Kendall, and Tessa. "Everything looks great. The repair looks solid and has healed much faster than we antici-pated. We'll ask you to wear a lightweight brace for the first practices with the team, but I feel confident that you are ready to return. I'm not putting any other re-strictions on your training regimen or your ability to play."

Drew let out the breath he'd been holding. He saw tears rising in Kendall's eyes.

"What's the good news, doctor?" she said.

"He's in great condition. You're going to have him around for a long time."

"That's what I want most," she said.

"One more thing," the doctor said. "If it works for you, I'd like to hold the baby for a few minutes."

Drew got up from his chair and transferred Tessa to the doctor's arms. She didn't stir.

"My daughter is due next month. It's our first grand-child. My wife has done a lot of shopping over the past few months," he joked.

Drew and Kendall both nodded. Their parents had done a little shopping too. Actually, more than a little. Tessa's wardrobe was complete until she was out of pre-school at least. When Drew and Kendall said Tessa was outfitted for years, the two grandmothers met up in Se-attle and sewed a "baby quilt" that could comfortably fit on a queen-sized bed.

The grandfathers bought Tessa her first tricycle.

Drew thought he had a lot to be thankful for before he met Kendall and they had Tessa. He had to admit he was the luckiest guy in the world now.

"Is there anything else we need to know?" Kendall said.

"It's all fine. I suppose I have to give the baby back now." The doctor cuddled their daughter and was re-warded with some cooing and another gummy smile.

"Not unless you'd like to move in with us, Dr. Kinkaid."

Nine months later

SMOKE FROM DRY ice swirled around the Sharks as they packed the tunnel to run out onto the field for the first game of the season at their home stadium. It was a per-fect, blue-skies day in Seattle: sunshine, sixty degrees, a soft breeze, with the underlying bite of fall in the air.

Fifty-three men ran in place, jumped up and down, and swung their arms to burn off the adrenaline and nerves as they waited to be announced.

In the alcove beside the entrance to the tunnel, a young man and his mother waited for their cue. He wore a McCoy jersey, Sharks warm-up pants, prototype shoes, and a lanyard with an all-access pass around his neck. The sound of a siren split the air, and the stadium shook with applause and shouts of "Go Sharks!" as the announcer called out, "For the first time this championship season, your Seattle Sharks!"

Drew paused to wait while the bulk of his teammates ran out onto the field. Nolan needed his grand entrance. Even more, Drew wanted to make sure every eye in the stadium would be riveted on the young man who'd won.

He reached out to grab Nolan's hand. Derrick had his other hand. Seth took Nolan's mom's hand.

"Are you ready?" Drew shouted. "Let's go!"

Derrick grabbed Nolan's mom's other hand as they emerged from the tunnel. The ovation from the sold-out stadium was deafening. The ground shook beneath them. His teammates had formed a line on either side of the tunnel to shout encouragement and slap Nolan on the back as they went by.

"Congratulations!"

"Good job!"

"You kicked cancer's ass!"

"That jersey is fresh. I wonder where I could get one," Seth Taylor joked.

The Sharks' QB, Tom Reed, reached out his hand to grab Nolan. "You ready?"

Nolan was beaming. The team clustered around him. They all put hands into the circle and Tom said to him, "It's all yours."

Nolan glanced up at the men surrounding him. "We're going to win today, because that's what we do. We win. We always win." He pulled in a breath. His cancer was in remission. He was still getting his strength back, but he didn't waver.

He shouted, "We always win," and fifty-three men shouted back, "GO SHARKS! GO SHARKS! GO SHARKS!"

Drew glanced at Nolan's mom, who still clung to Seth's hand. She was crying. Derrick was crying. Seth was brushing tears off of his face. The stadium rang with cheers, shouts, and stomping feet.

They won.

Author's Note

ONE OF THE subplots of *Covering Kendall* is how Kendall deals with a Miners player that attacks his girlfriend. Domestic violence is present in all segments of our society, and all women deserve a relationship without fear of violence against themselves and their children by a domestic partner or spouse.

If you are in a dangerous situation, please know there are people who want to help you. You are not alone. You are important and you matter.

Here are some resources:

Your local police department is always available at 911 in the United States.

The National Domestic Violence Hotline has both a phone number and a website. There are options to make a call, have an online chat, or look up information and resources at the following.

http://www.thehotline.org/

1-800-799-7233 | 1-800-787-3224 (TTY)

LifeWire is located on Seattle's Eastside, but there is important information on their website and they can point you toward resources in your community as well.

http://www.edvp.org/

1-425-746-1940 or 1-800-827-8840

If readers would like to help financially, the above organizations would be thrilled to get even a small donation for their very important work.

Again, if you're reading this and you need help, I know it is so hard to make that phone call or reach out to a friend. You deserve a life free of fear and full of love that doesn't hurt.

BLITZING EMILY

Love and Football, Book One

EMILY HAMILTON DOESN'T trust men. She's much more comfortable playing the romantic lead on stage in front of a packed house than in her own life. So, when NFL star and irresistible ladies' man Brandon McKenna acts as her personal white knight, she has no illusions he'll stick around. However, a misunderstanding with the press throws them together in a fake engagement that yields unexpected (and breathtaking) benefits.

Every time Brandon calls her "Sugar," Emily almost believes Brandon's playing for keeps, not just to score. Can she let down her defenses and get her own Happily Ever After?

RUSHING AMY

Love and Football, Book Two

FOR AMY HAMILTON, only three F's matter: Family, Football, and Flowers.

It might be nice to find someone to share Forever with too, but right now she's working double overtime while she gets her flower shop off the ground. The last thing she needs or wants is a distraction . . . or help, for that matter. Especially in the form of gorgeous and aggravatingly arrogant ex-NFL star Matt Stephens.

Matt lives by a playbook—*his* playbook. He never thought his toughest opponent would come in the form of a stunning florist with a stubborn streak to match his own. Since meeting her in the bar after her sister's wedding, he's known there's something between them. When she refuses, again and again, to go out with him, Matt will do anything to win her heart . . . But will Amy, who has everything to lose, let the clock run out on the one-yard line?

CATCHING CAMERON

Love and Football, Book Three

STAR SPORTS REPORTER Cameron Ondine has one firm rule: she does not date football players. Ever. She tangled with one years ago, and it did not end well. Been there, done that. But when Cameron comes face to face with the very man who shattered her heart—on camera, no less—her world is upended for a second time by recklessly handsome Seattle Shark Zach Anderson.

Zach has never been able to forget the gorgeous blonde who stole his breath away when he was still just a rookie. They've managed to give each other a wide berth for years, but when he and Cameron are suddenly forced to live in close quarters for a TV stunt, he knows he has to face his past once and for all. Because the more time they spend together, he's less focused on the action on the field and more concerned with catching Cameron.

CATCHING CAMERON

Love and Football Book Three

About the Author

Julie Brannagh has been writing since she was old enough to hold a pencil. She lives in a small town near Seattle, where she once served as a city council member and owned a yarn shop. She shares her home with a wonderful husband, two uncivilized Maine Coons, and a rambunctious chocolate lab.

Julie hasn't quite achieved the goal of owning a pro football team, so she created a fictional one: the Seattle Sharks. When she's not writing, she's reading, or armchair-quarterbacking her beloved Seattle Seahawks from the comfort of the family room couch. Julie is a Golden Heart finalist and the author of four contemporary sports romances.

Discover great authors, exclusive offers, and more at hc.com.

Give in to your impulses . . .
Read on for a sneak peek at six brand-new
e-book original tales of romance
from Avon Impulse.
Available now wherever e-books are sold.

BEAUTY AND THE BRIT
By Lizbeth Selvig

THE GOVERNESS CLUB: SARA
By Ellie Macdonald

CAUGHT IN THE ACT
Book Two: Independence Falls
By Sara Jane Stone

SINFUL REWARDS 1
A Billionaires and Bikers Novella
By Cynthia Sax

WHEN THE RANCHER CAME TO TOWN
A Valentine Valley Novella
By Emma Cane

LEARNING THE ROPES
By T. J. Kline

An Excerpt from

BEAUTY AND THE BRIT
by Lizbeth Selvig

Tough and self-reliant Rio Montoya has looked after her two siblings for most of their lives. But when a gang leader makes threats against her sister Bonnie, even Rio isn't prepared for the storm that could destroy her family. Rio seeks refuge for them all at a peaceful horse farm in the small town of Kennison Falls, Minnesota, but her budding romance with the stable's owner, handsome British ex-pat David Pitts-Matherson, feels as dangerous as her past.

"**D**id I ever tell you how much I hate British arrogance?" Chase grinned and captured the ball, dribbled it to the free-throw line, turned, and sank the shot. "Nothin' but net."

"Did I ever tell you how much I hate Americans showing off?"

"Yup. You have."

David laughed again and clapped Chase on the arm. Not quite a year before, Chase had married David's good friend and colleague Jill Carpenter, and this was the second time David had overnighted with Chase at Crossroads Youth and Community Center in Minneapolis. He was grateful for the camaraderie, and for the free lodging on his supply runs to the city, but mostly for the distraction from life at the stable back home in Kennison Falls. Here there were no bills staring up at him from his desk, no finances to finagle, no colicky horses. Here he could forget he was one disaster away from . . . well, disaster.

It also boggled his mind that he and Chase had an entire converted middle school to themselves.

"All right, play to thirty," Chase said, tossing him the ball. "Oughta take me no more'n three minutes to hang your limey ass out to dry."

"Bring it on, Nancy-boy."

A loud buzzer halted the game before it started.

"Isn't that the front door?" David asked.

"Yeah." Deep lines formed between Chase's brows.

The center had officially closed an hour before at nine o'clock. Members with I.D. pass cards could enter until eleven—but only did so for emergencies. David followed Chase toward the gymnasium doors. Voices echoed down the hallway.

"Stop pulling, Rio, you're worse than Hector. He's not going to follow us in here."

"It's Bonnie and Rio Montoya." Surprise colored Chase's voice. "Rio's one of the really good ones. Sane. Hardworking. I can't imagine why she's here."

Rio? David searched his memory but could only recall ever hearing the name in the Duran Duran song.

"Don't be an idiot." A second voice, filled with firm, angry notes, rang out clearly as David neared the source. "Of course they're following us. They may not come inside, but they'll be waiting, and you cannot handle either of them no matter how much you think you can. Dr. Preston's on duty tonight. He might be able to run interference."

"They won't listen to him. To them he's just a pretty face. Let me talk to Heco. You never gave me the chance."

"And I won't, even if I have to lock you in juvie for a year."

"God, Rio, you just don't get it."

"You're right, Bonnie Marie. I don't. What in God's name possessed you to meet Hector Black after curfew? Do you know what almost went down in that parking lot? Do you know who that other dude *was?*"

Chase hustled through the doorway. "Rio? Bonnie? Something happen?"

David followed five feet behind him. The hallway outside the gym glowed with harsh fluorescent lighting. Chase had the attention of both girls, but when David moved into view, one of them turned. A force field slammed him out of nowhere—a force field made up of amber-red hair and blazing blue eyes.

Frozen to the spot, he stared and she stared back. Her hair shone the color of new pennies on fire, and her complexion, more olive and exotic than a typical pale redhead's, captivated him. Her lips, parted and uncertain, were pinup-girl full. Her body, beneath a worn-to-softness plaid flannel shirt, was molded into the kind of feminine curves that got a shallow-thinking man in trouble. David normally prided himself on having left such loutishness behind in his university days, but he was rapidly reverting.

"Rio? You all right?" Chase called, and she broke the staring contest first.

David blinked.

"Fine," she said. "I'm sorry to come in so late. I needed a safe place for this one."

An Excerpt from

THE GOVERNESS CLUB: SARA
by Ellie Macdonald

Sweet Sara Collins is one of the founding members
of the Governess Club. But she has a secret:
She doesn't love teaching. She'd much prefer to
be a vicar's wife and help the local community.
Nathan Grant is the embodiment of everything
that frightens her. When Sara decides it's time
to take a chance and experience *all* that life has
to offer, Nathan is the first person she thinks of.
Will Sara's walk on the wild side ruin her chances
at a simple, happy life? Or has she just opened the
door to a once-in-a-lifetime chance at passion?

An Excerpt from

THE GOVERNESS CLUB: SARA
by Ellie Macdonald

Mr. Pomeroy helped her down from the gig, and Sara took a long look at Windent Hall. Curtains covering the windows shielded the interior from a visitor's view, lending the building a cold and unwelcoming front. Rotted trees and dead grass lined the driveway, and cracks were visible along the red brickwork. Piles of crumbled mortar littered the edge of the manor house, and even the front portico was listing to the side, on the verge of toppling over.

The place reeked of neglect, which was to be expected after thirty years of vacancy. What Sara hadn't expected was the blanket of loneliness that shrouded the house, adding to the chilly ambiance. She couldn't help feeling that it had been calling out to be noticed, only to be ignored that much longer.

She couldn't suppress the shiver that ran down her body.

Sara turned to Mr. Pomeroy as he offered his arm. "Are you certain we should be here? We are uninvited."

He led her gingerly up the front steps. "Even so, I feel it is my duty to welcome him to the community. One can see that taking on this place is a task of great proportions. He needs to know that he is welcomed here and be informed of the local tradesmen and laborers available."

His logic was sound. But she couldn't keep from wincing

when the door protested his banging with a loud crack down the middle. Mr. Pomeroy and Sara shared a glance. He grimaced apologetically.

The door creaked open, only to stop partway. A muffled curse was heard from the other side, and eight fingers appeared in the opening. Grunting started as whoever was on the far side started to pull. Mr. Pomeroy shrugged and added his efforts in pushing. With a loud squeal, the door inched open until Sara and the vicar were able to pass through.

They stepped into a dark foyer, dustcovers over everything, including a large chandelier and all the wall sconces. The man who had opened the door was walking away down a corridor on one side of the main staircase. "I don't get paid enuff fer this," they could hear him muttering. He pushed open a door and pointed into the room. "Youse wait in there." He disappeared farther down the corridor.

Sara stared. Mr. Pomeroy stared. They looked at each other. With another shrug, Mr. Pomeroy started down the corridor, and she had little choice but to follow.

It was a parlor, as far as Sara could tell, underneath all the dust. The pale green walls were faded and damaged, giving the impression of sickness. No paintings adorned them, and none of the other small pieces one expected in a room such as this were evident. The furniture that was not hidden by dustcovers was torn and did not appear strong enough to hold any weight whatsoever. She sat on the sofa gingerly, hoping it would not give out underneath her.

"Perhaps we should not have come today," she whispered to Mr. Pomeroy. "It does not appear Mr. Grant is prepared to receive visitors of any sort."

The vicar acknowledged her point with an incline of his head. "We are here now, however. We will not stay long, simply offer our welcome and depart."

They had been waiting in the sparse room for nearly twenty-five minutes before she heard a tapping out in the corridor. It drew closer, and Sara turned her head to the door, wondering what was causing the sound. A gold tip struck the floor at the threshold, and Sara's eyes followed a black shaft upward to a matching gold top shaped into the form of a wolf's head. The head was loosely grasped by lean fingers, confident of their ability to control the cane.

Her eyes continued to rise, taking in the brown coat, striped waistcoat, and snowy white cravat before reaching the gentleman's face. Her eyes widened in recognition, and her breath caught in her throat when she realized that the man was none other than the stranded traveler from a few days prior.

Up close and stationary, his icy blue eyes were even paler, and at this moment, the bloodshot orbs exuded barely concealed disdain that made her even more aware of their lack of an invitation to visit. She barely registered the ants in her throat, for she was too riveted by his face.

An Excerpt from

CAUGHT IN THE ACT
Book Two: Independence Falls
by *Sara Jane Stone*

For Liam Trulane, failure is not an option. He is determined to win a place in Katie Summers' life before she leaves Independence Falls for good. First, he needs to make amends for the last time they got down and dirty. But falling for his rivals' little sister could cost him everything in the second installment of a hot new series from contemporary romance writer Sara Jane Stone.

"What are you going to do with it?" Katie asked, drawing him back to the present and the piece of land that proved he was walking down the path marked success. The equity stake in Moore Timber his best friend had offered Liam in exchange for help running the company was one more milestone on that road—and one he had yet to prove he deserved.

"Thinking about building a home here someday," Liam said.

"A house? I would have thought you'd want to forget about this place. About us. After the way you ended it." Katie raised her hand to her mouth as if she couldn't believe she'd said those words out loud.

Liam stopped beside her, losing his grip on the goat's lead and allowing the animal to graze. "I messed up, Katie. I think we both know that. But I panicked when I realized how young you were, and how—"

"I was eighteen," she snapped.

"By a few weeks. You were so innocent. And I felt all kinds of guilt for not realizing it sooner."

"Not anymore," she said, her voice firm. Defiant. "I'm not innocent anymore."

"No." Liam knew every line, every angle of her face. There

were days he woke up dreaming about the soft feel of her skin. But it was the way Katie had looked at him after he'd gone too far, taken too much, that haunted his nightmares. In that moment, her green eyes had shone with hope and love.

Back then, when he was fresh out of college, returning home to build the life he'd dreamed about, that one look had sent him running scared. He wasn't ready for the weight of her emotions.

And he sure as hell wasn't ready now. Eric had given Liam one job since handing over part of the company—buy Summers Family Trucking. Liam couldn't let his best friend, now his business partner, down. Whatever lingering feelings he had for Katie needed to wait on the sidelines until after Liam finished negotiating with her brothers. There was too much at stake—including his vision of a secure future—to blow this deal over the girl who haunted his fantasies.

He drew the goat away from the overgrown grass and started toward the wooded area on the other side of the clearing. "We should go. Get you home before too late."

But Katie didn't follow. She marched down to the fir trees. "I'm twenty-five, Liam. I don't have a curfew. My brothers don't sit around waiting for me to come home."

"I know."

Brody, Chad, and Josh were waiting for him. Liam had been on his way to see her brothers when he'd spotted her car on the side of the road. They'd reluctantly agreed to an informal meeting to discuss selling to Moore Timber.

She spun to face him, hands on her hips. "I think you wanted to take a walk down memory lane."

"Katie—"

"Back then, you never held back." She closed the gap between them, the toes of her sandal-clad feet touching his boots. "So tell me, Liam, what are we doing here?"

He fought the urge to reach for her. He had no right. Not to mention bringing her here had confirmed one thing: After seven years, Katie Summers still held his mistakes against him.

She raised one hand, pressing her index finger to his chest. Damn, he wished he'd kept his leather jacket on. Her touch ignited years of flat-out need. No, he hadn't lived like a saint for seven years, but no one else turned him on like Katie Summers.

An Excerpt from

SINFUL REWARDS 1
A Billionaires and Bikers Novella
by Cynthia Sax

Belinda "Bee" Carter is a good girl; at least, that's
what she tells herself. And a good girl deserves
a nice guy—just like the gorgeous and moody
billionaire Nicolas Rainer. Or so she thinks,
until she takes a look through her telescope
and sees a naked, tattooed man on the balcony
across the courtyard. He has been watching
her, and that makes him all the more enticing.
But when a mysterious and anonymous text
message dares her to do something bad, she
must decide if she is really the good girl she has
always claimed to be, or if she's willing to risk
everything for her secret fantasy of being watched.

An Avon Red Novella

I'd told Cyndi I'd never use it, that it was an instrument purchased by perverts to spy on their neighbors. She'd laughed and called me a prude, not knowing that I was one of those perverts, that I secretly yearned to watch and be watched, to care and be cared for.

If I'm cautious, and I'm always cautious, she'll never realize I used her telescope this morning. I swing the tube toward the bench and adjust the knob, bringing the mysterious object into focus.

It's a phone. Nicolas's phone. I bounce on the balls of my feet. This is a sign, another declaration from fate that we belong together. I'll return Nicolas's much-needed device to him. As a thank you, he'll invite me to dinner. We'll talk. He'll realize how perfect I am for him, fall in love with me, marry me.

Cyndi will find a fiancé also—everyone loves her—and we'll have a double wedding, as sisters of the heart often do. It'll be the first wedding my family has had in generations.

Everyone will watch us as we walk down the aisle. I'll wear a strapless white Vera Wang mermaid gown with organza and lace details, crystal and pearl embroidery accents, the bodice fitted, and the skirt hemmed for my shorter height. My hair will be swept up. My shoes—

Voices murmur outside the condo's door, the sound piercing my delightful daydream. I swing the telescope upward, not wanting to be caught using it. The snippets of conversation drift away.

I don't relax. If the telescope isn't positioned in the same way as it was last night, Cyndi will realize I've been using it. She'll tease me about being a fellow pervert, sharing the story, embellished for dramatic effect, with her stern, serious dad—or, worse, with Angel, that snobby friend of hers.

I'll die. It'll be worse than being the butt of jokes in high school because that ridicule was about my clothes and this will center on the part of my soul I've always kept hidden. It'll also be the truth, and I won't be able to deny it. I am a pervert.

I have to return the telescope to its original position. This is the only acceptable solution. I tap the metal tube.

Last night, my man-crazy roommate was giggling over the new guy in three-eleven north. The previous occupant was a gray-haired, bowtie-wearing tax auditor, his luxurious accommodations supplied by Nicolas. The most exciting thing he ever did was drink his tea on the balcony.

According to Cyndi, the new occupant is a delicious piece of man candy—tattooed, buff, and head-to-toe lickable. He was completing armcurls outside, and she enthusiastically counted his reps, oohing and aahing over his bulging biceps, calling to me to take a look.

I resisted that temptation, focusing on making macaroni and cheese for the two of us, the recipe snagged from the diner my mom works in. After we scarfed down dinner, Cyndi licking her plate clean, she left for the club and hasn't returned.

Three-eleven north is the mirror condo to ours. I

straighten the telescope. That position looks about right, but then, the imitation UGGs I bought in my second year of college looked about right also. The first time I wore the boots in the rain, the sheepskin fell apart, leaving me barefoot in Economics 201.

Unwilling to risk Cyndi's friendship on "about right," I gaze through the eyepiece. The view consists of rippling golden planes, almost like . . .

Tanned skin pulled over defined abs.

I blink. It can't be. I take another look. A perfect pearl of perspiration clings to a puckered scar. The drop elongates more and more, stretching, snapping. It trickles downward, navigating the swells and valleys of a man's honed torso.

No. I straighten. This is wrong. I shouldn't watch our sexy neighbor as he stands on his balcony. If anyone catches me . . .

Parts 1, 2, and 3 available now!

An Excerpt from

WHEN THE RANCHER CAME TO TOWN
A Valentine Valley Novella

by Emma Cane

Welcome to Valentine Valley! Emma Cane
returns to the amazing and romantic town for
the latest installment in her sparkling series.
When an ex-rodeo star falls in love with an
agoraphobic B&B owner, he must pull out
all the stops to get her out of her shell.

With the pie in the oven, Amanda set the timer on her phone, changed into old clothes suitable for gardening, smeared on sunscreen, and headed outside. The grounds of the B&B took just as much work as the inside. She'd hired a landscaper for some of the major stuff like lawn and tree care, but the flowers, shrubs, and design work were all hers. She felt at peace in her garden, with the high bushes that formed walls on either side. The terraced lawn sloped down amidst rock gardens to Silver Creek, where she kept kayaks, canoes, and paddleboards for her guests. She had little hidden walkways between tall shrubs, where unusual fountains greeted visitors as a reward for their curiosity. She'd strung lights between the trees, and at night, her garden was like her own private fairy world.

One she had to share with guests, of course.

As she headed across the deck that was partially covered by an arbor, she glanced toward the hot tub beneath the gazebo—and did a double take. Mason Lopez sat alone on the edge of the tub, his jeans rolled up to his knees, his feet immersed. Though he was staring at the bubbling water, he seemed to be looking inward.

She must have made a sound, because he suddenly turned

his head. For a moment, she was pinned by his gaze, aware of him as a man in a way she hadn't felt about anyone in a long time.

She shook it off and said, "Sorry to disturb you." She was about to leave him in peace, but found herself saying instead, "Is everything all right?"

He smiled, white teeth gleaming out of the shadows of the gazebo, but it was a tired smile that quickly died.

"Sure, everything's fine. My meeting just didn't go as expected."

She felt frozen, unable to simply leave him when he'd said something so personal. "I bet you'll be able to work it out."

A corner of his mouth quirked upward. "I'm glad you're sure of that."

"You're not?" Where had that come from? And then she walked toward him, when she should have been giving him his privacy. But he looked so alone.

"Will you join me?" he asked.

She was surprised to hear a thread of hope in his voice. As a person who *enjoyed* being alone, this felt foreign to her, but the need to help a guest overruled that. She sat down cross-legged beside him. They didn't talk at first, and she watched him rub his shoulder.

He noticed her stare and gave a chagrinned smile. "I injured it years ago. It still occasionally aches."

"I imagine the hard work of ranching contributes to that."

"Yeah, it does, but it's worth it. I love working the land that's been in my family for almost seventy-five years. But we've been going through a tough time, and it's been pretty obvious we need a championship bull to invigorate our breeding program. I thought if I met with some of the ranchers here, we could find some investment partners."

"That was what your meeting today was about?"

"Yeah. But the Sweetheart Ranch is a large operation, and it's all they want to handle right now."

"We have other ranches around here."

He glanced at her and grinned. "Yeah, I have more meetings tomorrow."

"I'm sure you'll be successful." She looked away from him, the magnetism of his smile making her feel overheated though she was sitting in the shade. Or maybe it was the proximity of the hot tub, she told herself.

An Excerpt from

LEARNING THE ROPES
by T. J. Kline

From author T. J. Kline comes the stunning
follow-up to *Rodeo Queen*. When former
rodeo queen Alicia falls for perpetual playboy
Chris, she must find a way to tame him.

Alicia Kanani slapped the reins against her horse's rump as he stretched out, practically flying between the barrels down the length of the rodeo arena, dirt clods rising behind them as the paint gelding ate up the ground with his long stride. She glanced at the clock as she pulled him up, circling to slow him to a jog as a cowboy opened the back gate, allowing her to exit. 14.45. It was only good enough for second place right now. If only she'd been able to cut the first barrel closer, it might have taken another tenth of a second off her time.

She walked her favorite gelding, Beast, back to the trailer and hooked his halter around his neck before loosening his cinch. She heard the twitter of female laughter before she actually recognized the pair of women behind her trailer and cringed. Delilah had been a thorn in her side ever since high school, when Alicia had first arrived in West Hills. There'd never been a lack of competition between them, but it seemed, years later, only one of them had matured at all.

"Look, Dallas, there's Miss Runner-Up." Delilah jerked her chin at Alicia's trailer. "Came in second again, huh?" She flipped her long blonde waves over her shoulder. "I guess you can't win them all . . . oh, wait." She giggled. "You don't seem to win any, do you? That would be me." The pair laughed as if it were the funniest joke ever.

"Isn't it hard to ride a broom *and* a horse at the same time, Delilah?" Alicia tipped her head to the side innocently as Delilah glared at her and stormed away, pulling Dallas with her.

Alicia snidely imitated Delilah's laugh to her horse as she pulled the saddle from his back and put it into the trailer. "She thinks she's so funny. 'You haven't won. I have,' " she mimicked in a nasally voice. "Witch," she muttered as she rubbed the curry comb over Beast's neck and back.

"I sure hope you don't kiss your mother with that mouth."

Alicia spun to see Chris Thomas, her best friend Sydney's brother, walking toward her trailer. She'd rodeoed with Chris and Sydney for years, until Chris had gone pro with his team roping partner. For the last few years, they'd all been pursuing the same goal, the National Finals Rodeo, in their respective events. So far their paths hadn't crossed since Sydney's wedding nearly two years before. She'd suspected she might see him here since they were so close to home and this rodeo boasted a huge purse for team ropers.

"Chris!" She hurried over and gave him a bear hug. "Did you rope already?"

"Tonight during the slack." Most of the team ropers would be competing tonight before the barbecue and dance. "I see Delilah's still giving you a hard time."

She shrugged and smirked. "She's still mad I beat her out for rodeo queen when Sydney gave up the title."

"That was a long time ago. You'd think she'd let it go." Chris stuffed his hands into his pockets and leaned against the side of her trailer, patting Beast's neck. "Maybe you should put Nair in her shampoo like she did to you."

Alicia cringed at the memory. "It was a good thing I smelled it before I put it on my head. That could've been traumatizing, but I got her back."

"That's right. Didn't you put liniment in her lip gloss?" She smiled at the reminder of the prank, and Chris laughed. They'd had some good times together in the past. She wondered how they'd managed to drift apart over the past few years. She missed his laugh and the way he always seemed to bring the playful side of her personality to the surface.

"So, how'd you do?"

"Second—so far," she clarified. "Again."

He chuckled and crossed his arms over his chest. His biceps bulged against the material of his Western shirt, and she couldn't help but notice how much he'd filled out since she'd last seen him. And in all the right places. "Second's nothing to complain about."

"It's nothing to brag about either," she pointed out, tearing her eyes away from his broad chest. She finished brushing down the horse, feeling slightly uncomfortable with the way he continued to silently watch her, as if he wanted to say something but wasn't sure how to bring it up. Finally she turned and faced him. "What?"